Henry C. Lodge

Ballads and Lyrics

Henry C. Lodge

Ballads and Lyrics

ISBN/EAN: 9783744787918

Printed in Europe, USA, Canada, Australia, Japan

Cover: Foto ©Andreas Hilbeck / pixelio.de

More available books at **www.hansebooks.com**

BALLADS AND LYRICS.

SELECTED AND ARRANGED BY

HENRY CABOT LODGE.

BOSTON:

HOUGHTON, OSGOOD AND COMPANY.

The Riverside Press, Cambridge.

1880.

RIVERSIDE, CAMBRIDGE:
STEREOTYPED AND PRINTED BY
H. O. HOUGHTON AND COMPANY.

PREFACE.

THIS collection is intended for boys and girls between the ages of twelve and eighteen, in our public and private schools, and especially in the former. This class of readers, I need hardly say, covers not only a wide variety of age, capacity, and disposition, but a still wider range of opportunity and association, from children who have every advantage, both at home and in school, to obtain books and know about literature, to those who unfortunately have books only in school and must go, for more extended reading, without a guide to our public libraries. The poem which will appeal without explanation to one child is dumb to another, and it is for this reason that this collection ranges from the "Soldier from Bingen" and the "Old Sergeant" to Milton's "L'Allegro" and the Songs of Shakespeare. If children will read the former, or can be induced to do so, there is no reason why they cannot be led on through all the intervening stages to the highest kind of poetry.

The main purpose of the book, therefore, is of course educational. It is designed to breed a liking for good poetry, and to suggest more extended reading in the works, both in prose and in verse, of the best authors. With these objects, and for this class of readers, my choice has been somewhat limited, and the rules which I have followed in making the selection, although few, have required strict observance. The first essential point was to awaken interest, without which all attempts to teach are vain, and this will explain the variety in the style of the poems and in their arrangement. Simplicity of thought and diction has been required in every poem which has been admitted, and this has led to the introduction of a large proportion of narrative poems or ballads, which are also, as it seemed to me, best fitted to interest children. The lyrics which have been selected are, so far as possible, the simplest of their kind both in form and in idea.

I am well aware that the collection is very far from comprising all the best ballads and lyrics in the language, and I also know that many of those contained in the collection are inferior to others which have been omitted. But many of our most beautiful lyrics are too complicated and too refined in thought and expression for boys and girls, and are suited only to men and women whose minds are more mature and cultivated. Another very large class of lyrics of the greatest beauty deals wholly with love, and is too intense in feeling for children, especially in schools where both sexes are represented. Still another class, a much smaller, but a very important one, has been omitted on account of its sectarian fervor. Then, too, many poems not of the highest order of merit have been chosen because, as I have said, they would interest children when finer and more difficult ones might not, and would thus serve to pave the way and draw the reader on to better things.

I believe not only that there are in the collection many of the finest poems of their kind in the language, but also that there is nothing which is not good in itself, simple, true, and, with the possible exception of Poe's "Raven," which has found a place because of its wide renown and because no other example would do anything like justice to the author, nothing that is not thoroughly wholesome. The great difficulty has been to avoid making the collection too sober in tone, and I am far from being satisfied in this respect. But the number of really humorous poems of genuine and enduring merit is wofully small, most of them being either perfectly ephemeral or of a kind which would not appeal to children. This holds true,

also, of light and occasional verses and of satire,
all of which abound in English poetry, and are of
the highest merit, but which are, as a rule, in their
nature unsuited to children, and fit only for more
mature minds.   The notes are simply the bare out-
lines of the biography of each poet, and are merely
intended to give to children who desire it knowledge sufficient to enable them to obtain more and
better information.

The collection will fully serve its purpose if it
tends to develop a taste for good poetry, or if it
helps to open to children the splendid and unbounded resources of English literature.

H. C. LODGE.

CONTENTS.

viii   *CONTENTS.*

CONTENTS. ix

CONTENTS.

BALLADS AND LYRICS.

CHEVY CHASE.[1]

God prosper long our noble King,
Our lives and safeties all!
A woeful hunting once there did
In Chevy Chase befall.

To drive the deer with hound and horn
Earl Percy took the way:
The child may rue that is unborn
The hunting of that day!

The stout Earl of Northumberland
A vow to God did make,
His pleasure in the Scottish woods
Three summer's days to take;

The chiefest harts in Chevy Chase
To kill and bear away.

[1] This famous ballad was written probably during the fifteenth century. It may refer to the battle of Pepperden, fought in 1436, between the Earl of Northumberland and the Earl Douglas of Angus, but this is uncertain. The Percies and the Douglas family were always coming in conflict, and this ballad is the great epic of the continual warfare which was waged for centuries on the English and Scottish border. The version given here is from Bishop Percy's Folio MSS., vol. ii., p. 7.

These tidings to Earl Douglas came
 In Scotland where he lay,

Who sent Earl Percy present word
 He would prevent his sport.
The English Earl, not fearing that,
 Did to the woods resort

With fifteen hundred bowmen bold,
 All chosen men of might,
Who knew full well in time of need
 To aim their shafts aright.

The gallant grey hound swiftly ran
 To chase the fallow deer;
On Monday they began to hunt
 Ere day-light did appear;

And long before high noon they had
 An hundred fat bucks slain.
Then having dined, the drovers went
 To rouse the deer again.

The hounds ran swiftly through the woods
 The nimble deer to take,
And with their cries the hills and dales
 An echo shrill did make.

Lord Percy to the Quarry went
 To view the tender deer;
Quoth he, " Earl Douglas promised once
 This day to meet me here;

" But if I thought he would not come,
 No longer would I stay."

With that a brave young gentleman
　　Thus to the Earl did say,

" Lo, yonder doth Earl Douglas come,
　　His men in armor bright,
Full twenty hundred Scottish spears
　　All marching in our sight,

" All pleasant men of Teviotdale
　　Fast by the river Tweed."
" O cease your sports !" Earl Percy said,
　　" And take your bows with speed,

" And now with me, my countrymen,
　　Your courage forth advance !
For there was never champion yet
　　In Scotland nor in France

" That ever did on horseback come,
　　But if my hap it were,
I durst encounter man for man,
　　With him to break a spear."

Earl Douglas on his milk-white steed,
　　Most like a Baron bold,
Rode foremost of his company,
　　Whose armor shone like gold :

" Show me," said he, " whose men you be
　　That hunt so boldly here,
And, without my consent, do chase
　　And kill my fallow deer."

The first man that did answer make
　　Was noble Percy he,

Who said, " We list not to declare,
  Nor show whose men we be,

" Yet we will spend our dearest blood
    Thy chiefest harts to slay."
Then Douglas swore a solemn oath,
    And thus in rage did say,

" Ere thus I will out-bravèd be,
    One of us two shall die!
  I know thee well! An Earl thou art,
    Lord Percy! So am I;

" But trust me, Percy, pity 't were,
    And great offence, to kill
Any of these our guiltless men,
    For they have done no ill;

" Let thou and I the battle try,
    And set our men aside."
" Accursed be he!" Earl Percy said,
    " By whom it is denied."

Then stepped a gallant Squire forth, —
    Witherington was his name, —
Who said, "I would not have it told
    To Henry our King, for shame,

" That e'er my captain fought on foot,
    And I stand looking on:
You be two Earls," quoth Witherington,
    " And I a Squire alone.

" I 'll do the best that do I may,
    While I have power to stand!

While I have power to wield my sword,
  I 'll fight with heart and hand!''

Our English archers bent their bows —
  Their hearts were good and true, —
At the first flight of arrows sent,
  Full four score Scots they slew.

To drive the deer with hound and horn,
  Douglas bade on the bent;
Two Captains moved with mickle might,
  Their spears to shivers went.

They closed full fast on every side,
  No slackness there was found,
But many a gallant gentleman
  Lay gasping on the ground.

O Christ ! it was great grief to see
  How each man chose his spear,
And how the blood out of their breasts
  Did gush like water clear!

At last these two stout Earls did meet
  Like Captains of great might;
Like lions' moods they laid on load,
  They made a cruel fight.

They fought until they both did sweat,
  With swords of tempered steel,
Till blood adown their cheeks like rain
  They trickling down did feel.

" O yield thee, Percy!" Douglas said,
  " And in faith I will thee bring

Where thou shalt high advancèd be
  By James, our Scottish King;

"Thy ransom I will freely give,
  And this report of thee,
Thou art the most courageous Knight
  That ever I did see."

"No, Douglas!" quoth Earl Percy then,
  "Thy proffer I do scorn;
I will not yield to any Scot
  That ever yet was born!"

With that there came an arrow keen
  Out of an English bow,
Which struck Earl Douglas on the breast
  A deep and deadly blow;

Who never said more words than these,
  "Fight on, my merry men all!
For why, my life is at an end,
  Lord Percy sees my fall."

Then leaving life, Earl Percy took
  The dead man by the hand;
And said, "Earl Douglas! for thy sake
  Would I had lost my land!

"O Christ! my very heart doth bleed
  With sorrow for thy sake!
For sure, a more renownèd Knight
  Mischance could never take!"

A Knight amongst the Scots there was,
  Who saw Earl Douglas die,

And straight in heart did vow revenge
Upon the Lord Percy.

Sir Hugh Montgomery was he called,
Who, with a spear full bright,
Well mounted on a gallant steed,
Ran fiercely through the fight,

And past the English archers all
With naught of dread or fear,
And through Earl Percy's body then
He thrust his hateful spear

With such a vehement force and might
That his body he did gore,
The staff ran through the other side
A large cloth yard and more.

So thus did both those Nobles die,
Whose courage none could stain.
An English archer then perceived
The noble Earl was slain.

He had a good bow in his hand
Made of a trusty tree ;
An arrow of a cloth yard long
To the hard head halèd he.

Against Sir Hugh Montgomery
His shaft full right he set;
The grey goose wing that was thereon
In his heart's blood was wet.

This fight from break of day did last
Till setting of the sun,

For when they rung the Evening bell
   The Battle scarce was done.

With stout Earl Percy there was slain
   Sir John of Egerton,
Sir Robert Harcliffe and Sir William,
   Sir James that bold baròn ;

And with Sir George and with Sir James,
   Both Knights of good account ;
And good Sir Ralph Rabby there was slain,
   Whose prowess did surmount.

For Witherington needs must I wail
   As one in doleful dumps,
For when his legs were smitten off,
   He fought upon his stumps.

And with Earl Douglas there was slain
   Sir Hugh Montgomery,
And Sir Charles Murray that from field
   One foot would never flee ;

Sir Roger Hever of Harcliffe, too, —
   His sister's son was he, —
Sir David Lamb so well esteemed,
   But saved he could not be ;

And the Lord Maxwell in like case
   With Douglas he did die ;
Of twenty hundred Scottish spears,
   Scarce fifty-five did fly ;

Of fifteen hundred Englishmen
   Went home but fifty-three ;

The rest in Chevy Chase were slain,
  Under the greenwood tree.

Next day did many widows come
  Their husbands to bewail;
They washed their wounds in brinish tears,
  But all would not prevail.

Their bodies, bathed in purple blood,
  They bore with them away,
They kissed them dead a thousand times
  Ere they were clad in clay.

The news was brought to Edinborough
  Where Scotland's king did reign,
That brave Earl Douglas suddenly
  Was with an arrow slain.

" O heavy news!" King James can say,
  " Scotland may witness be
I have not any Captain more
  Of such account as he!"

Like tidings to King Henry came
  Within as short a space,
That Percy of Northumberland
  Was slain in Chevy Chase.

" Now God be with him!" said our king,
  " Sith it will no better be,
I trust I have within my realm
  Five hundred as good as he!

" Yet shall not Scots nor Scotland say
  But I will vengeance take,

And be revengèd on them all
  For brave Earl Percy's sake.''

This vow the king did well perform
  After, on Humble down;
In one day fifty knights were slain,
  With lords of great renown.

And of the rest, of small account,
  Did many hundreds die:
Thus endeth the hunting in Chevy Chase
  Made by the Earl Percy.

God save our King, and bless this land
  With plenty, joy, and peace;
And grant henceforth that foul debate
  'Twixt noble men may cease!

ANONYMOUS.
Old Ballad.

SIR PATRICK SPENS.[1]

THE king sits in Dunfermline town,
  Drinking the blude-red wine:
" O where will I get a skeely skipper
  To sail this new ship of mine? ''

[1] This is an old Scotch ballad of great antiquity. There is no historical incident which corresponds exactly to that narrated in the ballad, but the story belongs to the period of Alexander the Third, of Scotland, who died in 1285, and whose daughter married Eric, King of Norway. The daughter of Eric by this marriage, who was named Margaret and called the maid of Norway, became the heiress of the Scottish crown, and an effort was

O up and spake an eldern knight,
    Sat at the king's right knee:
" Sir Patrick Spens is the best sailor
    That ever sailed the sea."

Our king has written a braid letter,
    And sealed it with his hand,
And sent it to Sir Patrick Spens,
    Was walking on the strand.

" To Noroway, to Noroway,
    To Noroway o'er the faem;
The king's daughter of Noroway,
    'T is thou maun bring her hame!"

The first word that Sir Patrick read,
    Sae loud, loud laughed he,
The neist word that Sir Patrick read,
    The tear blindit his e'e.

" O wha is this has done this deed,
    And tauld the king o' me,
To send us out at this time of the year,
    To sail upon the sea?

" Be it wind, be it weet, be it hail, be it sleet,
    Our ship must sail the faem;
The king's daughter of Noroway,
    'T is we must fetch her hame."

made to marry her to Edward, son of Edward I. of England; but she died before her return to Scotland. She is the princess referred to in the ballad, and for whom Sir Patrick Spens was sent, according to the tradition. The version given here is taken from Sir Walter Scott's *Minstrelsy of the Scottish Border*, vol. i., p. 3.

They hoysed their sails on Monenday morn
　Wi' a' the speed they may;
They hae landed in Noroway
　Upon a Wodensday.

They hadna been a week, a week
　In Noroway, but twae,
When that the lords o' Noroway
　Began aloud to say:

"Ye Scottishmen spend a' our king's gowd
　And a' our queenè's fee."
"Ye lie, ye lie, ye liars loud!
　Fu' loud I hear ye lie!

"For I hae brought as much white monie
　As gane my men and me,
And I brought a half-fou o' gude red gowd
　Out oure the sea wi' me.

"Make ready, make ready, my merry men a'!
　Our gude ship sails the morn."
"Now, ever alake! my master dear,
　I fear a deadly storm!

"I saw the new moon, late yestreen,
　Wi' the auld moon in her arm;
And if we gang to sea, master,
　I fear we 'll come to harm."

They hadna sailed a league, a league,
　A league, but barely three,
When the lift grew dark, and the wind blew loud,
　And gurly grew the sea.

The ankers brak, and the topmasts lap,
    It was sic a deadly storm;
And the waves came o'er the broken ship
    Till a' her sides were torn.

" O where will I get a gude sailor
    To take my helm in hand,
Till I get up to the tall topmast,
    To see if I can spy land? "

" O here am I, a sailor gude,
    To take the helm in hand,
Till you go up to the tall topmast, —
    But I fear you 'll ne'er spy land."

He hadna gane a step, a step,
    A step, but barely ane,
When a boult flew out of our goodly ship,
    And the salt sea it came in.

" Gae fetch a web o' the silken claith,
    Another o' the twine,
And wap them into our ship's side
    And let na the sea come in."

They fetched a web o' the silken claith,
    Another o' the twine,
And they wapped them roun' that gude ship's side,
    But still the sea came in.

O laith, laith were our gude Scots lords
    To weet their cork-heeled shoon!
But lang or a' the play was played,
    They wat their hats aboon.

And mony was the feather-bed
  That floated on the faem,
And mony was the gude lord's son
  That never mair cam hame.

The ladyes wrange their fingers white,
  The maidens tore their hair;
A' for the sake of their true loves,
  For them they 'll see na mair.

O lang, lang may the ladyes sit,
  Wi' their fans into their hand,
Before they see Sir Patrick Spens
  Come sailing to the strand!

And lang, lang may the maidens sit,
  Wi' their gowd kaims in their hair,
A' waiting for their ain dear loves,
  For them they 'll see na mair.

'O forty miles off Aberdeen
  'T is fifty fathoms deep,
And there lies gude Sir Patrick Spens
  Wi' the Scots lords at his feet.

ANONYMOUS.
Old Ballad.

ARIEL'S SONG.

Come unto these yellow sands,
  And then take hands:
Courtsied when you have and kiss'd
  The wild waves whist,
Foot it featly here and there;
  And, sweet sprites, the burthen bear.
    Burthen : Hark, hark !
                Bow-wow.
    The watch-dogs bark :
                Bow-wow.
Hark, hark ! I hear
The strain of strutting chanticleer
Cry, Cock-a-diddle-dow.
          WILLIAM SHAKESPEARE.[1]
               The Tempest.

[1] WILLIAM SHAKESPEARE. Very little is known in regard to Shakespeare's life. He was the son of John and Mary Shakespeare, of Stratford-upon-Avon, where he was born about April 23, 1564. In his eighteenth year he married Anne Hathaway, of Shottery, a neighboring village. His wife was eight years older than he, and tradition says that the marriage was an unhappy one. About the year 1587 he left Stratford to seek his fortune in London as an actor and playwright. In 1589 he became a partner in the Blackfriars Theatre. He prospered in London, made money, and secured a competence, purchased property, about the beginning of the seventeenth century, in Stratford, and soon after returned there to live, a rich man for those days. There in his native village he died of a violent fever on April 23, 1616, his fifty-third birthday, probably, and while still in the prime of life. He was buried in the parish church and his tomb remains unaltered. Between his arrival in London and his death at Stratford he wrote the marvellous plays, and hardly less marvellous sonnets, which prove him to have been the greatest writer of any age, nation, or language. The poems in this collection are all taken from the plays in which they occur.

A SEA DIRGE.

Full fathom five thy father lies;
 Of his bones are coral made;
Those are pearls that were his eyes:
 Nothing of him that doth fade
But doth suffer a sea change
Into something rich and strange.
Sea-nymphs hourly ring his knell:
Hark ! now I hear them, — Ding-dong, bell.
 WILLIAM SHAKESPEARE.
 The Tempest.

ARIEL'S SONG.

Where the bee sucks there suck I:
In a cowslip's bell I lie;
There I couch when owls do cry.
On the bat's back I do fly
After summer merrily.
Merrily, merrily shall I live now,
Under the blossom that hangs on the bough.
 WILLIAM SHAKESPEARE.
 The Tempest.

SONG.

Pack, clouds, away, and welcome day,
 With night we banish sorrow;
Sweet air, blow soft; mount, larks, aloft
 To give my Love good-morrow !
Wings from the wind to please her mind,
 Notes from the lark, I 'll borrow ;

Bird, prune thy wing, nightingale, sing,
  To give my Love good-morrow;
    To give my Love good-morrow
    Notes from them both I'll borrow.

Wake from thy nest, Robin-red-breast;
  Sing, birds, in every furrow;
And from each hill let music shrill
  Give my fair Love good-morrow!
Blackbird and thrush in every bush,
  Stare, linnet, and cock-sparrow!
You pretty elves, amongst yourselves
  Sing my fair Love good-morrow;
    To give my Love good-morrow
    Sing, birds, in every furrow!
               Thomas Heywood.[1]

SONG.

Under the greenwood tree
Who loves to lie with me,
And turn his merry note
Unto the sweet bird's throat,
Come hither, come hither, come hither:
  Here shall he see
  No enemy
But winter and rough weather.

  Who doth ambition shun
  And loves to live i' the sun,

---

1 Thomas Heywood was an actor and a prolific dramatist
and prose writer of the Elizabethan school, who flourished in
London during the reigns of Elizabeth, James I., and Charles I.
His fame rests upon his plays, of which he said he had written
wholly or in part no less than two hundred and twenty.

Seeking the food he eats
And pleased with what he gets,
Come hither, come hither, come hither :
Here shall he see
No enemy
But winter and rough weather.

WILLIAM SHAKESPEARE.
As You Like It.

CHARACTER OF A HAPPY LIFE.

How happy is he born and taught
That serveth not another's will;
Whose armor is his honest thought
And simple truth his utmost skill!

Whose passions not his masters are,
Whose soul is still prepared for death,
Not tied unto the world with care
Of public fame, or private breath;

Who envies none that chance doth raise,
Or vice; who never understood
How deepest wounds are given by praise;
Nor rules of state, but rules of good:

Who hath his life from rumors freed,
Whose conscience is his strong retreat;
Whose state can neither flatterers feed,
Nor ruin make accusers great;

Who God doth late and early pray
More of his grace than gifts to lend;
And entertains the harmless day
With a well-chosen book or friend;

This man is freed from servile bands
Of hope to rise, or fear to fall;
Lord of himself, though not of lands;
And, having nothing, yet hath all.
SIR HENRY WOTTON.[1]

WINTER.

WHEN icicles hang by the wall
  And Dick the shepherd blows his nail
And Tom bears logs into the hall
  And milk comes frozen home in pail,
When blood is nipp'd and ways be foul,
Then nightly sings the staring owl,

Tu-whit;

Tu-who, a merry note,
While greasy Joan doth keel the pot.

When all aloud the wind doth blow
  And coughing drowns the parson's saw

---

1 SIR HENRY WOTTON was born at Boughton Hall, Kent (England), in 1568. He was educated at Oxford, where he showed a taste for poetry. After graduation he was employed in the diplomatic service and passed nine years on the Continent. On his return he became secretary to the Earl of Essex, and retired to Italy when his patron fell from power and was beheaded. He again returned to England on the accession of James I., who knighted him and employed him on several important foreign missions. He was made Provost of Eton College in 1627, and retained this office until his death, in 1639. He is best known as a statesman and diplomatist. His prose writings included political essays and memoirs. His poems were composed solely for his own amusement, but several of them, like that in the **text,** have great beauty of thought.

And birds sit brooding in the snow,
  And Marian's nose looks red and raw,
When roasted crabs hiss in the bowl,
Then nightly sings the staring owl,
                Tu-whit;
Tu-who, a merry note,
While greasy Joan doth keel the pot.
          WILLIAM SHAKESPEARE.
             Love's Labour 's Lost.

SONG.

TELL me where is fancy bred,
Or in the heart or in the head ?
How begot, how nourishèd ?
    Reply, reply.
It is engender'd in the eyes,
With gazing fed; and fancy dies
In the cradle where it lies.
    Let us all ring fancy's knell:
    I 'll begin it, — Ding-dong, bell.
          WILLIAM SHAKESPEARE.
            Merchant of Venice.

FAIRY'S SONG.

OVER hill, over dale,
  Thorough bush, thorough brier,
Over park, over pale,
  Thorough flood, thorough fire,
I do wander everywhere,
Swifter than the moon's sphere;

And I serve the fairy queen,
To dew her orbs upon the green.
The cowslips tall her pensioners be:
In their gold coats spots you see;
Those be rubies, fairy favors,
In those freckles live their savors:
I must go seek some dewdrops here
And hang a pearl in every cowslip's ear.
Farewell, thou lob of spirits; I 'll be gone:
Our queen and all our elves come here anon.

WILLIAM SHAKESPEARE.
Midsummer Night's Dream.

SONG OF THE FAIRIES.

You spotted snakes with double tongue,
   Thorny hedgehogs, be not seen;
Newts and blind-worms, do no wrong,
   Come not near our fairy queen.
   Philomel, with melody
   Sing in our sweet lullaby:
Lulla, lulla, lullaby, lulla, lulla, lullaby:
    Never harm,
    Nor spell nor charm,
   Come our lovely lady nigh;
   So good-night, with lullaby.

Weaving spiders, come not here;
   Hence, you long-legg'd spinners, hence!
Beetles black, approach not near;
   Worm nor snail, do no offence.
   Philomel, with melody, etc.

WILLIAM SHAKESPEARE.
Midsummer Night's Dream.

PUCK'S SONG.

Now the hungry lion roars,
    And the wolf behowls the moon ;
Whilst the heavy ploughman snores,
    All with weary task fordone.
Now the wasted brands do glow,
    Whilst the screech-owl, screeching loud,
Puts the wretch that lies in woe
    In remembrance of a shroud.
Now it is the time of night
    That the graves all gaping wide,
Every one lets forth his sprite
    In the church-way paths to glide:
And we fairies, that do run
    By the triple Hecate's team,
From the presence of the sun,
    Following darkness like a dream,
Now are frolic: not a mouse
Shall disturb this hallow'd house:
I am sent with broom before,
To sweep the dust behind the door.

            WILLIAM SHAKESPEARE.
              Midsummer Night's Dream.

SONG.

HARK, hark! the lark at heaven's gate sings,
    And Phœbus 'gins arise,
His steeds to water at those springs
    On chaliced flowers that lies ;
And winking Mary-buds begin

To ope their golden eyes:
With everything that pretty is,
My lady sweet, arise;
  Arise, arise.
          WILLIAM SHAKESPEARE.
                        Cymbeline.

SONG.

BLOW, blow, thou winter wind,
Thou art not so unkind
    As man's ingratitude;
Thy tooth is not so keen,
Because thou art not seen,
    Although thy breath be rude.
Heigh-ho! sing, heigh-ho! unto the green holly:
Most friendship is feigning, most loving mere folly:
    Then, heigh-ho, the holly!
    This life is most jolly.

Freeze, freeze, thou bitter sky,
That dost not bite so nigh
    As benefits forgot:
Though thou the waters warp,
Thy sting is not so sharp
    As friend remember'd not.
Heigh-ho! sing, heigh-ho! unto the green holly:
Most friendship is feigning, most loving mere folly:
    Then, heigh-ho, the holly!
    This life is most jolly.
          WILLIAM SHAKESPEARE.
                    As You Like It.

SONG.

FEAR no more the heat o' the sun,
　　Nor the furious winter's rages ;
Thou thy worldly task hast done,
　　Home art gone, and ta'en thy wages :
Golden lads and girls all must,
As chimney-sweepers, come to dust.

Fear no more the frown o' the great ;
　　Thou art past the tyrant's stroke ;
Care no more to clothe and eat ;
　　To thee, the reed is as the oak :
The sceptre, learning, physic, must
All follow this, and come to dust.

Fear no more the lightning-flash,
　　Nor the all-dreaded thunder-stone ;
Fear not slander, censure rash ;
　　Thou hast finish'd joy and moan :
All lovers young, all lovers must
Consign to thee, and come to dust.

　　No exorciser harm thee !
　　Nor no witchcraft charm thee !
　　Ghost unlaid forbear thee !
　　Nothing ill come near thee !
　　Quiet consummation have !
　　And renownèd be thy grave !
WILLIAM SHAKESPEARE.
Cymbeline.

SONG.

How should I your true love know
From another one ?
By his cockle hat and staff,
And his sandal shoon.

He is dead and gone, lady,
He is dead and gone;
At his head a grass-green turf,
At his heels a stone.

White his shroud as the mountain snow
Larded with sweet flowers;
Which bewept to the grave did go
With true-love showers.

WILLIAM SHAKESPEARE.
Hamlet.

THE NOBLE NATURE.

It is not growing like a tree
In bulk, doth make man better be;
Or standing long an oak, three hundred year,
To fall a log at last, dry, bald, and sere :
A lily of a day
Is fairer far in May,
Although it fall and die that night —
It was the plant and flower of Light.
In small proportions we just beauties see ;
And in short measures life may perfect be.

BEN JONSON.[1]

[1] BEN JONSON was born in Westminster in 1573.   His family

VIRTUE.

Sweet Day, so cool, so calm, so bright,
The bridal of the earth and sky,
The dew shall weep thy fall to-night;
           For thou must die.

Sweet Rose, whose hue angry and brave
Bids the rash gazer wipe his eye,
Thy root is ever in its grave,
           And thou must die.

Sweet Spring, full of sweet days and roses,
A box where sweets compacted lie,
My music shows ye have your closes,
           And all must die.

was of humble condition and he appears to have been taught the trade of a bricklayer. He received his education at Westminster School, and then went to Cambridge. He did not remain at the university, however, more than a month, but turned soldier in his sixteenth year and served in the wars in the Low Countries, where he gained distinction by his bravery. When he was nineteen he returned to England, married, and became an actor, and then a playwright. He was a friend of Shakespeare, and next to him, though at long distance, the most famous of the brilliant school of Elizabethan dramatists. In 1616 he was made poet-laureate of England, and died in 1637. He wrote many plays, of which the best and most famous are his early comedies. He was a witty, agreeable man, hot-tempered and quarrelsome, and always in conflict with his literary brethren. He was also a free liver, jovial and extravagant, and given to a profuse hospitality, so that despite his position as poet-laureate, and the success of his plays, he was always in money difficulties, and died in extreme poverty. Besides his plays, he wrote many short poems of great beauty of thought, language, and expression, of which the one given in this collection is an admirable example.

Only a sweet and virtuous soul,
Like season'd timber, never gives;
But, though the whole world turn to coal,
   Then chiefly lives.
     GEORGE HERBERT.[1]

TO BLOSSOMS.

FAIR pledges of a fruitful tree,
 Why do ye fall so fast ?
 Your date is not so past,
But you may stay yet here a while,
 To blush and gently smile;
   And go at last.

What, were ye born to be
 An hour or half's delight;
 And so to bid good-night ?
'T was pity Nature brought ye forth
 Merely to show your worth,
   And lose you quite.

But you are lovely leaves, where we
 May read how soon things have
 Their end, though ne'er so brave:

[1] GEORGE HERBERT was a descendant of the Earls of Pembroke and younger brother of the famous Lord Herbert of Cherbury. He was born at Montgomery Castle in Wales, in 1593, and was educated at Westminster School and at Trinity College, Cambridge. After graduation he took holy orders, became a minister of the Established Church and prebendary of Layton. In 1630 he was presented by King Charles I. to the living of Bemerton, and died while still a young man, in 1632. He wrote a great deal, both prose and verse, but always on religious and moral subjects, and was a man of gentle and devout nature and pure life.

And after they have shown their pride,
　Like you, a while, they glide
　　Into the grave.
　　　　　　Robert Herrick.[1]

TO LUCASTA, ON GOING TO THE WARS.

Tell me not, Sweet, I am unkind,
　That from the nunnery
Of thy chaste breast and quiet mind,
　To war and arms I fly.

True, a new mistress now I chase,
　The first foe in the field;
And with a stronger faith embrace
　A sword, a horse, a shield.

Yet this inconstancy is such
　As you too shall adore;
I could not love thee, Dear, so much,
　Loved I not Honor more.
　　　　　　Richard Lovelace.[2]

[1] Robert Herrick was born in London in 1591. He was a student at Cambridge, took orders, and was presented by Charles I. to the living of Dean Prior in Devonshire in 1629. He was deprived of his living by Cromwell in 1648. He then returned to London and lived in retirement, believing his connection with the church to be wholly severed, but on the restoration of Charles II. in 1660 he was reinstated in his living, which he held until his death, about the year 1674. He was eminent both as a divine and as a poet. His poems are chiefly secular and many very light, but it is as the author of them that he is chiefly remembered, although he wrote some verses on sacred subjects. Almost all his poems are very short, but they are very perfect and highly finished and many are among the very best of their kind.

[2] Richard Lovelace, the son of Sir William Lovelace, of

TO DAFFODILS.

FAIR daffodils, we weep to see
　　You haste away so soon:
As yet the early-rising sun
　　Has not attain'd his noon.
　　　　　Stay, stay,
　　Until the hasting day
　　　　　Has run
　　But to the even-song;
And, having prayed together, we
　　Will go with you along.

We have short time to stay, as you,
　　We have as short a spring;
As quick a growth to meet decay,
　　As you, or any thing.
　　　　　We die,
　　As your hours do, and dry
　　　　　Away,
　　Like to the summer's rain;
Or as the pearls of morning's dew,
　　Ne'er to be found again.

　　　　　　　ROBERT HERRICK.

Woolwich, Kent, was born in 1618. He came of age just at the outbreak of the civil war between king and Parliament. He at once embraced the royal cause, and after its defeat took service with the king of France and commanded a regiment when he was wounded at Dunkirk. He returned to England only to be thrown into prison, and after his release lingered in London in obscurity and poverty, and died there in 1658, a victim to the political troubles of the time. He was a handsome, gallant cavalier, and a good soldier as well as a poet. Most of his poems have little merit, but there are one or two besides that given here which have preserved his name from oblivion.

GO, LOVELY ROSE.

Go, lovely Rose!
Tell her, that wastes her time and me,
    That now she knows,
When I resemble her to thee,
How sweet and fair she seems to be.

Tell her that 's young
And shuns to have her graces spied,
    That hadst thou sprung
In deserts, where no men abide,
Thou must have uncommended died.

Small is the worth
Of beauty from the light retired:
    Bid her come forth,
Suffer herself to be desired,
And not blush so to be admired.

Then die! that she
The common fate of all things rare
    May read in thee:
How small a part of time they share
That are so wondrous sweet and fair!

EDMUND WALLER.[1]

[1] EDMUND WALLER was born in 1605. He was of good family, a connection of both John Hampden and Oliver Cromwell, and was a man of property. He was educated at Eton and Cambridge, entered Parliament in 1621, and, with occasional intervals, continued there through life, being elected the last time in 1685, as member for Saltash in the only Parliament of James II. In 1643 he was discovered in a plot against the Long Parliament, made abject submission, was fined £10,000, and forced into exile. He returned in 1653, and made terms with Crom-

"I'LL NEVER LOVE THEE MORE."

I.

My dear and only love, I pray
   That little world of thee
Be governed by no other sway
   Than purest monarchy;
For if confusion have a part,
   Which virtuous souls abhor,
And hold a *synod* in thine heart,
   I 'll never love thee more.

II.

As Alexander I will reign,
   And I will reign alone;
My thoughts did evermore disdain
   A rival on my throne.
He either fears his fate too much,
   Or his deserts are small,
That dares not put it to the touch,
   To gain or lose it all.

III.

But I will reign and govern still,
   And always give the law,
And have each subject at my will,
   And all to stand in awe;
But 'gainst my batteries if I find
   Thou kick, or vex me sore,
As that thou set me up a blind,
   I 'll never love thee more.

well, by whom he was protected. On the Restoration he again changed sides, and made his peace with Charles II., during whose reign he continued to flourish. He died in 1687. As a politician he was sharp, mean, and time-serving; as a poet, graceful and witty. He wrote much, both prose and verse.

IV.

And in the empire of thine heart,
   Where I should solely be,
If others do pretend a part,
   Or dare to vie with me,
Or if *committees* thou erect,
   And go on such a score,
I 'll laugh and sing at thy neglect,
   And never love thee more.

V.

But if thou wilt prove faithful, then,
   And constant of thy word,
I 'll make thee glorious by my pen,
   And famous by my sword;
I 'll serve thee in such noble ways
   Was never heard before;
I 'll crown and deck thee all with bays,
   And love thee more and more.
            MARQUIS OF MONTROSE.[1]

L'ALLEGRO.

HENCE, loathèd Melancholy,
   Of Cerberus and blackest Midnight born,
   In Stygian cave forlorn,

[1] JAMES GRAHAME, Marquis of Montrose, was born at Edinburgh in 1612. He took up arms for the king in the civil wars, and was made commander-in-chief of the Scottish forces by Charles I. in 1644. After a campaign of great brilliancy he was finally defeated by the Covenanters under Leslie at Philiphaugh, in 1645. He fled to the Continent, but soon returned to Scotland and again took arms. He was defeated, taken prisoner, and executed at Edinburgh in May, 1650. He was the most remarkable and the most successful of the Cavalier generals.

'Mongst horrid shapes, and shrieks, and sights un-
    holy !
Find out some uncouth cell
    Where brooding Darkness spreads his jealous wings
And the night-raven sings;
    There under ebon shades, and low-brow'd rocks
As ragged as thy locks,
    In dark Cimmerian desert ever dwell.

But come, thou Goddess fair and free,
In heaven yclep'd Euphrosyne,
And by men, heart-easing Mirth,
Whom lovely Venus at a birth
With two sister Graces more
To ivy-crownèd Bacchus bore:
Or whether (as some sager sing)
The frolic wind that breathes the spring,
Zephyr, with Aurora playing,
As he met her once a-Maying,
There on beds of violets blue
And fresh-blown roses wash'd in dew
Fill'd·her with thee, a daughter fair,
So buxom, blithe, and debonair.

Haste thee, Nymph, and bring with thee
Jest, and youthful jollity,
Quips, and cranks, and wanton wiles,
Nods, and becks, and wreathèd smiles
Such as hang on Hebe's cheek
And love to live in dimple sleek ;
Sport that wrinkled Care derides,
And Laughter holding both his sides, —
Come, and trip it as you go
On the light fantastic toe ;
And in thy right hand lead with thee

The mountain-nymph, sweet Liberty;
And if I give thee honor due,
Mirth, admit me of thy crew,
To live with her, and live with thee,
In unreprovèd pleasures free;
To hear the lark begin his flight
And singing startle the dull night
From· his watch-tower in the skies
Till the dappled dawn doth rise ;
Then to come, in spite of sorrow,
And at my window bid good-morrow
Through the sweet-briar, or the vine,
Or the twisted eglantine:
While the cock with lively din
Scatters the rear of darkness thin,
And to the stack, or the barn-door,
Stoutly struts his dames before:
Oft listening how the hounds and horn
Cheerly rouse the slumbering morn,
From the side of some hoar hill,
Through the high wood echoing shrill.
Sometime walking, not unseen,
By hedge-row elms, on hillocks green,
Right against the eastern gate
Where the great Sun begins his state
Robed in flames and amber light,
The clouds in thousand liveries dight;
While the ploughman, near at hand,
Whistles o'er the furrow'd land,
And the milkmaid singeth blithe,
And the mower whets his scythe,
And every shepherd tells his tale
Under the hawthorn in the dale.
  Straight mine eye hath caught new pleasures
Whilst the landscape round it measures;

Russet lawns, and fallows gray,
Where the nibbling flocks do stray;
Mountains on whose barren breast
The laboring clouds do often rest;
Meadows trim with daisies pied,
Shallow brooks, and rivers wide;
Towers and battlements it sees
Bosom'd high in tufted trees,
Where perhaps some Beauty lies,
The cynosure of neighboring eyes.
Hard by, a cottage chimney smokes
From betwixt two aged oaks,
Where Corydon and Thyrsis, met,
Are at their savory dinner set
Of herbs and other country messes
Which the neat-handed Phillis dresses;
And then in haste her bower she leaves
With Thestylis to bind the sheaves;
Or, if the earlier season lead,
To the tann'd haycock in the mead.
   Sometimes with secure delight
The upland hamlets will invite,
When the merry bells ring round,
And the jocund rebecks sound
To many a youth and many a maid,
Dancing in the chequer'd shade;
And young and old come forth to play
On a sun-shine holy-day,
Till the live-long daylight fail;
Then to the spicy nut-brown ale,
With stories told of many a feat,
How faery Mab the junkets eat;
She was pinch'd and pull'd, she said;
And he, by friar's lantern led,
Tells how the drudging Goblin sweat

To earn his cream-bowl duly set,
When in one night, ere glimpse of morn,
His shadowy flail hath thresh'd the corn
That ten day-laborers could not end;
Then lies him down the lubber fiend,
And, stretch'd out all the chimney's length,
Basks at the fire his hairy strength;
And crop-full out of doors he flings,
Ere the first cock his matin rings.
　　Thus done the tales, to bed they creep,
By whispering winds soon lull'd asleep.
　　Tower'd cities please us then,
And the busy hum of men,
Where throngs of knights and barons bold
In weeds of peace high triumphs hold,
With store of ladies, whose bright eyes
Rain influence, and judge the prize
Of wit or arms, while both contend
To win her grace, whom all commend.
There let Hymen oft appear
In saffron robe, with taper clear,
And pomp, and feast, and revelry;
With mask, and antique pageantry;
Such sights as youthful poets dream
On summer eves by haunted stream.
Then to the well-trod stage anon,
If Jonson's learned sock be on,
Or sweetest Shakespeare, Fancy's child,
Warble his native wood-notes wild.
　　And ever against eating cares
Lap me in soft Lydian airs
Married to immortal verse,
Such as the meeting soul may pierce
In notes, with many a winding bout
Of linkèd sweetness long drawn out,

With wanton heed and giddy cunning,
The melting voice through mazes running,
Untwisting all the chains that tie
The hidden soul of harmony,
That Orpheus' self may heave his head
From golden slumber on a bed
Of heap'd Elysian flowers, and hear
Such strains as would have won the ear
Of Pluto, to have quite set free
His half-regained Eurydice.
    These delights if thou canst give,
Mirth, with thee I mean to live.

JOHN MILTON.[1]

[1] JOHN MILTON, the son of a scrivener of the same name, was born in London, in Bread Street, December 9, 1608. He was educated by Dr. Young, a famous Puritan divine, then at St. Paul's School, and finally at Christ's College, where he first wrote verses in Latin and English. After a brief stay at his father's, when were written some of his more famous short poems, including the two given here, he travelled in Italy, where he met Galileo. In 1639 he returned to England and soon drifted into the great struggle between king and Parliament then just beginning. He soon won the foremost place as a writer on political and religious questions, and in 1649 was made Latin Secretary of the Commonwealth, a post which he continued to hold under Cromwell. He was the chief defender, with the pen, of the Commonwealth and the Protector. About 1653 he became totally blind, owing to incessant work, made necessary by his continual controversies. At the Restoration his life was spared, but he was obliged to live in obscurity. It was at this period that he returned to poetry and wrote *Paradise Lost* and *Paradise Regained*, the greatest epic poems in the English language, and which have caused him to be ranked next to Shakespeare among English poets. He was a man of profound learning and a wonderful linguist. His prose writings were voluminous and chiefly controversial. The style seems heavy and involved, if judged by the standard of the present day, but it is nevertheless magnificent, rich, and powerful. It is as the great literary genius of Puritan England, and as the

IL PENSEROSO.

HENCE, vain deluding joys,
  The brood of Folly without father bred !
How little you bestead
  Or fill the fixèd mind with all your toys !
Dwell in some idle brain,
  And fancies fond with gaudy shapes possess
As thick and numberless
  As the gay motes that people the sunbeams,
Or likest hovering dreams,
  The fickle pensioners of Morpheus' train.

But hail, thou goddess sage and holy,
Hail, divinest Melancholy !
Whose saintly visage is too bright
To hit the sense of human sight,
And therefore to our weaker view
O'erlaid with black, staid wisdom's hue;
Black, but such as in esteem
Prince Memnon's sister might beseem,
Or that starr'd Ethiop queen that strove
To set her beauty's praise above
The sea-nymphs, and their powers offended:
Yet thou art higher far descended:
Thee bright-haired Vesta, long of yore,
To solitary Saturn bore;
His daughter she; in Saturn's reign
Such mixture was not held a stain:
Oft in glimmering bowers and glades
He met her, and in secret shades
Of woody Ida's inmost grove,
While yet there was no fear of Jove.

poet of Puritanism, that Milton is most interesting. He died in
November, 1674, at his home in Bunhill Fields.

Come, pensive nun, devout and pure,
Sober, steadfast, and demure,
All in a robe of darkest grain
Flowing with majestic train,
And sable stole of cypres lawn
Over thy decent shoulders drawn:
Come, but keep thy wonted state,
With even step, and musing gait,
And looks commercing with the skies,
Thy rapt soul sitting in thine eyes:
There, held in holy passion still,
Forget thyself to marble, till
With a sad leaden downward cast
Thou fix them on the earth as fast:
And join with thee calm Peace and Quiet,
Spare Fast that oft with gods doth diet,
And hears the Muses in a ring
Aye round about Jove's altar sing:
And add to these retirèd Leisure,
That in trim gardens takes his pleasure:
But first, and chiefest, with thee bring
Him that yon soars on golden wing,
Guiding the fiery-wheelèd throne,
The cherub Contemplatiòn;
And the mute Silence hist along,
'Less Philomel will deign a song
In her sweetest, saddest plight,
Smoothing the rugged brow of night,
While Cynthia checks her dragon yoke
Gently o'er the accustom'd oak.
Sweet bird, that shunn'st the noise of folly,
Most musical, most melancholy!
Thee, chantress, oft, the woods among,
I woo, to hear thy even-song;
And missing thee, I walk unseen

On the dry, smooth-shaven green,
To behold the wandering moon
Riding near her highest noon,
Like one that had been led astray
Through the heavens' wide pathless way,
And oft, as if her head she bow'd,
Stooping through a fleecy cloud.
   Oft, on a plat of rising ground,
I hear the far-off curfeu sound
Over some wide-water'd shore,
Swinging slow with sullen roar:
Or, if the air will not permit,
Some still removèd place will fit,
Where glowing embers through the room
Teach light to counterfeit a gloom;
Far from all resort of mirth,
Save the cricket on the hearth,
Or the bellman's drowsy charm
To bless the doors from nightly harm.
   Or let my lamp at midnight hour
Be seen in some high lonely tower,
Where I may oft out-watch the Bear
With thrice-great Hermes, or unsphere
The spirit of Plato, to unfold
What worlds or what vast regions hold
The immortal mind that hath forsook
Her mansion in this fleshly nook:
And of those demons that are found
In fire, air, flood, or under-ground,
Whose power hath a true consent
With planet, or with element.
Some time let gorgeous Tragedy
In sceptred pall come sweeping by,
Presenting Thebes, or Pelops' line,
Or the tale of Troy divine;

Or what (though rare) of later age
Ennobled hath the buskin'd stage.
　　But, O sad Virgin, that thy power
Might raise Musæus from his bower,
Or bid the soul of Orpheus sing
Such notes as, warbled to the string,
Drew iron tears down Pluto's cheek
And made Hell grant what Love did seek!
Or call up him that left half-told
The story of Cambuscan bold,
Of Camball, and of Algarsife,
And who had Canace to wife
That own'd the virtuous ring and glass;
And of the wondrous horse of brass
On which the Tartar king did ride:
And if aught else great bards beside
In sage and solemn tunes have sung
Of turneys, and of trophies hung,
Of forests, and enchantments drear,
Where more is meant than meets the ear.
　　Thus, Night, oft see me in thy pale career,
Till civil-suited Morn appear,
Not trick'd and frounced as she was wont
With the Attic Boy to hunt,
But kerchieft in a comely cloud,
While rocking winds are piping loud,
Or usher'd with a shower still,
When the gust hath blown his fill,
Ending on the rustling leaves
With minute drops from off the eaves.
And when the sun begins to fling
His flaring beams, me, Goddess, bring
To archèd walks of twilight groves,
And shadows brown, that Sylvan loves,
Of pine, or monumental oak,

Where the rude axe, with heavèd stroke,
Was never heard the nymphs to daunt
Or fright them from their hallow'd haunt;
There in close covert by some brook
Where no profaner eye may look,
Hide me from day's garish eye,
While the bee with honey'd thigh
That at her flowery work doth sing,
And the waters murmuring,
With such concert as they keep,
Entice the dewy-feather'd Sleep;
And let some strange mysterious dream
Wave at his wings in aery stream
Of lively portraiture display'd,
Softly on my eyelids laid:
And, as I wake, sweet music breathe
Above, about, or underneath,
Sent by some spirit to mortals good,
Or the unseen genius of the wood.
    But let my due feet never fail
To walk the studious cloister's pale,
And love the high-embowèd roof,
With antique pillars massy proof,
And storied widows richly dight,
Casting a dim religious light:
There let the pealing organ blow
To the full-voiced quire below
In service high and anthems clear,
As may with sweetness, through mine ear,
Dissolve me into ecstasies
And bring all heaven before mine eyes.
    And may at last my weary age
Find out the peaceful hermitage,
The hairy gown and mossy cell,
Where I may sit and rightly spell

Of every star that heaven doth show,
And every herb that sips the dew;
Till old experience do attain
To something like prophetic strain.
    These pleasures, Melancholy, give,
And I with thee will choose to live.

JOHN MILTON.

"TO ALL YOU LADIES NOW ON LAND."

SONG WRITTEN AT SEA.

To all you ladies now on land,
    We men at sea indite ;
But first would have you understand
    How hard it is to write :
The Muses now, and Neptune too,
We must implore to write to you.

For tho' the Muses should prove kind,
    And fill our empty brain ;
Yet if rough Neptune rouse the wind,
    To wave the azure main,
Our paper, pen, and ink, and we
Roll up and down our ships at sea.

Then, if we write not by each post,
    Think not we are unkind ;
Nor yet conclude our ships are lost
    By Dutchmen or by wind ;
Our tears we 'll send a speedier way :
The tide shall bring them twice a day.

The king, with wonder and surprise,
    Will swear the seas grow bold ;

Because the tides will higher rise
   Than e'er they did of old :
But let him know it is our tears
Bring floods of grief to Whitehall-stairs.

Should foggy Opdam chance to know
   Our sad and dismal story,
The Dutch would scorn so weak a foe,
   And quit their fort at Goree;
For what resistance can they find
From men who 've left their hearts behind !

Let wind and weather do its worst,
   Be you to us but kind;
Let Dutchmen vapor, Spaniards curse,
   No sorrow we shall find :
'T is then no matter how things go,
Or who 's our friend, or who 's our foe

To pass our tedious hours away,
   We throw a merry main :
Or else at serious ombre play;
   But why should we in vain
Each other's ruin thus pursue ?
We were undone when we left you.

But now our fears tempestuous grow
   And cast our hopes away;
Whilst you, regardless of our wo,
   Sit careless at a play :
Perhaps permit some happier man
To kiss your hand, or flirt your fan.

When any mournful tune you hear,
   That dies in every note,

As if it sigh'd with each man's care
  For being so remote :
Think then how often love we 've made
To you, when all those tunes were play'd.

In justice, you cannot refuse
  To think of our distress,
When we for hopes of honor lose
  Our certain happiness ;
All these designs are but to prove
Ourselves more worthy of your love.

And now we 've told you all our loves,
  And likewise all our fears,
In hopes this declaration moves
  Some pity for our tears ;
Let 's hear of no inconstancy,
We have too much of that at sea.
      CHARLES SACKVILLE, *Earl of Dorset.*[1]

SONG FOR SAINT CECILIA'S DAY.

1687.

FROM Harmony, from heavenly Harmony
  This universal frame began :
When nature underneath a heap
  Of jarring atoms lay

[1] CHARLES SACKVILLE, Viscount Buckhurst, and afterwards Earl of Dorset, was born in 1637. In his youth he was one of the wildest and most debauched of all the courtiers who surrounded Charles II., but he was always a man of refined tastes, and a patron of literature. He died in 1706. This song, the best known of his poems, was written on board the English fleet at the time of the first war between Charles II. and the Dutch, and on the eve of battle.

And could not heave her head,
The tuneful voice was heard from high,
    Arise, ye more than dead!
Then cold, and hot, and moist, and dry,
In order to their stations leap,
    And Music's power obey.
From Harmony, from heavenly Harmony
    This universal frame began :
    From Harmony to Harmony
Through all the compass of the notes it ran,
The diapason closing full in man.

What passion cannot Music raise and quell ?
    When Jubal struck the chorded shell
    His listening brethren stood around,
    And, wondering, on their faces fell
    To worship that celestial sound.
Less than a God they thought there could not dwell
    Within the hollow of that shell
    That spoke so sweetly and so well.
What passion cannot Music raise and quell?

    The trumpet's loud clangor
        Excites us to arms,
    With shrill notes of anger
        And mortal alarms,
    The double double double beat
        Of the thundering drum
Cries, "Hark! the foes come;
Charge, charge, 't is too late to retreat ! "

    The soft complaining flute
    In dying notes discovers.
    The woes of hopeless lovers,
Whose dirge is whispered by the warbling lute.

Sharp violins proclaim
Their jealous pangs and desperation,
Fury, frantic indignation,
Depth of pains and height of passion
For the fair disdainful dame.

But Ó! what art can teach,
What human voice can reach,
      The sacred organ's praise?
Notes inspiring holy love,
Notes that wing their heavenly ways
      To mend the choirs above.

Orpheus could lead the savage race,
And trees uprooted left their place
      Sequacious of the lyre:
But bright Cecilia raised the wonder higher:
When to her organ vocal breath was given
An Angel heard, and straight appear'd —
      Mistaking Earth for Heaven!

GRAND CHORUS.

As from the power of sacred lays
      The spheres began to move,
And sung the great Creator's praise
      To all the blest above;
So when the last and dreadful hour
This crumbling pageant shall devour,
The trumpet shall be heard on high,
The dead shall live, the living die,
And music shall untune the sky.

JOHN DRYDEN.[1]

[1] JOHN DRYDEN, the most famous of the poets of the Restoration, was born in 1631, and educated at Westminster School and Trinity College, Cambridge. He was bred a Puritan, but went

VERSION OF THE NINETEENTH PSALM.

I.

THE spacious firmament on high,
With all the blue ethereal sky,
And spangled heavens, a shining frame,
Their great Original proclaim:
Th' unwearied sun from day to day
Does his Creator's power display,
And publishes to every land
The work of an Almighty hand.

II.

Soon as the evening shades prevail,
The moon takes up the wondrous tale,
And nightly to the list'ning earth
Repeats the story of her birth:
Whilst all the stars that round her burn,
And all the planets, in their turn,
Confirm the tidings as they roll,
And spread the truth from pole to pole.

III.

What though, in solemn silence, all
Move round the dark terrestrial ball?
What tho' nor real voice nor sound
Amid their radiant orbs be found?

over to Charles II. at the Restoration and became a playwright,
essayist, and poet. He was received into favor at court, and
was made poet-laureate in 1668. He wrote many plays, all of
which are now deservedly forgotten, and some prose essays. His
fame rests on his shorter poems, his satires of great force and
brilliancy, and his translation of Virgil. He died May 1, 1700,
and was buried in Westminster Abbey.

> In reason's ear they all rejoice,
> And utter forth a glorious voice,
> Forever singing, as they shine,
> " The hand that made us is divine."
> JOSEPH ADDISON.[1]

THE DYING CHRISTIAN TO HIS SOUL.

> VITAL Spark of heavenly flame,
> Quit, O quit this mortal frame!
> Trembling, hoping, lingering, flying,
> O the pain, the bliss of dying!
> Cease, fond nature, cease thy strife,
> And let me languish into life!
>
> Hark! they whisper; angels say,
> Sister spirit, come away.
> What is this absorbs me quite,
> Steals my senses, shuts my sight,

[1] JOSEPH ADDISON, the eldest son of Lancelot Addison, Dean of Lichfield, was born at Milston, Wiltshire, in 1672. He was educated at the Charter House, and afterwards at Oxford, where he had a high reputation for classical scholarship. He at once ventured into literature, and a successful poem gained him a pension from King William. He then travelled abroad, and on his return in 1704 attracted the notice of Queen Anne's government by a poem on the battle of Blenheim, entitled *The Campaign.* The favor thus gained soon bore fruit. He was made Commissioner of Appeals and under Secretary of State, and ably defended with his pen the Whig ministry. In 1716 he married the Countess of Warwick, and died at Holland House, London, in the forty-eighth year of his age. Addison wrote the tragedy of *Cato,* and some minor poems, but his literary fame rests on the essays contributed to the *Spectator* and *Tatler.* These essays, abounding in wit, humor, and refined criticism, give Addison his position as one of the first of English prose writers.

Drowns my spirits, draws my breath ?
Tell me, my Soul! can this be death?

The world recedes; it disappears ;
Heaven opens on my eyes ; my ears
With sounds seraphic ring:
Lend, lend your wings! I mount! I fly!
O grave! where is thy victory?
O death! where is thy sting?

ALEXANDER POPE.[1]

SOLITUDE.[2]

HAPPY the man whose wish and care
A few paternal acres bound,
Content to breathe his native air
In his own ground.

[1] ALEXANDER POPE, the son of a merchant, was born in London in May, 1688. He was deformed in body, and as his parents were Roman Catholics he was educated at home or at private schools. He was a boy of great precocity and began at an early period his literary career, to which he was wholly devoted. All his important works, including, of course, the translations of Homer, are in verse. Some are poems on fashionable society, others philosophical and critical, and others still are satire, in which Pope excelled. In the various fields of original poetry which he entered he has hardly ever been surpassed, and was, with the exception of Swift, the greatest of the remarkable group of literary men known as the school of Queen Anne. Pope passed his life quietly at Twickenham, in the neighborhood of London, where he saw the best society of the time, and carried on the bitter paper warfare into which his vanity and irritable temper constantly led him. He died at Twickenham in 1744.

[2] Written when the author was about twelve years old.

Whose herds with milk, whose fields with bread,
Whose flocks supply him with attire,
Whose trees in summer yield him shade,
In winter fire.

Bless'd who can unconcern'dly find
Hours, days, and years slide soft away,
In health of body, peace of mind,
Quiet by day;

Sound sleep by night; study and ease
Together mixed; sweet recreation;
And innocence, which most does please,
With meditation.

Thus let me live, unseen, unknown,
Thus unlamented let me die;
Steal from the world, and not a stone
Tell where I lie.

ALEXANDER POPE.

TO A CHILD OF QUALITY.[1]

LORDS, knights, and squires, the numerous band,
  That wear the fair Miss Mary's fetters,
Were summon'd by her high command,
  To show their passions by their letters.

My pen among the rest I took,
  Lest those bright eyes that cannot read
Should dart their kindling fires, and look
  The power they have to be obey'd.

[1] Five years old, 1704; the author then forty.

Nor quality, nor reputation,
　Forbid me yet my flame to tell,
Dear five years old befriends my passion,
　And I may write till she can spell.

For, while she makes her silk worms beds
　With all the tender things I swear,
Whilst all the house my passion reads,
　In papers round her baby's hair;

She may receive and own my flame,
　For, though the strictest prudes should know it,
She 'll pass for a most virtuous dame,
　And I for an unhappy poet.

Then too, alas ! when she shall tear
　The lines some younger rival sends,
She 'll give me leave to write, I fear,
　And we shall still continue friends.

For as our different ages move,
　'T is so ordained (would Fate but mend it!)
That I shall be past making love,
　When she begins to comprehend it.

MATTHEW PRIOR.[1]

[1] MATTHEW PRIOR was born in Devonshire in 1664 and adopted by his uncle, the landlord of a London tavern, who sent him to Westminster School. His cleverness and knowledge of Latin are said to have attracted the notice of Lord Dorset, who sent him to Cambridge, and who afterwards certainly pushed his fortunes. He entered politics, held many important offices. both at home and in diplomatic service, and finally rose to be minister at Paris, when Lord Bolingbroke was at the head of affairs, during the last years of Queen Anne. On the death of the queen and the fall of the Tories from power Prior was thrown into prison by the Whigs, but was discharged without a trial. He died at Wimpole

ELEGY WRITTEN IN A COUNTRY CHURCH-YARD.

THE curfew tolls the knell of parting day,
The lowing herd winds slowly o'er the lea,
The ploughman homeward plods his weary way,
And leaves the world to darkness and to me.

Now fades the glimmering landscape on the sight,
And all the air a solemn stillness holds,
Save where the beetle wheels his droning flight,
And drowsy tinklings lull the distant folds:

Save that from yonder ivy-mantled tower
The moping owl does to the moon complain
Of such as, wandering near her secret bower,
Molest her ancient solitary reign.

Beneath those rugged elms, that yew-tree's shade,
Where heaves the turf in many a mouldering heap,
Each in his narrow cell forever laid,
The rude forefathers of the hamlet sleep.

The breezy call of incense-breathing morn,
The swallow twittering from the straw-built shed,
The cock's shrill clarion, or the echoing horn,
No more shall rouse them from their lowly bed.

in 1721. During all his active life he never lost his taste for letters, or ceased to write both prose and verse. Besides his memoirs he left many poems, almost all of a light and easy character, but displaying wit, fancy, and humor. He was a genial man and agreeable companion, but he was a loose liver, extravagant, and had low tastes in some respects which he freely indulged.

For them no more the blazing hearth shall burn,
Or busy housewife ply her evening care:
No children run to lisp their sire's return,
Or climb his knees the envied kiss to share.

Oft did the harvest to their sickle yield,
Their furrow oft the stubborn glebe has broke;
How jocund did they drive their team afield!
How bow'd the woods beneath their sturdy stroke!

Let not Ambition mock their useful toil,
Their homely joys, and destiny obscure;
Nor Grandeur hear with a disdainful smile
The short and simple annals of the poor.

The boast of heraldry, the pomp of power,
And all that beauty, all that wealth e'er gave,
Await alike th' inevitable hour:
The paths of glory lead but to the grave.

Nor you, ye Proud, impute to these the fault
If Memory o'er their tomb no trophies raise,
Where through the long-drawn aisle and fretted vault
The pealing anthem swells the note of praise

Can storied urn or animated bust
Back to its mansion call the fleeting breath?
Can Honor's voice provoke the silent dust,
Or Flattery soothe the dull, cold ear of Death?

Perhaps in this neglected spot is laid
Some heart once pregnant with celestial fire;
Hands that the rod of Empire might have sway'd,
Or waked to ecstasy the living lyre:

But Knowledge to their eyes her ample page,
Rich with the spoils of time, did ne'er unroll;
Chill Penury repress'd their noble rage,
And froze the genial current of the soul.

Full many a gem of purest ray serene
The dark unfathom'd caves of ocean bear:
Full many a flower is born to blush unseen,
And waste its sweetness on the desert air.

Some village-Hampden, that with dauntless breast
The little tyrant of his fields withstood,
Some mute, inglorious Milton here may rest,
Some Cromwell, guiltless of his country's blood.

Th' applause of list'ning senates to command,
The threats of pain and ruin to despise,
To scatter plenty o'er a smiling land,
And read their history in a nation's eyes,

Their lot forbade; nor circumscribed alone
Their growing virtues, but their crimes confined;
Forbade to wade through slaughter to a throne,
And shut the gates of mercy on mankind;

The struggling pangs of conscious truth to hide,
To quench the blushes of ingenuous shame,
Or heap the shrine of Luxury and Pride
With incense kindled at the Muse's flame.

Far from the madding crowd's ignoble strife
Their sober wishes never learn'd to stray;
Along the cool, sequester'd vale of life
They kept the noiseless tenor of their way.

Yet e'en these bones from insult to protect,
Some frail memorial still erected nigh,
With uncouth rhymes and shapeless sculpture deck'd,
Implores the passing tribute of a sigh.

Their name, their years, spelt by th' unletter'd Muse,
The place of fame and elegy supply:
And many a holy text around she strews
That teach the rustic moralist to die.

For who, to dumb forgetfulness a prey,
This pleasing, anxious being e'er resign'd,
Left the warm precincts of the cheerful day,
Nor cast one longing, lingering look behind?

On some fond breast the parting soul relies,
Some pious drops the closing eye requires ;
E'en from the tomb the voice of Nature cries,
E'en in our ashes live their wonted fires.

For thee, who, mindful of th' unhonor'd dead,
Dost in these lines their artless tale relate;
If chance, by lonely Contemplation led,
Some kindred spirit shall inquire thy fate, —

Haply some hoary-headed swain may say,
Oft have we seen him at the peep of dawn
Brushing with hasty steps the dews away,
To meet the sun upon the upland lawn;

There, at the foot of yonder nodding beech
That wreathes its old fantastic roots so high,
His listless length at noontide would he stretch,
And pore upon the brook that babbles by.

Hard by yon wood, now smiling as in scorn,
Muttering his wayward fancies he would rove;
Now drooping, woeful-wan, like one forlorn,
Or crazed with care, or cross'd in hopeless love.

One morn I miss'd him on the custom'd hill,
Along the heath, and near his favorite tree;
Another came; nor yet beside the rill,
Nor up the lawn, nor at the wood was he;

The next, with dirges due in sad array
Slow through the church-way path we saw him borne,—
Approach and read (for thou canst read) the lay
Graved on the stone beneath yon aged thorn.

THE EPITAPH.

Here rests his head upon the lap of Earth
A Youth to Fortune and to Fame unknown;
Fair Science frown'd not on his humble birth,
And Melancholy mark'd him for her own.

Large was his bounty, and his soul sincere;
Heaven did a recompense as largely send:
He gave to Misery, all he had, a tear,
He gain'd from Heaven, 't was all he wish'd, a friend.

No farther seek his merits to disclose,
Or draw his frailties from their dread abode
(There they alike in trembling hope repose),
The bosom of his Father and his God.

THOMAS GRAY.[1]

[1] THOMAS GRAY was born in London, in December, 1716.
Through the care of his mother he received a good education,
first at Eton and then at Cambridge. After leaving the university he travelled on the Continent with Horace Walpole, return-

THE BARD.[1]

PINDARIC ODE.

" RUIN seize thee, ruthless King!
  Confusion on thy banners wait !
Tho' fanned by Conquest's crimson wing
  They mock the air with idle state.
Helm, nor hauberk's twisted mail,
Nor e'en thy virtues, tyrant, shall avail
To save thy secret soul from nightly fears,
From Cambria's curse, from Cambria's tears! ''
Such were the sounds that o'er the crested pride
  Of the first Edward scattered wild dismay,
As down the steep of Snowdon's shaggy side
  He wound with toilsome march his long array.
Stout Glo'ster stood aghast in speechless trance;
" To arms! " cried Mortimer, and couched his quiver-
      ing lance.

ing in 1741. The following year he settled at Cambridge, where, with the exception of occasional visits to London, he passed the remainder of his life. He refused the position of poet-laureate in 1757, and in 1769 was made professor of modern history. He died of an attack of the gout in 1771. He was a ripe scholar and led a retired life of learned leisure, which was most congenial to his modest disposition and studious tastes. He published but few poems, as he was never satisfied with his work, and passed an endless time in polishing everything he wrote. The few poems he did publish are all most perfect in execution, and the Elegy is one of the most famous poems in the language. It was of the Elegy that Wolfe remarked, when about to attack the French on the Heights of Abraham, that he would rather have written that poem than take Quebec.

1 This poem refers to the conquest of Wales by Edward I., and is supposed to be the prophecy of one of the bards or harpers who figured conspicuously among the Welsh.

On a rock, whose haughty brow
Frowns o'er cold Conway's foaming flood,
  Robed in the sable garb of woe,
With haggard eyes the Poet stood;
(Loose his beard and hoary hair
Stream'd, like a meteor, to the troubled air)
And with a master's hand, and prophet's fire,
Struck the deep sorrows of his lyre.
" Hark, how each giant oak, and desert-cave,
  Sighs to the torrent's awful voice beneath!
O'er thee, O King! their hundred arms they wave,
  Revenge on thee in hoarser murmurs breathe;
Vocal no more, since Cambria's fatal day,
To high-born Hoel's harp, or soft Llewellyn's lay.

  " Cold is Cadwallo's tongue,
  That hush'd the stormy main:
Brave Urien sleeps upon his craggy bed:
  Mountains, ye mourn in vain
  Modred, whose magic song
Made huge Plinlimmon bow his cloud-topt head.
  On dreary Arvon's shore they lie,
Smeared with gore, and ghastly pale:
Far, far aloof th' affrighted ravens sail;
  The famished eagle screams, and passes by.
Dear lost companions of my tuneful art,
  Dear as the light that visits these sad eyes,
Dear as the ruddy drops that warm my heart,
  Ye died amidst your dying country's cries —
No more I weep. They do not sleep.
  On yonder cliffs, a griesly band,
I see them sit, they linger yet,
  Avengers of their native land:
With me in dreadful harmony they join,
And weave with bloody hands the tissue of thy line.

"Weave the warp, and weave the woof,
    The winding-sheet of Edward's race.
Give ample room, and verge enough
    The characters of hell to trace.
Mark the year, and mark the night,
When Severn shall reëcho with affright
The shrieks of death thro' Berkley's roof that ring,
Shrieks of an agonizing king! [1]
    She-wolf of France, with unrelenting fangs,
That tear'st the bowels of thy mangled mate,
    From thee be born, who o'er thy country hangs
The scourge of heaven.   What terrors round him wait!
Amazement in his van, with flight combined,
And Sorrow's faded form, and Solitude behind.

" Mighty victor, mighty lord! [2]
    Low on his funeral couch he lies!
No pitying heart, no eye, afford
    A tear to grace his obsequies.
Is the sable warrior fled? [3]
Thy son is gone.   He rests among the dead.
The swarm that in thy noontide beam were born?
Gone to salute the rising morn.
Fair laughs the morn, and soft the zephyr blows,
    While proudly riding o'er the azure realm
In gallant trim the gilded vessel goes,
    Youth on the prow, and Pleasure at the helm,
Regardless of the sweeping whirlwind's sway,
That, hush'd in grim repose, expects his ev'ning prey.

[1] This stanza refers to Edward II., son of the conqueror of
Wales, who was murdered in Berkley Castle at the instigation
of his Queen Isabella, referred to below as "she-wolf of France."

[2] Edward III., conqueror of France, said to have been neglected and deserted in his last moments and after his death.

[3] The Black Prince, son of Edward III., who died at Bordeaux.

" Fill high the sparkling bowl,
The rich repast prepare;
    Reft of a crown, he yet may share the feast:[1]
Close by the regal chair
    Fell Thirst and Famine scowl
    A baleful smile upon their baffled guest.
Heard ye the din of battle bray,
    Lance to lance, and horse to horse?
    Long years of havoc urge their destined course,
And thro' the kindred squadrons mow their way.[2]
    Ye towers of Julius, London's lasting shame,
With many a foul and midnight murder fed,
    Revere his Consort's faith, his father's fame,
And spare the meek usurper's holy head.[3]
Above, below, the rose of snow,
    Twined with her blushing foe, we spread :
The bristled boar in infant gore
    Wallows beneath the thorny shade.[4]
Now, brothers, bending o'er the accursèd loom,
Stamp we our vengeance deep, and ratify his doom.

" Edward, lo! to sudden fate
    (Weave we the woof.   The thread is spun.)
Half of thy heart we consecrate.
    (The web is wove.   The work is done.)
Stay, O stay! nor thus forlorn
Leave me unblessed, unpitied, here to mourn:

[1] Richard II., son of the Black Prince, who was forced to ab-
dicate by the Duke of Lancaster, afterwards Henry IV.

[2] This passage refers to the long and bloody Wars of the Roses
between the rival houses of York and Lancaster.

[3] Henry VI., murdered in the Tower and succeeded by Edward IV., of the house of York.

[4] The Duke of Gloucester, afterwards Richard III., who is
supposed to have murdered, in the Tower of London, his nephews
Edward V. and the young Duke of York, sons of Edward IV.

In yon bright track, that fires the western skies,
They melt, they vanish from my eyes.
But O! what solemn scenes on Snowdon's height
   Descending slow their glittering skirts unroll?
Visions of glory, spare my aching sight!
   Ye unborn ages, crowd not on my soul!
No more our long-lost Arthur we bewail.
All hail, ye genuine kings, Britannia's issue, hail!

  "Girt with many a baron bold
Sublime their starry fronts they rear;
   And gorgeous dames, and statesmen old
In bearded majesty, appear.
In the midst a form divine!
Her eye proclaims her of the Briton-Line: [1]
Her lion-port, her awe-commanding face,
Attemper'd sweet to virgin-grace.
What strings symphonious tremble in the air,
   What strains of vocal transport round her play.
Hear from the grave, great Taliessin, hear;
   They breathe a soul to animate thy clay.
Bright Rapture calls, and, soaring as she sings,
Waves in the eye of heaven her many-color'd wings.

  "The verse adorn again
   Fierce war, and faithful love,
And truth severe by fairy fiction drest.
   In buskin'd measures move
Pale grief, and pleasing pain,
With horror, tyrant of the throbbing breast.
A voice, as of the cherub-choir,
   Gales from blooming Eden bear;
   And distant warblings lessen on my ear,
That lost in long futurity expire.

            [1] Queen Elizabeth.

Fond impious man, think'st thou yon sanguine cloud,
  Raised by thy breath, has quench'd the orb of day?
To-morrow he repairs the golden flood,
  And warms the nations with redoubled ray.
Enough for me, with joy I see
  The different doom our fates assign.
Be thine despair and sceptred care,
  To triumph, and to die, are mine."
He spoke, and headlong from the mountain's height
Deep in the roaring tide he plunged to endless night.

THOMAS GRAY.

ODE WRITTEN IN MDCCXLVI.[1]

How sleep the Brave who sink to rest
By all their Country's wishes blest!
When Spring, with dewy fingers cold,
Returns to deck their hallow'd mould,
She there shall dress a sweeter sod
Than Fancy's feet have ever trod.

By fairy hands their knell is rung,
By forms unseen their dirge is sung:
There Honor comes, a pilgrim gray,
To bless the turf that wraps their clay,
And Freedom shall awhile repair
To dwell a weeping hermit there!

WILLIAM COLLINS.[2]

[1] This was the period of the war between Great Britain and Spain.

[2] WILLIAM COLLINS was born in Chichester in 1720, and educated at Winchester School and Oxford. While still in college he wrote some of his best poems, the *Persian Eclogues*. He did not succeed, however, as a literary man, and the effects of his fail-

ON A FAVORITE CAT, DROWNED IN A TUB OF GOLD FISHES.

'T was on a lofty vase's side
Where China's gayest art had dyed
  The azure flowers that blow;
Demurest of the tabby kind,
The pensive Selima, reclined,
  Gazed on the lake below.

Her conscious tail her joy declared;
The fair round face, the snowy beard,
  The velvet of her paws,
Her coat, that with the tortoise vies,
Her ears of jet, and emerald eyes,
  She saw; and purr'd applause.

Still had she gazed; but 'midst the tide
Two angel forms were seen to glide,
  The Genii of the stream :
Their scaly armor's Tyrian hue
Through richest purple to the view
  Betray'd a golden gleam.

The hapless nymph with wonder saw:
A whisker first, and then a claw,
  With many an ardent wish,
She stretch'd, in vain, to reach the prize.
What female heart can gold despise ?
  What Cat 's averse to fish ?

ure and his irregular life brought on a settled melancholy. He
travelled on the Continent, but returned only to become the in-
mate of a lunatic asylum, and died soon after his discharge, in
1756. His life was sad and an apparent failure, but his lyrics
hold a high place in English literature.

Presumptuous maid! with looks intent
Again she stretch'd, again she bent,
   Nor knew the gulf between.
(Malignant Fate sat by and smiled.)
The slippery verge her feet beguiled,
   She tumbled headlong in.

Eight times emerging from the flood
She mew'd to every watery God
   Some speedy aid to send :
No Dolphin came, no Nereid stirr'd,
Nor cruel Tom, nor Susan heard.
   A fav'rite has no friend !

From hence, ye beauties, undeceived,
Know one false step is ne'er retrieved,
   And be with caution bold.
Not all that tempts your wandering eyes
And heedless hearts is lawful prize,
   Nor all, that glisters, gold!

THOMAS GRAY.

ELEGY

ON THE DEATH OF A MAD DOG.

GOOD people all, of every sort,
   Give ear unto my song;
And if you find it wondrous short, —
   It cannot hold you long.

In Islington there was a man,
   Of whom the world might say,

That still a godly race he ran, —
　Whene'er he went to pray.

A kind and gentle heart he had,
　To comfort friends and foes ;
The naked every day he clad, —
　When he put on his clothes.

And in that town a dog was found,
　As many dogs there be,
Both mongrel, puppy, whelp, and hound,
　And curs of low degree.

This dog and man at first were friends,
　But then a pique began ;
The dog, to gain some private ends,
　Went mad, and bit the man.

Around from all the neighboring streets
　The wondering neighbors ran,
And swore the dog had lost his wits,
　To bite so good a man.

The wound it seem'd both sore and sad
　To every Christian eye ;
And while they swore the dog was mad,
　They swore the man would die.

But soon a wonder came to light,
　That show'd the rogues they lied :
The man recover'd of the bite,
　The dog it was that died.

OLIVER GOLDSMITH.[1]

[1] OLIVER GOLDSMITH, the son of a clergyman, was born in
Longford County, Ireland, in 1728. After such an education as

AN ELEGY

ON THAT GLORY OF HER SEX, MRS. MARY BLAIZE.

GOOD people all, with one accord,
    Lament for Madame Blaize,
Who never wanted a good word —
    From those who spoke her praise.

The needy seldom pass'd her door,
    And always found her kind;
She freely lent to all the poor, —
    Who left a pledge behind.

She strove the neighborhood to please,
    With manners wond'rous winning;
And never follow'd wicked ways, —
    Unless when she was sinning.

At church, in silks and satins new,
    With hoop of monstrous size;
She never slumber'd in her pew, —
    But when she shut her eyes.

could be obtained at the village school, he entered Dublin College, and graduated, after some mishaps, in 1749. His life was one long and bitter struggle to maintain himself by his pen. He was always in debt and lived loosely. He was a warm-hearted and humorous Irishman, and a brilliant writer. Amid a mass of hack work which he produced to gain his daily bread, were some of the best works of their kind in the language, notably, the *Vicar of Wakefield*, a novel possessing the most enduring charm which humor and pathos combined can give. He wrote also many essays and some plays and poems, and was the friend of Samuel Johnson, Sir Joshua Reynolds, Edmund Burke, and others of the most brilliant men of his time. He died in London, in 1774, when at the height of his fame.

Her love was sought, I do aver,
  By twenty beaux and more;
The king himself has follow'd her, —
  When she has walk'd before.

But now her wealth and finery fled,
  Her hangers-on cut short all;
The doctors found, when she was dead, —
  Her last disorder mortal.

Let us lament, in sorrow sore,
  For Kent Street well may say,
That had she liv'd a twelve-month more,—
  She had not died to-day.

OLIVER GOLDSMITH.

LOSS OF THE ROYAL GEORGE.[1]

Toll for the Brave!
The brave that are no more!
All sunk beneath the wave
Fast by their native shore!

Eight hundred of the brave.
Whose courage well was tried,
Had made the vessel heel
And laid her on her side.

A land-breeze shook the shrouds
And she was overset;

[1] The Royal George, a first rate man-of-war, was overset while lying at anchor at Spithead, by the guns rolling to one side when the vessel was careened to be repaired. Rear Admiral Kempenfelt was drowned with all on board, about six hundred persons. The disaster occurred August 29, 1782.

Down went the Royal George,
With all her crew complete.

Toll for the brave!
Brave Kempenfelt is gone;
His last sea-fight is fought,
His work of glory done.

It was not in the battle;
No tempest gave the shock;
She sprang no fatal leak,
She ran upon no rock.

His sword was in its sheath,
His fingers held the pen,
When Kempenfelt went down
With twice four hundred men.

Weigh the vessel up
Once dreaded by our foes!
And mingle with our cup
The tear that England owes.

Her timbers yet are sound,
And she may float again
Full charged with England's thunder,
And plough the distant main:

But Kempenfelt is gone,
His victories are o'er;
And he and his eight hundred
Shall plough the wave no more.

WILLIAM COWPER.[1]

[1] WILLIAM COWPER, son of the Rev. John Cowper, of the
family of Earl Cowper, was born at Berkhampstead, November

IS THERE, FOR HONEST POVERTY.

Is there, for honest poverty,
 That hangs his head, and a' that?
The coward slave, we pass him by,
 We dare be poor for a' that!
For a' that, and a' that,
 Our toils obscure, and a' that ;
The rank is but the guinea's stamp,
 The man 's the gowd for a' that!

What tho' on hamely fare we dine,
 Wear hoddin gray, and a' that;
Gie fools their silks, and knaves their wine,
 A man 's a man, for a' that!
For a' that, and a' that,
 Their tinsel show, and a' that;
The honest man, though e'er sae poor,
 Is king o' men for a' that!

Ye see yon birkie, ca'd a lord,
 Wha struts, and stares, and a' that ;

26, 1731. He was a delicate child, and after leaving Westminster
School, where he had a good reputation for scholarship, entered
a lawyer's office and took chambers subsequently, intending to
practise at the bar. His health, however, gave way, and his
mind was seriously affected. The disease took the form of religious mania and melancholy, and recurred, at intervals, with
greater or less acuteness through his life. Incapacitated for active pursuits Cowper retired to the country, and passed his life
in the little village of Olney, in the house of Mrs. Unwin, who
befriended him and to whom some of his most beautiful lyrics
were addressed. He devoted himself to literature in his retirement, where he passed a peaceful life. He died in 1800.

Though hundreds worship at his word,
  He 's but a coof for a' that:
For a' that, and a' that,
  His riband, star, and a' that,
The man of independent mind,
  He looks and laughs at a' that!

A king can mak a belted knight,
  A marquis, duke, and a' that;
But an honest man 's aboon his might,
  Guid faith he mauna fa' that!
For a' that, and a' that,
  Their dignities, and a' that,
The pith o' sense, and pride o' worth,
  Are higher ranks than a' that.

Then let us pray that come it may —
  As come it will for a' that —
That sense and worth, o'er a' the earth,
  May bear the gree, and a' that;
For a' that, and a' that,
  It 's comin' yet for a' that,
That man to man, the warld o'er,
  Shall brothers be for a' that!

ROBERT BURNS.[1]

1 ROBERT BURNS was the son of a small farmer in Alloway, Scotland. He was born in 1759, and received a meagre education at the village school. But the love of knowledge there awakened led him to pursue his studies and educate himself so far as possible by every means in his power. He began to write verses at the age of sixteen, and was then brought into notice and received at Edinburgh, where he first fell into the habits of excessive drinking which proved his curse. He was appointed an exciseman or gauger, which tended to increase his intemperate habits, and although he afterwards returned to farming, his excesses had undermined his constitution and he

THE SOLITUDE OF ALEXANDER SELKIRK.[1]

I AM monarch of all I survey;
My right there is none to dispute;
From the centre all round to the sea
I am lord of the fowl and the brute.
O Solitude! where are the charms
That sages have seen in thy face?
Better dwell in the midst of alarms
Than reign in this horrible place.

I am out of humanity's reach,
I must finish my journey alone,
Never hear the sweet music of speech;
I start at the sound of my own.
The beasts that roam over the plain
My form with indifference see;
They are so unacquainted with man,
Their tameness is shocking to me.

Society, Friendship, and Love,
Divinely bestow'd upon man,
O had I the wings of a dove
How soon would I taste you again!

died of a fever in 1796, at the age of thirty-seven. His lyrics
are among the best in the language, in sentiment and expression, and some of his longer poems abound in rollicking humor as well as deep and simple feeling. He wrote sometimes
in English, but his best work was done in his native Scotch
dialect.

[1] Selkirk was a Scotch sailor who was cast away upon the un-
inhabited island of Juan Fernandez, off the west coast of South
America, in 1704. Here he remained in utter solitude for four
years, when he was taken off by an English ship. His advent-
ures suggested to Defoe his famous story of Robinson Crusoe.

My sorrows I then might assuage
In the ways of religion and truth,
Might learn from the wisdom of age,
And be cheer'd by the sallies of youth.

Ye winds that have made me your sport,
Convey to this desolate shore
Some cordial, endearing report
Of a land I shall visit no more:
My friends, do they now and then send
A wish or a thought after me?
O tell me I yet have a friend,
Though a friend I am never to see.

How fleet is a glance of the mind!
Compared with the speed of its flight,
The tempest itself lags behind,
And the swift-wingèd arrows of light.
When I think of my own native land
In a moment I seem to be there;
But alas! recollection at hand
Soon hurries me back to despair.

But the seafowl is gone to her nest,
The beast is laid down in his lair;
Even here is a season of rest,
And I to my cabin repair.
There 's mercy in every place,
And mercy, encouraging thought!
Gives even affliction a grace
And reconciles man to his lot.

WILLIAM COWPER.

MY HEART'S IN THE HIGHLANDS.

I.

My heart's in the Highlands, my heart is not here;
My heart's in the Highlands a chasing the deer;
Chasing the wild deer, and following the roe —
My heart's in the Highlands wherever I go.
Farewell to the Highlands, farewell to the North,
The birthplace of valor, the country of worth;
Wherever I wander, wherever I rove,
The hills of the Highlands forever I love.

II.

Farewell to the mountains high cover'd with snow;
Farewell to the straths and green vallies below:
Farewell to the forests and wild-hanging woods;
Farewell to the torrents and loud-pouring floods.
My heart's in the Highlands, my heart is not here,
My heart's in the Highlands a chasing the deer:
Chasing the wild deer, and following the roe —
My heart's in the Highlands, wherever I go.

ROBERT BURNS.

THE DIVERTING HISTORY OF JOHN GILPIN,

SHOWING HOW HE WENT FARTHER THAN HE INTENDED, AND CAME SAFE HOME AGAIN.

JOHN GILPIN was a citizen
Of credit and renown,
A train-band Captain eke was he
Of famous London town.

John Gilpin's spouse said to her dear,
  Though wedded we have been
These twice ten tedious years, yet we
  No holiday have seen.

To-morrow is our wedding-day,
  And we will then repair
Unto the Bell at Edmonton,
  All in a chaise and pair.

My sister and my sister's child,
  Myself and children three,
Will fill the chaise, so you must ride
  On horseback after we.

He soon replied — I do admire
  Of womankind but one,
And you are she, my dearest dear,
  Therefore it shall be done.

I am a linen-draper bold,
  As all the world doth know.
And my good friend the Callender
  Will lend his horse to go.

Quoth Mrs. Gilpin — That 's well said;
  And for that wine is dear,
We will be furnish'd with our own,
  Which is both bright and clear.

John Gilpin kiss'd his loving wife,
  O'erjoyed was he to find
That though on pleasure she was bent,
  She had a frugal mind.

The morning came, the chaise was brought,
   But yet was not allow'd
To drive up to the door, lest all
   Should say that she was proud.

So three doors off the chaise was stay'd,
   Where they did all get in,
Six precious souls, and all agog
   To dash through thick and thin.

Smack went the whip, round went the wheel,
   Were never folk so glad,
The stones did rattle underneath
   As if Cheapside were mad.

John Gilpin at his horse's side
   Seized fast the flowing mane,
And up he got in haste to ride,
   But soon came down again.

For saddle-tree scarce reach'd had he,
   His journey to begin,
When turning round his head he saw
   Three customers come in.

So down he came, for loss of time,
   Although it grieved him sore,
Yet loss of pence, full well he knew,
   Would trouble him much more.

'T was long before the customers
   Were suited to their mind,
When Betty screaming came down stairs,
   " The wine is left behind."

Good lack ! quoth he, yet bring it me,
  My leathern belt likewise,
In which I bear my trusty sword
  When I do exercise.

Now Mistress Gilpin, careful soul,
  Had two stone bottles found,
To hold the liquor that she loved,
  And keep it safe and sound.

Each bottle had a curling ear,
  Through which the belt he drew,
And hung a bottle on each side
  To make his balance true.

Then over all, that he might be
  Equipped from top to toe,
His long red cloak well brush'd and neat
  He manfully did throw.

Now see him mounted once again
  Upon his nimble steed,
Full slowly pacing o'er the stones
  With caution and good heed.

But finding soon a smoother road
  Beneath his well-shod feet,
The snorting beast began to trot,
  Which galled him in his seat.

So, Fair and softly, John he cried,
  But John he cried in vain,
That trot became a gallop soon
  In spite of curb and rein.

So stooping down, as needs he must
  Who cannot sit upright,
He grasp'd the mane with both his hands
  And eke with all his might.

His horse, who never in that sort
  Had handled been before,
What thing upon his back had got
  Did wonder more and more.

Away went Gilpin, neck or nought,
  Away went hat and wig,
He little dreamt when he set out
  Of running such a rig.

The wind did blow, the cloak did fly,
  Like streamer long and gay,
Till loop and button failing both,
  At last it flew away.

Then might all people well discern
  The bottles he had slung,
A bottle swinging at each side
  As hath been said or sung.

The dogs did bark, the children scream'd,
  Up flew the windows all,
And every soul cried out, Well done!
  As loud as he could bawl.

Away went Gilpin — who but he;
  His fame soon spread around —
He carries weight, he rides a race,
  'T is for a thousand pound.

And still as fast as he drew near,
  'T was wonderful to view
How in a trice the turnpike-men
  Their gates wide open threw.

And now as he went bowing down
  His reeking head full low,
The bottles twain behind his back
  Were shatter'd at a blow.

Down ran the wine into the road,
  Most piteous to be seen,
Which made his horse's flanks to smoke
  As they had basted been.

But still he seem'd to carry weight,
  With leathern girdle braced,
For all might see the bottle-necks
  Still dangling at his waist.

Thus all through merry Islington
  These gambols he did play,
And till he came into the Wash
  Of Edmonton so gay.

And there he threw the Wash about
  On both sides of the way,
Just like unto a trundling mop,
  Or a wild-goose at play.

At Edmonton his loving wife
  From the balcony spied
Her tender husband, wondering much
  To see how he did ride.

Stop, stop, John Gilpin! — Here's the house —
     They all at once did cry,
The dinner waits, and we are tired :
     Said Gilpin — so am I.

But yet his horse was not a whit
     Inclined to tarry there,
For why? his owner had a house
     Full ten miles off, at Ware.

So like an arrow swift he flew
     Shot by an archer strong,
So did he fly — which brings me to
     The middle of my song.

Away went Gilpin, out of breath,
     And sore against his will,
Till at his friend's the Callender's
     His horse at last stood still.

The Callender, amazed to see
     His neighbor in such trim,
Laid down his pipe, flew to the gate,
     And thus accosted him —

What news? what news? your tidings tell,
     Tell me you must and shall —
Say why bare-headed you are come,
     Or why you come at all?

Now Gilpin had a pleasant wit
     And loved a timely joke,
And thus unto the Callender
     In merry guise he spoke —

I came because your horse would come;
   And if I well forebode,
My hat and wig will soon be here,
   They are upon the road.

The Callender, right glad to find
   His friend in merry pin,
Return'd him not a single word,
   But to the house went in.

Whence straight he came with hat and wig,
   A wig that flow'd behind,
A hat not much the worse for wear,
   Each comely in its kind.

He held them up and in his turn
   Thus show'd his ready wit,
— My head is twice as big as yours,
   They therefore needs must fit.

But let me scrape the dirt away
   That hangs upon your face;
And stop and eat, for well you may
   Be in a hungry case.

Said John — It is my wedding-day,
   And all the world would stare,
If wife should dine at Edmonton
   And I should dine at Ware.

So turning to his horse, he said,
   I am in haste to dine,
'T was for your pleasure you came here,
   You shall go back for mine.

Ah, luckless speech, and bootless boast!
  For which he paid full dear;
For while he spake a braying ass
  Did sing most loud and clear.

Whereat his horse did snort as he
  Had heard a lion roar,
And gallop'd off with all his might
  As he had done before.

Away went Gilpin, and away
  Went Gilpin's hat and wig;
He lost them sooner than at first,
  For why? they were too big.

Now Mistress Gilpin, when she saw
  Her husband posting down
Into the country far away,
  She pull'd out half a crown;

And thus unto the youth she said
  That drove them to the Bell,
This shall be yours when you bring back
  My husband safe and well.

The youth did ride, and soon did meet
  John coming back amain,
Whom in a trice he tried to stop
  By catching at his rein.

But not performing what he meant,
  And gladly would have done,
The frighted steed he frighted more,
  And made him faster run.

Away went Gilpin, and away
  Went post-boy at his heels,
The post-boy's horse right glad to miss
  The lumbering of the wheels.

Six gentlemen upon the road
  Thus seeing Gilpin fly,
With post-boy scampering in the rear,
  They raised the hue and cry.

Stop thief, stop thief — a highwayman!
  Not one of them was mute,
And all and each that pass'd that way
  Did join in the pursuit.

And now the turnpike gates again
  Flew open in short space,
The toll men thinking as before
  That Gilpin rode a race.

And so he did, and won it too,
  For he got first to town,
Nor stopp'd till where he had got up
  He did again get down.

Now let us sing, Long live the king,
  And Gilpin, long live he,
And when he next doth ride abroad,
  May I be there to see!

WILLIAM COWPER.

MY BONNIE MARY:

Go fetch to me a pint o' wine,
  And fill it in a silver tassie;
That I may drink, before I go,
  A service to my bonnie lassie;
The boat rocks at the pier o' Leith;
  Fu' loud the wind blaws frae the ferry;
The ship rides by the Berwick-law,
  And I maun leave my bonnie Mary.

The trumpets sound, the banners fly,
  The glittering spears are rankèd ready;
The shouts o' war are heard afar,
  The battle closes thick and bloody;
But it 's not the war o' sea or shore
  Wad make me langer wish to tarry;
Nor shouts o' war that 's heard afar —
  It 's leaving thee, my bonnie Mary.

ROBERT BURNS.

THE SLEEPING BEAUTY.

SLEEP on, and dream of Heaven awhile —
Tho' shut so close thy laughing eyes,
Thy rosy lips still wear a smile,
And move, and breathe delicious sighs!

Ah, now soft blushes tinge her cheeks
And mantle o'er her neck of snow:
Ah, now she murmurs, now she speaks
What most I wish — and fear to know!

She starts, she trembles, and she weeps!
Her fair hands folded on her breast:
— And now, how like a saint she sleeps!
A seraph in the realms of rest!

Sleep on secure! Above control
Thy thoughts belong to Heaven and thee:
And may the secret of thy soul
Remain within its sanctuary!

SAMUEL ROGERS.[1]

JOHN ANDERSON.

JOHN Anderson my jo, John,
  When we were first acquent;
Your locks were like the raven,
  Your bonnie brow was brent;
But now your brow is beld, John,
  Your locks are like the snaw;
But blessings on your frosty pow,
  John Anderson my jo.

John Anderson my jo, John,
  We clamb the hill thegither;

---

[1] SAMUEL ROGERS was the son of a London banker and born in 1763. He succeeded to his father's business in 1793, but after a few years retired with a sufficient fortune to live a life of leisure, and gratify his literary tastes and the love of poetry, which he had shown from his earliest years. He published a long descriptive poem, *Italy*, and a volume of short poems. He was best known, however, during his long life, as a wit and man of society, and was for two generations one of the most conspicuous figures in London life. He died in 1855.

And mony a canty day, John,
  We 've had wi' ane anither:
Now we maun totter down, John,
  But hand in hand we 'll go,
And sleep thegither at the foot,
  John Anderson my jo.

ROBERT BURNS.

BRUCE TO HIS MEN AT BANNOCKBURN.[1]

SCOTS, wha hae wi' Wallace bled,
Scots, wham Bruce has aften led;
Welcome to your gory bed,
      Or to victorie!

Now 's the day, and now 's the hour;
See the front o' battle lour:
See approach proud Edward's pow'r —
      Chains and slaverie!

Wha will be a traitor-knave?
Wha can fill a coward's grave?
Wha sae base as be a slave?
      Let him turn and flee!

Wha for Scotland's King and law
Freedom's sword will strongly draw,
Freeman stand or freeman fa'?
      Let him follow me!

[1] The battle of Bannockburn was fought on June 24, 1314, between the Scotch, under Robert Bruce, and the English, under Edward II. It resulted in the total defeat of the English.

By oppression's woes and pains!
By our sons in servile chains!
We will drain our dearest veins,
   But they shall be free!

Lay the proud usurpers low!
Tyrants fall in every foe!
Liberty 's in every blow!—
   Let us do or die!
      ROBERT BURNS.

BRUCE AND THE ABBOT.[1]

THE Abbot on the threshold stood,
And in his hand the holy rood.
Then, cloaking hate with fiery zeal,
Proud Lorn first answered the appeal:
  " Thou comest, O holy man,
True sons of blessèd Church to greet,
But little deeming here to meet
  A wretch, beneath the ban
Of Pope and Church, for murder done
E'en on the sacred altar stone!
Well may'st thou wonder we should know
Such miscreant here, nor lay him low,
Or dream of greeting, peace, or truce,
With excommunicated Bruce!
Yet well I grant to end debate,
Thy sainted voice decide his fate."

---

[1] This is an extract from the *Lord of the Isles*, one of Scott's
longer poems.

The Abbot seemed with eye severe
The hardy chieftain's speech to hear;
Then on King Robert turned the monk, —
But twice his courage came and sunk,
Confronted with the hero's look ;
Twice fell his eye, his accents shook.
Like man by prodigy amazed,
Upon the King the Abbot gazed ;
Then o'er his pallid features glance
Convulsions of ecstatic trance ;
His breathing came more thick and fast,
And from his pale blue eyes were cast
Strange rays of wild and wandering light;
Uprise his locks of silver white,
Flushed is his brow; through every vein
In azure tide the currents strain,
And undistinguished accents broke
The awful silence ere he spoke.

" De Bruce ! I rose with purpose dread
To speak my curse upon thy head,
And give thee as an outcast o'er
To him who burns to shed thy gore;
But, like the Midianite of old,
Who stood on Zophim, Heaven-controlled,
I feel within mine aged breast
A power that will not be repressed;
It prompts my voice, it swells my veins,
It burns, it maddens, it constrains!
De Bruce, thy sacrilegious blow
Hath at God's altar slain thy foe:
O'ermastered yet by high behest,
I bless thee, and thou shalt be blessed! "
He spoke, and o'er the astonished throng
Was silence, awful, deep, and long.

Again that light has fired his eye,
Again his form swells bold and high,
The broken voice of age is gone,
'T is vigorous manhood's lofty tone:
" Thrice vanquished on the battle plain, —
Thy followers slaughtered, fled, or ta'en, —
A hunted wanderer on the wild,
On foreign shores a man exiled,
Disowned, deserted, and distressed, —
I bless thee, and thou shalt be blessed!
Blessed in the hall and in the field,
Under the mantle as the shield.
Avenger of thy country's shame,
Restorer of her injured fame,
Blessed in thy sceptre and thy sword, —
De Bruce, fair Scotland's rightful lord,
Blessed in thy deeds and in thy fame,
What lengthened honors wait thy name!
In distant ages, sire to son
Shall tell thy tale of freedom won,
And teach his infants, in the use
Of earliest speech, to falter Bruce.
Go, then, triumphant! sweep along
Thy course, the theme of many a song!
The Power, whose dictates swell my breast,
Hath blessed thee, and thou shalt be blessed!"

Sir Walter Scott.[1]

[1] Sir Walter Scott, the greatest, perhaps, of all modern English writers, was the son of Walter Scott, a writer to the *Signet*, and was born in Edinburgh in 1771. Although his health in childhood was delicate, he displayed extraordinary talents at a very early age. He was educated at the high school and University of Edinburgh, was admitted to the bar, and held several profitable and important legal appointments. He was married in 1797, and soon after published his first

CLAUD HALCRO'S SONG.

FAREWELL to Northmaven,
    Gray Hillswicke, farewell!
To the calms of thy haven,
    The storms on thy fell;
To each breeze that can vary
    The mood of thy main,
And to thee, bonny Mary!
    We meet not again.

Farewell the wild ferry,
    Which Hacon could brave,
When the peaks of the Skerry
    Were white in the wave.

volume of poems and translations. These were followed by his longer poems, such as *Marmion* and the *Lady of the Lake,* which gave him a wide reputation. In 1814 he published, anonymously, *Waverley,* the first of the great series of novels bearing that name, and which gave him world-wide renown and a foremost place in English literature, and which have never been surpassed. He wrote much and well on other subjects also, and was a man of great learning in our older literature. He had an almost superhuman power of production, and made vast sums by his novels. But the money thus gained was wasted, and a partnership with his publishers ended in financial ruin. He finally extricated himself from his most pressing difficulties, but never regained his wealth. He died in 1832. No biographical paragraph can do justice to his vast and versatile genius, or even give any idea of it. In poetry and romance alike he achieved a success which it is given to few men to attain in either. The lyrics in this collection are taken from the longer poems, and from the novels through which they were scattered with a lavish hand. They are among the most beautiful in the whole range of English literature.

There 's a maid may look over
    These wild waves in vain,
For the skiff of her lover —
    He comes not again!

The vows thou hast broke,
    On the wild currents fling them;
On the quicksand and rock
    Let the mermaidens sing them;
New sweetness they 'll give her
    Bewildering strain;
But there 's one who will never
    Believe them again.

O were there an island,
    Though ever so wild,
Where woman could smile, and
    No man be beguiled —
Too tempting a snare
    To poor mortals were given;
And the hope would fix there,
    That should anchor in heaven.

SIR WALTER SCOTT.
The Pirate.

THE SONG OF HAROLD HARFAGER.[1]

THE sun is rising dimly red,
The wind is wailing low and dread;
From his cliff the eagle sallies,
Leaves the wolf his darksome valleys;

---

[1] Harold Härfager or Harold Fair Hair, the most famous of
the early kings of Norway, 885-894.

In the mist the ravens hover,
Peep the wild dogs from the cover,
Screaming, croaking, baying, yelling,
Each in his wild accents telling,
" Soon we feast on dead and dying,
Fair-haired Harold's flag is flying."

Many a crest on air is streaming,
Many a helmet darkly gleaming,
Many an arm the axe uprears,
Doomed to hew the wood of spears.
All along the crowded ranks
Horses neigh and armor clanks;
Chiefs are shouting, clarions ringing,
Louder still the bards are singing:
" Gather, footmen! gather, horsemen!
To the field, ye valiant Norsemen!

" Halt ye not for food or slumber,
View not vantage, count not number;
Jolly reapers, forward still.
Grow the crop on vale or hill,
Thick or scattered, stiff or lithe,
It shall down before the scythe.
Forward with your sickles bright,
Reap the harvest of the fight;
Onward, footmen! onward, horsemen!
To the charge, ye gallant Norsemen!

Fatal choosers of the Slaughter,
O'er you hovers Odin's daughter;
Hear the choice she spreads before ye, —
Victory, and wealth, and glory;
Or old Valhalla's roaring hail,
Her ever-circling mead and ale,

Where for eternity unite
The joys of wassail and of fight.
Headlong forward, foot and horsemen,
Charge and fight, and die like Norsemen!"

SIR WALTER SCOTT.
The Pirate.

HUNTING SONG.

WAKEN, lords and ladies gay,
On the mountain dawns the day,
All the jolly chase is here,
With hawk, and horse, and hunting spear
Hounds are in their couples yelling,
Hawks are whistling, horns are knelling,
Merrily, merrily, mingle they,
" Waken, lords and ladies gay."

Waken, lords and ladies gay,
The mist has left the mountain gray,
Springlets in the dawn are steaming,
Diamonds on the brake are gleaming;
And foresters have busy been,
To track the buck in thicket green;
Now we come to chant our lay,
" Waken, lords and ladies gay."

Waken, lords and ladies gay,
To the greenwood haste away;
We can show you where he lies,
Fleet of foot, and tall of size;
We can show the marks he made,
When 'gainst the oak his antlers frayed;

You shall see him brought to bay,
" Waken, lords and ladies gay."

Louder, louder chant the lay,
Waken, lords and ladies gay !
Tell them youth, and mirth, and glee
Run a course as well as we;
Time, stern huntsman! who can balk,
Staunch as hound, and fleet as hawk;
Think of this, and rise with day,
Gentle lords and ladies gay.

SIR WALTER SCOTT.

SONG: COUNTY GUY.

AH! County Guy, the hour is nigh,
  The sun has left the lea,
The orange-flower perfumes the bower,
  The breeze is on the sea.
The lark, his lay who trilled all day,
  Sits hushed his partner nigh ;
Breeze, bird, and flower confess the hour,
  But where is County Guy?

The village maid steals through the shade,
  Her shepherd's suit to hear;
To beauty shy, by lattice high,
  Sings high-born Cavalier.
The star of Love, all stars above,
  Now reigns o'er earth and sky;
And high and low the influence know —
  But where is County Guy?

SIR WALTER SCOTT.
Quentin Durward.

MACPHERSON'S FAREWELL.

Farewell, ye dungeons dark and strong,
   The wretch's destinie!
Macpherson's time will not be long
   On yonder gallows-tree.
     Sae rantingly, sae wantonly,
      Sae dauntingly gaed he;
     He play'd a spring, and danc'd it round,
      Below the gallows-tree.

O, what is death but parting breath?
   On many a bloody plain
I've dar'd his face, and in this place
   I scorn him yet again!

Untie these bands from off my hands,
   And bring to me my sword;
And there's no a man in all Scotland,
   But I'll brave him at a word.

I've liv'd a life of sturt and strife;
   I die by treacherie:
It burns my heart I must depart,
   And not avengèd be.

Now farewell light, thou sunshine bright,
   And all beneath the sky!
May coward shame distain his name,
   The wretch that dares not die!
     Sae rantingly, sae wantonly, etc.

Robert Burns.

THE POPLAR FIELD.

THE poplars are fell'd, farewell to the shade
And the whispering sound of the cool colonnade;
The winds play no longer and sing in the leaves,
Nor Ouse on his bosom their image receives.

Twelve years have elapsed since I last took a view
Of my favorite field, and the bank where they grew:
And now in the grass behold they are laid,
And the tree is my seat that once lent me a shade.

The blackbird has fled to another retreat
Where the hazels afford him a screen from the heat;
And the scene where his melody charm'd me before
Resounds with his sweet-flowing ditty no more.

My fugitive years are all hasting away,
And I must erelong lie as lowly as they,
With a turf on my breast and a stone at my head
Ere another such grove shall arise in its stead.

'T is a sight to engage me, if anything can,
To muse on the perishing pleasures of man;
Short-lived as we are, our enjoyments, I see,
Have a still shorter date, and die sooner than we.

WILLIAM COWPER.

A WISH.

MINE be a cot beside the hill;
A bee-hive's hum shall soothe my ear;
A willowy brook, that turns a mill,
With many a fall shall linger near.

The swallow, oft, beneath my thatch
Shall twitter from her clay-built nest;
Oft shall the pilgrm lift the latch,
And share my meal, a welcome guest.

Around my ivied porch shall spring
Each fragrant flower that drinks the dew;
And Lucy, at her wheel, shall sing
In russet gown and apron blue.

The village church among the trees,
Where first our marriage vows were given,
With merry peals shall swell the breeze
And point with taper spire to Heaven.

SAMUEL ROGERS.

THE BANKS O' DOON.

I.

YE banks and braes o' bonnie Doon,
How can ye bloom sae fresh and fair;
How can ye chant, ye little birds,
And I sae weary, fu' o' care!
Thou 'lt break my heart, thou warbling bird,
That wantons thro' the flowering thorn:
Thou minds me o' departed joys,
Departed — never to return !

II.

Aft hae I rov'd by bonnie Doon,
To see the rose and woodbine twine;
And ilka bird sang o' its luve,
And fondly sae did I o' mine.

Wi' lightsome heart I pu'd a rose,
  Fu' sweet upon its thorny tree;
And my fause luver stole my rose,
  But, ah! he left the thorn wi' me.

ROBERT BURNS.

EVENING.

THE sun upon the lake is low,
  The wild birds hush their song,
The hills have evening's deepest glow,
  Yet Leonard tarries long.
Now all whom varied toil and care
  From home and love divide,
In the calm sunset may repair
  Each to the loved one's side.

The noble dame on turret high,
  Who waits her gallant knight,
Looks to the western beam to spy
  The flash of armor bright.
The village maid, with hand on brow
  The level ray to shade,
Upon the footpath watches now
  For Colin's darkening plaid.

Now to their mates the wild swans row,
  By day they swam apart,
And to the thicket wanders slow
  The hind beside the hart.
The woodlark at his partner's side
  Twitters his closing song —
All meet whom day and care divide,
  But Leonard tarries long !

SIR WALTER SCOTT.

SONG.

THERE is mist on the mountain and night on the vale,
But more dark is the sleep of the sons of the Gael.
A stranger commanded — it sunk on the land,
It has frozen each heart, and benumbed every hand!

The dirk and the target lie sordid with dust,
The bloodless claymore is but reddened with rust:
On the hill or the glen if a gun should appear,
It is only to war with the heath-cock or deer.

The deeds of our sires if our bards should rehearse,
Let a blush or a blow be the meed of their verse!
Be mute every string, and be hushed every tone,
That shall bid us remember the fame that is flown.

But the dark hours of night and of slumber are past,
The morn on our mountains is dawning at last;
Glenaladale's peaks are illumed with the rays,
And the streams of Glenfinnan leap bright in the blaze.

O high-minded Moray! — the exiled — the dear!
In the blush of the dawning the Standard uprear!
Wide, wide to the winds of the north let it fly,
Like the sun's latest flash when the tempest is nigh!

Ye sons of the strong, when that dawning shall break,
Need the harp of the aged remind you to wake?
That dawn never beamed on your forefathers' eye,
But it roused each high chieftain to vanquish or die.

O sprung from the Kings who in Islay kept state,
Proud chiefs of Clan-Ranald, Glengary, and Sleat!

Combine like three streams from one mountain of snow,
And resistless in union rush down on the foe!

True son of Sir Evan, undaunted Lochiel,
Place thy targe on thy shoulder and burnish thy steel!
Rough Keppoch, give breath to thy bugle's bold swell,
Till far Coryarrick resound to the knell!

Stern son of Lord Kenneth, high chief of Kintail,
Let the stag in thy standard bound wild in the gale!
May the race of Clan-Gillian, the fearless and free,
Remember Glenlivet, Harlaw, and Dundee!

Let the clan of gray Fingon, whose offspring has given
Such heroes to earth, and such martyrs to heaven,
Unite with the race of renowned Rori More,
To launch the long galley, and stretch to the oar!

How Mac-Shimei will joy when their chief shall display
The yew-crested bonnet o'er tresses of gray!
How the race of wronged Alpine and murdered Glencoe
Shall shout for revenge when they pour on the foe!

Ye sons of brown Dermid, who slew the wild boar,
Resume the pure faith of the great Callum-More!
Mac-Neil of the Islands, and Moy of the Lake,
For honor, for freedom, for vengeance awake!

Awake on your hills, on your islands awake!
Brave sons of the mountain, the frith, and the lake!
'T is the bugle — but not for the chase is the call;
'T is the pibroch's shrill summons — but not to the hall.

'T is the summons of heroes for conquest or death,
When the banners are blazing on mountain and heath;

They call to the dirk, the claymore, and the targe,
To the march and the muster, the line and the charge.

Be the brand of each chieftain like Fin's in his ire!
May the blood through his veins flow like currents of
    fire!
Burst the base foreign yoke as your sires did of yore!
Or die, like your sires, and endure it no more!
Sir Walter Scott.
Waverley.

GLENARA.

O heard ye yon pibroch sound sad in the gale,
Where a band cometh slowly with weeping and wail?
'T is the chief of Glenara laments for his dear;
And her sire, and the people, are call'd to her bier.

Glenara came first with the mourners and shroud;
Her kinsmen they follow'd, but mourned not aloud:
Their plaids all their bosoms were folded around:
They march'd all in silence, — they looked on the
    ground.

In silence they reach'd over mountain and moor,
To a heath, where the oak-tree grew lonely and hoar:
" Now here let us place the gray stone of her cairn;
Why speak ye no word?" said Glenara the stern.

" And tell me, I charge you! ye clan of my spouse,
Why fold ye your mantles? why cloud ye your brows?"
So spake the rude chieftain: no answer is made,
But each mantle unfolding a dagger display'd.
8

"I dreamt of my lady, I dreamt of her shroud,"
Cried a voice from the kinsmen, all wrathful and loud;
"And empty that shroud and that coffin did seem:
Glenara! Glenara! now read me my dream!"

O! pale grew the cheek of that chieftain, I ween,
When the shroud was unclosed, and no lady was seen;
When a voice from the kinsmen spoke louder in scorn,
'T was the youth who had loved the fair Ellen of
    Lorn:

"I dreamt of my lady, I dreamt of her grief,
I dreamt that her lord was a barbarous chief:
On a rock of the ocean fair Ellen did seem;
Glenara! Glenara! now read me my dream!"

In dust, low the traitor has knelt to the ground,
And the desert reveal'd where his lady was found;
From a rock of the ocean that beauty is borne, —
Now joy to the house of fair Ellen of Lorn!

THOMAS CAMPBELL.[1]

[1] THOMAS CAMPBELL, born in Glasgow in 1777, graduated at
the university of his native town, and made an early reputation
as a poet by the publication of his *Pleasures of Hope*. After
a journey on the Continent, where he witnessed the battle of
Hohenlinden, he returned to London, where he passed the rest of
his life. His prose writings, which were extensive and profitable, and gained for him a pension from the government, are
now forgotten, but his lyric poetry holds a high place. He died
n 1844.

LOCHINVAR.

O, YOUNG Lochinvar is come out of the West,
Through all the wide border his steed was the best;
And save his good broadsword he weapons had none,
He rode all unarmed, and he rode all alone.
So faithful in love, and so dauntless in war,
There never was knight like the young Lochinvar.

He staid not for brake, and he stopped not for stone,
He swam the Eske river where ford there was none;
But, ere he alighted at Netherby gate,
The bride had consented, the gallant came late:
For a laggard in love, and a dastard in war,
Was to wed the fair Ellen of brave Lochinvar.

So boldly he entered the Netherby hall,
Among bride's-men, and kinsmen, and brothers and
    all:
Then spoke the bride's father, his hand on his
    sword
(For the poor craven bridegroom said never a word),
" O come ye in peace here, or come ye in war,
Or to dance at our bridal, young Lord Lochinvar? "

" I long woo'd your daughter, my suit you denied;
Love swells like the Solway, but ebbs like its tide;
And now am I come, with this lost love of mine,
To lead but one measure, drink one cup of wine.
There are maidens in Scotland, more lovely by far,
That would gladly be bride to the young Lochin-
    var."

The bride kissed the goblet; the knight took it up,
He quaffed off the wine, and he threw down the cup.

She looked down to blush, and she looked up to
　　sigh,
With a smile on her lips, and a tear in her eye.
He took her soft hand, ere her mother could bar, —
"Now tread we a measure!" said young Lochinvar.

So stately his form, and so lovely his face,
That never a hall such a galliard did grace;
While her mother did fret, and her father did fume,
And the bridegroom stood dangling his bonnet and
　　plume;
And the bride-maidens whispered, " 'T were better
　　by far
To have matched our fair cousin with young Loch-
　　invar."

One touch to her hand, and one word in her ear,
When they reached the hall-door, and the charger
　　stood near;
So light to the croupe the fair lady he swung,
So light to the saddle before her he sprung!
"She is won! we are gone, over bank, bush, and
　　scaur;
They 'll have fleet steeds that follow," quoth young
　　Lochinvar.

There was mounting 'mong Graemes of the Netherby
　　clan;
Forsters, Fenwicks, and Musgraves, they rode and
　　they ran:
There was racing and chasing, on Cannobie Lee,
But the lost bride of Netherby ne'er did they see.
So daring in love, and so dauntless in war,
Have ye e'er heard of gallant like young Lochinvar?
Sir Walter Scott.

LORD ULLIN'S DAUGHTER.

A CHIEFTAIN, to the Highlands bound,
Cries, " Boatman, do not tarry !
And I 'll give thee a silver pound,
To row us o'er the ferry."

" Now who be ye, would cross Lochgyle,
This dark and stormy water?"
" O I 'm the chief of Ulva's isle,
And this Lord Ullin's daughter.

" And fast before her father's men
Three days we 've fled together,
For should he find us in the glen,
My blood would stain the heather.

" His horsemen hard behind us ride;
Should they our steps discover,
Then who will cheer my bonny bride
When they have slain her lover?"

Out spoke the hardy Highland wight,
" I 'll go, my chief — I 'm ready:
It is not for your silver bright,
But for your winsome lady:

" And by my word! the bonny bird
In danger shall not tarry;
So, though the waves are raging white,
I 'll row you o'er the ferry."

By this the storm grew loud apace,
The water-wraith [1] was shrieking;

[1] The evil spirit of the waters.

And in the scowl of heaven each face
  Grew dark as they were speaking.

But still as wilder blew the wind,
  And as the night grew drearer,
Adown the glen rode armèd men,
  Their trampling sounded nearer.

" O haste thee, haste! " the lady cries,
  " Though tempests round us gather;
I 'll meet the raging of the skies,
  But not an angry father."

The boat has left a stormy land,
  A stormy sea before her, —
When, O! too strong for human hand,
  The tempest gather'd o'er her.

And still they row'd amidst the roar
  Of waters fast prevailing :
Lord Ullin reach'd that fatal shore,
  His wrath was changed to wailing.

For sore dismay'd, through storm and shade,
  His child he did discover :
One lovely hand she stretched for aid,
  And one was round her lover.

" Come back ! come back !" he cried in grief,
  " Across this stormy water :
And I 'll forgive your Highland chief,
  My daughter ! — O my daughter ! "

'T was vain; the loud waves lashed the shore,
  Return or aid preventing :

The waters wild went o'er his child, —
And he was left lamenting.
THOMAS CAMPBELL.

THE CRUSADER'S RETURN.

I.

HIGH deeds achieved of knightly fame,
From Palestine the champion came ;
The cross upon his shoulders borne
Battle and blast had dimmed and torn ;
Each dint upon his battered shield
Was token of a foughten field;
And thus, beneath his lady's bower,
He sung, as fell the twilight hour:

II.

" Joy to the fair ! — thy knight behold,
Returned from yonder land of gold;
No wealth he brings, nor wealth can need,
Save his good arms and battle-steed ;
His spurs to dash against a foe,
His lance and sword to lay him low;
Such all the trophies of his toil,
Such — and the hope of Tekla's smile !

III.

" Joy to the fair! whose constant knight
Her favor fired to feats of might !
Unnoted shall she not remain
Where meet the bright and noble train;
Minstrel shall sing, and herald tell —
' Mark yonder maid of beauty well,

'T is she for whose bright eyes was won
The listed field of Ascalon!

IV.

" ' Note well her smile ! — it edged the blade
Which fifty wives to widows made,
When, vain his strength and Mahound's spell,
Iconium's turbaned Soldan fell.
Seest thou her locks, whose sunny glow
Half shows, half shades, her neck of snow?
Twines not of them one golden thread,
But for its sake a Paynim bled ! '

V.

" Joy to the fair ! — My name unknown,
Each deed, and all its praise, thine own ;
Then, O ! unbar this churlish gate,
The night-dew falls, the hour is late.
Inured to Syria's glowing breath,
I feel the north breeze chill as death ;
Let grateful love quell maiden shame,
And grant him bliss who brings thee fame."

SIR WALTER SCOTT.
Ivanhoe.

ELSPETH'S BALLAD.

Now haud your tongue, baith wife and carle,
 And listen great and sma',
And I will sing of Glenallan's Earl
 That fought on the red Harlaw.

The cronach 's cried on Bennachie,
 And down the Don and a',

And hicland and lawland may mournfu' be
For the sair field of Harlaw.

They saddled a hundred milk-white steeds,
They hae bridled a hundred black,
With a chafron of steel on each horse's head,
And a good knight upon his back.

They hadna ridden a mile, a mile,
A mile but barely ten,
When Donald came branking down the brae
Wi' twenty thousand men.

Their tartans they were waving wide,
Their glaives were glancing clear,
The pibrochs rung frae side to side,
Would deafen ye to hear.

The great Earl in his stirrups stood,
That Highland host to see:
" Now here a knight that 's stout and good
May prove a jeopardie:

" What wouldst thou do, my squire so gay,
That rides beside my rein, —
Were ye Glenallan's Earl the day,
And I were Roland Cheyne?

" To turn the rein were sin and shame,
To fight were wondrous peril, —
What would ye do now, Roland Cheyne,
Were ye Glenallan's Earl? "

" Were I Glenallan's Earl this tide,
And ye were Roland Cheyne,

The spear should be in my horse's side,
  And the bridle upon his mane.

" If they hae twenty thousand blades,
  And we twice ten times ten,
Yet they hae but their tartan plaids,
  And we are mail-clad men.

" My horse shall ride through ranks sae rude,
  As through the moorland fern, —
Then ne'er let the gentle Norman blude
  Grow cauld for Highland kerne."
                    SIR WALTER SCOTT.
                        The Antiquary.

HOHENLINDEN.[1]

On Linden, when the sun was low,
All bloodless lay the untrodden snow,
And dark as winter was the flow
Of Iser, rolling rapidly.

But Linden saw another sight,
When the drum beat, at dead of night,
Commanding fires of death to light
The darkness of her scenery.

By torch and trumpet fast array'd,
Each horseman drew his battle-blade,

[1] The battle of Hohenlinden was fought between the French and Bavarians, under Moreau, and the Austrians, under the Archduke John, December 3, 1800, and resulted in the defeat of the Austrians.

And furious every charger neigh'd,
To join the dreadful revelry.

Then shook the hills with thunder riven,
Then rush'd the steed to battle driven,
And louder than the bolts of heaven,
Far flash'd the red artillery.

But redder yet that light shall glow,
On Linden's hills of stainèd snow,
And bloodier yet the torrent flow
Of Iser, rolling rapidly.

'T is morn, but scarce yon level sun
Can pierce the war-clouds, rolling dun,
Where furious Frank, and fiery Hun,
Shout in their sulph'rous canopy.

The combat deepens. On, ye brave,
Who rush to glory, or the grave!
Wave, Munich! all thy banners wave!
And charge with all thy chivalry!

Few, few shall part where many meet!
The snow shall be their winding-sheet,
And every turf beneath their feet
Shall be a soldier's sepulchre.

THOMAS CAMPBELL.

SONG: THE CAVALIER.

WHILE the dawn on the mountain was misty and gray,
My true love has mounted his steed and away,
Over hill, over valley, o'er dale and o'er down;
Heaven shield the brave gallant that fights for the
    crown!

He has doffed the silk doublet the breast-plate to
    bear,
He has placed the steel-cap o'er his long flowing hair,
From his belt to his stirrup his broadsword hangs
    down.
Heaven shield the brave gallant that fights for the
    crown!

For the rights of fair England that broadsword he
    draws,
Her king is his leader, her church is his cause;
His watch-word is honor, his pay is renown, —
God strike with the gallant that strikes for the crown!

They may boast of their Fairfax, their Waller, and
    all
The roundheaded rebels of Westminster-hall;
But tell these bold traitors of London's proud town,
That the spears of the north have encircled the crown.

There 's Derby and Cavendish, dread of their foes;
There 's Erin's high Ormond, and Scotland's Mont-
    rose!
Would you match the base Skippon, and Massy, and
    Brown,
With the barons of England that fight for the crown?

Now joy to the crest of the brave cavalier!
Be his banner unconquered, resistless his spear,
Till in peace and in triumph his toils he may drown,
In a pledge to fair England, her church, and her crown!
Sir Walter Scott.

GLEE FOR KING CHARLES.

Bring the bowl which you boast,
   Fill it up to the brim;
'T is to him we love most,
   And to all who love him.
Brave gallants, stand up,
   And avaunt, ye base carles!
Were there death in the cup,
   Here 's a Health to King Charles!

Though he wanders through dangers,
   Unaided, unknown,
Dependent on strangers,
   Estranged from his own;
Though 't is under our breath,
   Amidst forfeits and perils,
Here 's to honor and faith,
   And a Health to King Charles!

Let such honors abound
   As the time can afford,
The knee on the ground,
   And the hand on the sword;
But the time shall come round,
   When, 'mid Lords, Dukes, and Earls,

The loud trumpet shall sound,
Here 's a Health to King Charles!

Sir Walter Scott.

Woodstock.

THE SOLDIER'S DREAM.

Our bugles sang truce — for the night-cloud had
    lower'd,
And the sentinel stars set their watch in the sky;
And thousands had sunk on the ground overpower'd,
    The weary to sleep, and the wounded to die.

When reposing that night on my pallet of straw,
    By the wolf-scaring fagot that guarded the slain,
At the dead of the night a sweet vision I saw,
    And thrice ere the morning I dreamt it again.

Methought from the battle-field's dreadful array,
    Far, far I had roam'd on a desolate track;
'T was autumn, — and sunshine arose on the way
    To the home of my fathers, that welcomed me back.

I flew to the pleasant fields traversed so oft
    In life's morning march, when my bosom was young;
I heard my own mountain-goats bleating aloft,
    And knew the sweet strain that the corn-reapers
    sung.

Then pledged we the wine-cup, and fondly I swore,
    From my home and my weeping friends never to
    part;

My little ones kiss'd me a thousand times o'er,
  And my wife sobb'd aloud in her fulness of heart.

Stay, stay with us — rest, thou art weary and worn;
  And fain was their war-broken soldier to stay; —
But sorrow return'd with the dawning of morn,
  And the voice in my dreaming ear melted away.
THOMAS CAMPBELL.

ROSABELLE.

O LISTEN, listen, ladies gay!
  No haughty feat of arms I tell;
Soft is the note, and sad the lay,
  That mourns the lovely Rosabelle.

"Moor, moor the barge, ye gallant crew!
  And, gentle lady, deign to stay!
Rest thee in Castle Ravensheuch,
  Nor tempt the stormy firth to-day.

"The blackening wave is edged with white;
  To inch and rock the sea-mews fly;
The fishers have heard the water-sprite,
  Whose screams forebode that wreck is nigh.

"Last night the gifted seer did view
  A wet shroud swathed round lady gay;
Then stay thee, Fair, in Ravensheuch:
  Why cross the gloomy firth to-day?"

"'T is not because Lord Lindesay's heir
  To-night at Roslin leads the ball,

But that my lady-mother there
　　Sits lonely in her castle-hall.

" 'T is not because the ring they ride,
　　And Lindesay at the ring rides well,
But that my sire the wine will chide,
　　If 't is not filled by Rosabelle."

O'er Roslin all that dreary night
　　A wondrous blaze was seen to gleam:
'T was broader than the watch-fire's light,
　　And redder than the bright moonbeam.

It glared on Roslin's castled rock,
　　It ruddied all the copse-wood glen;
'T was seen from Dryden's groves of oak,
　　And seen from caverned Hawthornden.

Seemed all on fire that chapel proud,
　　Where Roslin's chiefs uncoffined lie;
Each baron, for a sable shroud,
　　Sheathed in his iron panoply.

Seemed all on fire, within, around,
　　Deep sacristry and altar's pale:
Shone every pillar foliage-bound,
　　And glimmered all the dead men's mail.

Blazed battlement and pinnet high,
　　Blazed every rose-carved buttress fair, —
So still they blaze, when fate is nigh
　　The lordly line of high St. Clair.

There are twenty of Roslin's barons bold
　　Lie buried within that proud chapelle:

Each one the holy vault doth hold, —
But the sea holds lovely Rosabelle!

And each St. Clair was buried there,
  With candle, with book, and with knell;
But the sea-caves rung, and the wild winds sung
  The dirge of lovely Rosabelle.
                              SIR WALTER SCOTT.

PIBROCH OF DONUIL DHU.

PIBROCH of Donuil Dhu,
    Pibroch of Donuil,
Wake thy wild voice anew,
    Summon Clan-Conuil.
Come away, come away,
    Hark to the summons!
Come in your war array,
    Gentles and commons.

Come from deep glen, and
    From mountain so rocky,
The war-pipe and pennon
    Are at Inverlochy:
Come every hill-plaid, and
    True heart that wears one,
Come every steel blade, and
    Strong hand that bears one.

Leave untended the herd,
    The flock without shelter;
Leave the corpse uninterr'd,
    The bride at the altar;

Leave the deer, leave the steer,
   Leave nets and barges;
Come with your fighting gear,
   Broadswords and targes.

Come as the winds come, when
   Forests are rended;
Come as the waves come, when
   Navies are stranded;
Faster come, faster come,
   Faster and faster,
Chief, vassal, page, and groom,
   Tenant and master.

Fast they come, fast they come ;
   See how they gather!
Wide waves the eagle plume,
   Blended with heather.
Cast your plaids, draw your blades,
   Forward each man set!
Pibroch of Donuil Dhu,
   Knell for the onset!

Sir Walter Scott.

LOVE OF COUNTRY.[1]

Breathes there the man, with soul so dead,
Who never to himself hath said,
   This is my own, my native land!
Whose heart hath ne'er within him burned,
As home his footsteps he hath turned,
   From wandering on a foreign strand?

[1] This is an extract from the *Lay of the Last Minstrel.*

If such there breathe, go, mark him well:
For him no minstrel raptures swell;
High though his titles, proud his name,
Boundless his wealth as wish can claim;
Despite those titles, power, and pelf,
The wretch, concentred all in self,
Living, shall forfeit fair renown,
And, doubly dying, shall go down
To the vile dust, from whence he sprung,
Unwept, unhonored, and unsung.

SIR WALTER SCOTT.

LIFE AND DEATH.

LIFE! I know not what thou art,
But know that thou and I must part;
And when, or how, or where we met
I own to me 's a secret yet.

Life! we 've been long together
Through pleasant and through cloudy weather;
'T is hard to part when friends are dear, —
Perhaps 't will cost a sigh, a tear;
Then steal away, give little warning,
   Choose thine own time;
Say not Good Night, — but in some brighter clime
   Bid me Good Morning.

ANNA LÆTITIA BARBAULD.[1]

[1] ANNA LÆTITIA BARBAULD, the daughter of the Rev. John Aikin, was born in 1743, and married in 1774 to the Rev. Rochemont Barbauld, a dissenting minister. She was a prolific writer, chiefly for children and on educational and political subjects. Some of her poems have considerable merit. She died in 1825.

THE BURIAL OF SIR JOHN MOORE, AT CORUNNA.[1]

Not a drum was heard, not a funeral note,
  As his corpse to the ramparts we hurried;
Not a soldier discharged his farewell shot
  O'er the grave where our hero we buried.

We buried him darkly at dead of night,
  The sods with our bayonets turning;
By the struggling moonbeam's misty light
  And the lantern dimly burning.

No useless coffin enclosed his breast,
  Not in sheet nor in shroud we wound him;
But he lay like a warrior taking his rest
  With his martial cloak around him.

Few and short were the prayers we said,
  And we spoke not a word of sorrow,
But we steadfastly gazed on the face that was dead,
  And we bitterly thought of the morrow.

We thought as we hollow'd his narrow bed
  And smoothed down his lonely pillow,
That the foe and the stranger would tread o'er his
    head,
  And we far away on the billow!

[1] The British army, under Sir John Moore, entered Spain in
1808. They were forced to retreat before the French to Corunna,
where they made a gallant stand, and after hard fighting re-
pulsed the French, January 16, 1809. Sir John Moore was fa-
tally wounded in this battle and buried the same night. The
next day the army was safely embarked on board the British
fleet.

Lightly they 'll talk of the spirit that 's gone,
  And o'er his cold ashes upbraid him, —
But little he 'll reck if they let him sleep on
  In the grave where a Briton has laid him.

But half of our heavy task was done
  When the clock struck the hour for retiring;
And we heard the distant and random gun
  That the foe was sullenly firing.

Slowly and sadly we laid him down,
  From the field of his fame fresh and gory;
We carved not a line, and we raised not a stone, —
  But we left him alone with his glory.

CHARLES WOLFE.[1]

BOAT SONG.

HAIL to the chief who in triumph advances!
  Honored and blessed be the evergreen pine!
Long may the tree in his banner that glances
  Flourish, the shelter and grace of our line!
        Heaven send it happy dew,
        Earth lend it sap anew,
  Gayly to bourgeon, and broadly to grow;
        While every highland glen
        Sends our shout back again,
" Roderigh Vich Alpine dhu, ho! ieroe! "

---

[1] CHARLES WOLFE, a connection of General James Wolfe, the hero of Quebec, was born in Dublin, 1791, and educated at Dublin University. He entered the church and became curate of Donoughmore. He wrote, besides sermons, various essays and some poetry, but has secured a lasting remembrance by this single famous poem. He died at Cork in 1823.

Ours is no sapling, chance-sown by the fountain,
　Blooming at Beltane, in winter to fade;
When the whirlwind has stripped every leaf on the
　　mountain,
　The more shall Clan-Alpine exult in her shade.
　　　　Moored in the rifted rock,
　　　　Proof to the tempest's shock,
　Firmer he roots him the ruder it blow;
　　　　Menteith and Breadalbane, then,
　　　　Echo his praise again,
" Roderigh Vich Alpine dhu, ho! ieroe!"

Proudly our pibroch has thrilled in Glen Fruin,
　And Bannachar's groans to our slogan replied,
Glen Luss and Ross-dhu, they are smoking in ruin,
　And the best of Loch-Lomond lie dead on her side.
　　　　Widow and Saxon maid
　　　　Long shall lament our aid,
　Think of Clan-Alpine with fear and with wo;
　　　　Lennox and Leven-glen
　　　　Shake when they hear again,
" Roderigh Vich Alpine dhu, ho! ieroe !"

Row, vassals, row, for the pride of the highlands!
　Stretch to your oars for the evergreen pine!
O that the rose-bud that graces yon islands
　Were wreathed in a garland around him to twine!
　　　　O that some seedling gem,
　　　　Worthy such noble stem,
　Honored and blessed in their shadow might grow!
　　　　Loud should Clan-Alpine then
　　　　Ring from the deepmost glen,
" Roderigh Vich Alpine dhu, ho! ieroe!"
Sir Walter Scott.

SEA-SONG.

A WET sheet and a flowing sea,
  A wind that follows fast
And fills the white and rustling sail
  And bends the gallant mast;
And bends the gallant mast, my boys,
  While, like the eagle free,
Away the good ship flies, and leaves
  Old England on the lee.

O for a soft and gentle wind!
  I heard a fair one cry ;
But give to me the snoring breeze,
  And white waves heaving high;
And white waves heaving high, my lads,
  The good ship tight and free, —
The world of waters is our home,
  And merry men are we.

There 's tempest in yon hornèd moon,
  And lightning in yon cloud ;
But hark the music, mariners!
  The wind is piping loud;
The wind is piping loud, my boys,
  The lightning flashes free, —
While the hollow oak our palace is,
  Our heritage the sea.

ALLAN CUNNINGHAM.[1]

[1] ALLAN CUNNINGHAM, born in Scotland in 1785, was the son of a gardener. In 1810 he removed to London, where he wrote for the press, and in 1814 obtained the position of clerk to Sir Francis Chantrey, the celebrated sculptor, with whom he remained until 1841. He wrote romances, some poems of considerable length, and many beautiful and spirited songs. He died in 1842.

SONG.

O, BRIGNAL banks are wild and fair,
  And Greta woods are green,
And you may gather garlands there,
  Would grace a summer queen.
And as I rode by Dalton-hall,
  Beneath the turrets high,
A maiden on the castle wall
  Was singing merrily, —

" O, Brignal banks are fresh and fair,
  And Greta woods are green;
I 'd rather rove with Edmund there,
  Than reign our English queen."

" If, maiden, thou wouldst wend with me,
  To leave both tower and town,
Thou first must guess what life lead we,
  That dwell by dale and down.
And if thou canst that riddle read,
  As read full well you may,
Then to the greenwood shalt thou speed,
  As blithe as queen of May."

Yet sung she, " Brignal banks are fair,
  And Greta woods are green;
I 'd rather rove with Edmund there,
  Than reign our English queen.

" I read you, by your bugle horn,
  And by your palfrey good,
I read you for a ranger sworn,
  To keep the king's greenwood."

"A ranger, lady, winds his horn,
  And 't is at peep of light;
His blast is heard at merry morn,
  And mine at dead of night."

Yet sung she, "Brignal banks are fair,
  And Greta woods are gay,
I would I were with Edmund there,
  To reign his queen of May!

"With burnished brand and musquetoon,
  So gallantly you come,
I read you for a bold dragoon,
  That lists the tuck of drum."
"I list no more the tuck of drum,
  No more the trumpet hear;
But when the beetle sounds his hum,
  My comrades take the spear.

"And O! though Brignal banks be fair,
  And Greta woods be gay,
Yet mickle must the maiden dare,
  Would reign my queen of May!

"Maiden! a nameless life I lead,
  A nameless death I 'll die;
The fiend whose lantern lights the mead
  Were better mate than I!
And when I 'm with my comrades met,
  Beneath the greenwood bough,
What once we were we all forget,
  Nor think what we are now.

"Yet Brignal banks are fresh and fair,
  And Greta woods are green,

And you may gather garlands there,
Would grace a summer queen."
SIR WALTER SCOTT.

SONG.

"A WEARY lot is thine, fair maid,
A weary lot is thine!
To pull the thorn, thy brow to braid,
And press the rue for wine!
A lightsome eye, a soldier's mien,
A feather of the blue,
A doublet of the Lincoln green, —
No more of me you knew,
My love!
No more of me you knew.

"This morn is merry June, I trow,
The rose is budding fain,
But she shall bloom in winter snow,
Ere we two meet again."
He turned his charger as he spake,
Upon the river shore,
He gave his bridle reins a shake,
Said, "Adieu for evermore,
My love !
And adieu for evermore."
SIR WALTER SCOTT.

BATTLE OF THE BALTIC.[1]

Of Nelson and the North,
Sing the glorious day's renown,
When to battle fierce came forth
All the might of Denmark's crown,
And her arms along the deep proudly shone;
By each gun the lighted brand,
In a bold determined hand,
And the Prince of all the land
Led them on.

Like leviathans afloat,
Lay their bulwarks on the brine;
While the sign of battle flew
On the lofty British line :
It was ten of April morn by the chime :
As they drifted on their path,
There was silence deep as death;
And the boldest held his breath,
For a time.

But the might of England flush'd
To anticipate the scene;
And her van the fleeter rush'd
O'er the deadly space between.
" Hearts of oak ! " our captains cried : when each gun
From its adamantine lips
Spread a death-shade round the ships,
Like the hurricane eclipse
Of the sun.

1 Copenhagen was bombarded by the English fleet, under Lord
Nelson and Admiral Parker, in April, 1801, and the Danish fleet
was almost totally destroyed in the engagement.

Again! again! again!
And the havoc did not slack,
Till a feeble cheer the Dane
To our cheering sent us back;
Their shots along the deep slowly boom:
Then ceased — and all is wail,
As they strike the shatter'd sail
Or, in conflagration pale,
Light the gloom.

Out spoke the victor then,
As he hail'd them o'er the wave;
" Ye are brothers! ye are men!
And we conquer but to save:
So peace instead of death let us bring;
But yield, proud foe, thy fleet,
With the crews, at England's feet,
And make submission meet
To our King."

Then Denmark blest our chief,
That he gave her wounds repose;
And the sounds of joy and grief
From her people wildly rose,
As death withdrew his shades from the day.
While the sun look'd smiling bright
O'er a wide and woeful sight,
Where the fires of funeral light
Died away.

Now joy, old England, raise!
For the tidings of thy might,
By the festal cities' blaze,
While the wine-cup shines in light;
And yet amidst that joy and uproar,

Let us think of them that sleep,
Full many a fathom deep,
By thy wild and stormy steep,
Elsinore !

Brave hearts! to Britain's pride
Once so faithful and so true,
On the deck of fame that died,
With the gallant good Riou : [1]
Soft sigh the winds of Heaven o'er their grave!
While the billow mournful rolls
And the mermaid's song condoles,
Singing glory to the souls
Of the brave!

THOMAS CAMPBELL.

YE MARINERS OF ENGLAND.

I.

YE mariners of England!
That guard our native seas;
Whose flag has braved, a thousand years,
The battle and the breeze!
Your glorious standard launch again
To match another foe !
And sweep through the deep,
While the stormy tempests blow;
While the battle rages loud and long,
And the stormy tempests blow.

[1] Captain Riou, justly entitled the gallant and the good by
Lord Nelson, when he wrote home his dispatches.

II.

The spirits of your fathers
Shall start from every wave!—
For the deck it was their field of fame,
And ocean was their grave:
Where Blake and mighty Nelson fell,
Your manly hearts shall glow,
As ye sweep through the deep,
While the stormy tempests blow;
While the battle rages loud and long,
And the stormy tempests blow.

III.

Britannia needs no bulwark,
No towers along the steep;
Her march is o'er the mountain-waves,
Her home is on the deep.
With thunders from her native oak,
She quells the floods below, —
As they roar on the shore,
When the stormy tempests blow;
When the battle rages loud and long,
And the stormy tempests blow.

IV.

The meteor flag of England
Shall yet terrific burn;
Till danger's troubled night depart,
And the star of peace return.
Then, then, ye ocean-warriors!
Our song and feast shall flow
To the fame of your name,
When the storm has ceased to blow;
When the fiery fight is heard no more,
And the storm has ceased to blow.

THOMAS CAMPBELL.

BORDER BALLAD.

MARCH, march, Ettrick and Teviotdale,
  Why the deil dinna ye march forward in order?
March, march, Eskdale and Liddesdale,
  All the Blue Bonnets are bound for the Border
      Many a banner spread
      Flutters above your head,
Many a crest that is famous in story.
      Mount and make ready then,
      Sons of the mountain glen,
Fight for the Queen and our old Scottish glory.

Come from the hills where your hirsels are grazing,
  Come from the glen of the buck and the roe;
Come to the crag where the beacon is blazing,
  Come with the buckler, the lance, and the bow.
      Trumpets are sounding,
      War-steeds are bounding,
Stand to your arms, then, and march in good order,
      England shall many a day
      Tell of the bloody fray,
When the Blue Bonnets came over the Border.
SIR WALTER SCOTT.
The Monastery.

THE FORAY.

THE last of our steers on the board has been spread,
And the last flask of wine in our goblet is red ;
Up! up, my brave kinsmen! belt swords and begone,
There are dangers to dare, and there 's spoil to be won.

The eyes that so lately mixed glances with ours
For a space must be dim, as they gaze from the towers,
And strive to distinguish, through tempest and gloom,
The prance of the steed and the toss of the plume.

The rain is descending; the wind rises loud;
And the moon her red beacon has veiled with a cloud;
'T is the better, my mates! for the warder's dull eye
Shall in confidence slumber, nor dream we are nigh.

Our steeds are impatient! I hear my blithe Gray!
There is life in his hoof-clang, and hope in his neigh;
Like the flash of a meteor, the glance of his mane
Shall marshal your march through the darkness and
      rain.

The drawbridge has dropped, the bugle has blown;
One pledge is to quaff yet — then mount and be-
      gone !
To their honor and peace, that shall rest with the slain,
To their health and their glee, that see Teviot again!
SIR WALTER SCOTT.

THE JOURNEY ONWARDS.

As slow our ship her foamy track
  Against the wind was cleaving,
Her trembling pennant still look'd back
  To that dear isle 't was leaving.
So loath we part from all we love,
  From all the links that bind us;
So turn our hearts, as on we rove,
  To those we 've left behind us!

When, round the bowl, of vanish'd years
   We talk with joyous seeming —
With smiles that might as well be tears,
   So faint, so sad their beaming;
While memory brings us back again
   Each early tie that twined us,
O, sweet 's the cup that circles then
   To those we 've left behind us!

And when, in other climes, we meet
   Some isle or vale enchanting,
Where all looks flowery wild and sweet,
   And nought but love is wanting;
We think how great had been our bliss
   If Heaven had but assign'd us
To live and die in scenes like this,
   With some we 've left behind us!

As travellers oft look back at eve
   When eastward darkly going,
To gaze upon that light they leave
   Still faint behind them glowing, —
So, when the close of pleasure's day
   To gloom hath near consign'd us,
We turn to catch one fading ray
   Of joy that 's left behind us.

THOMAS MOORE.[1]

[1] THOMAS MOORE, the son of a respectable Roman Catholic grocer, was born in Dublin, in May, 1779. He was educated at the Dublin schools and at Trinity College, Dublin. He began to write verses and love songs at an early age, and on going to London to study law, after leaving college, he returned to his early love for literature. He soon abandoned the law, obtained a place under government, travelled in America, and finally settled in England to lead a literary life. He made money from his writings, and received a pension from the government. He

JOCK OF HAZELDEAN.

I.

" Why weep ye by the tide, ladie?
   Why weep ye by the tide?
I 'll wed ye to my youngest son,
   And ye sall be his bride :
And ye sall be his bride, ladie,
   Sae comely to be seen " —
But aye she loot the tears down fa'
   For Jock of Hazeldean.

II.

" Now let this wilfu' grief be done,
   And dry that cheek so pale :
Young Frank is chief of Errington,
   And lord of Langley-dale;
His step is first in peaceful ha',
   His sword in battle keen " —
But aye she loot the tears down fa'
   For Jock of Hazeldean.

III.

" A chain of gold ye sall not lack,
   Nor braid to bind your hair;
Nor mettled hound, nor managed hawk,
   Nor palfrey fresh and fair;
And you, the foremost o' them a',
   Shall ride our forest queen " —
But aye she loot the tears down fa'
   For Jock of Hazeldean.

was the intimate friend of Lord Byron, and of many of the men
of the day most famous in politics and literature. His most
ambitious work was *Lalla Rookh*, but his fame rests chiefly on
his songs and lyrics. He died in 1852.

IV.

The kirk was decked at morning-tide,
   The tapers glimmered fair;
The priest and bridegroom wait the bride,
   And dame and knight were there.
They sought her baith by bower and ha';
   The ladie was not seen!
She 's o'er the Border, and awa'
   Wi' Jock of Hazeldean.

SIR WALTER SCOTT.

THE INCHCAPE ROCK.

No stir in the air, no stir in the sea,
The ship was still as she could be;
Her sails from heaven received no motion;
Her keel was steady in the ocean.

Without either sign or sound of their shock,
The waves flowed over the Inchcape Rock;
So little they rose, so little they fell,
They did not move the Inchcape Bell.

The Abbot of Aberbrothok
Had placed that Bell on the Inchcape Rock;
On a buoy in the storm it floated and swung,
And over the waves its warning rung.

When the Rock was hid by the surge's swell,
The mariners heard the warning bell;
And then they knew the perilous Rock,
And blest the Abbot of Aberbrothok.

The sun in heaven was shining gay;
All things were joyful on that day;

The sea-birds screamed as they wheeled round,
And there was joyance in their sound.

The buoy of the Inchcape Bell was seen,
A darker speck on the ocean green:
Sir Ralph the Rover walked his deck,
And he fixed his eye on the darker speck.

He felt the cheering power of spring;
It made him whistle, it made him sing:
His heart was mirthful to excess,
But the Rover's mirth was wickedness.

His eye was on the Inchcape float;
Quoth he, " My men, put out the boat,
And row me to the Inchcape Rock,
And I 'll plague the Abbot of Aberbrothok."

The boat is lowered, the boatmen row,
And to the Inchcape Rock they go ;
Sir Ralph bent over from the boat,
And he cut the bell from the Inchcape float.

Down sunk the Bell with a gurgling sound;
The bubbles rose and burst around:
Quoth Sir Ralph, " The next who comes to the rock
Won't bless the Abbot of Aberbrothok."

Sir Ralph the Rover sailed away ;
He scoured the seas for many a day;
And now, grown rich with plundered store,
He steers his course for Scotland's shore.

So thick a haze o'erspreads the sky,
They cannot see the sun on high:

The wind hath blown a gale all day;
At evening it hath died away.

On the deck the Rover takes his stand;
So dark it is, they see no land.
Quoth Sir Ralph, " It will be lighter soon,
For there is the dawn of the rising moon."

" Canst hear," said one, " the breakers roar?
For methinks we should be near the shore."
" Now where we are I cannot tell,
But I wish I could hear the Inchcape Bell."

They hear no sound; the swell is strong;
Though the wind hath fallen, they drift along,
Till the vessel strikes with a shivering shock:
" O Christ! it is the Inchcape Rock!"

Sir Ralph the Rover tore his hair;
He cursed himself in his despair:
The waves rush in on every side;
The ship is sinking beneath the tide.

But, even in his dying fear,
One dreadful sound could the Rover hear, —
A sound as if, with the Inchcape Bell,
The Devil below was ringing his knell.

ROBERT SOUTHEY.[1]

---

[1] ROBERT SOUTHEY, the son of a linen draper of Bristol, was born in 1774, educated at Bristol and Westminster, and at Baliol College, Oxford. He tried the law, held a few offices, and then betook himself to literature, to which he devoted his life. He was made poet-laureate in 1813, and held this post until his death, in 1843. His works, both in prose and in verse, are very numerous, and are nearly all unread at the present day.

THE LAMENTATION FOR CELIN.

At the gate of old Granada, when all its bolts are
    barred,
At twilight, at the Vega-gate, there is a trampling
    heard;
There is a trampling heard, as of horses treading slow,
And a weeping voice of women, and a heavy sound of
    woe!
" What tower is fallen, what star is set, what chief
    come these bewailing? "
" A tower is fallen, a star is set! — Alas! alas for
    Celin!"

Three times they knock, three times they cry, — and
    wide the doors they throw;
Dejectedly they enter, and mournfully they go;
In gloomy lines they mustering stand, beneath the hol-
    low porch,
Each horseman grasping in his hand a black and flam-
    ing torch;
Wet is each eye as they go by, and all around is wail-
    ing,
For all have heard the misery. — " Alas! alas for
    Celin!"

Him, yesterday, a Moor did slay, of Bencerraje's
    blood, —
'Twas at the solemn jousting — around the nobles
    stood;
The nobles of the land were by, and ladies bright and
    fair
Looked from their latticed windows, the haughty sight
    to share;

But now the nobles all lament — the ladies are bewail-
    ing —
For he was Granada's darling knight. — " Alas! alas
    for Celin!"

Before him ride his vassals, in order two by two,
With ashes on their turbans spread, most pitiful to
    view;
Behind him his four sisters, each wrapped in sable veil,
Between the tambour's dismal strokes take up their
    doleful tale;
When stops the muffled drum, ye hear their brother-
    less bewailing,
And all the people, far and near, cry — " Alas! alas
    for Celin!"

O! lovely lies he on the bier, above the purple pall,
The flower of all Granada's youth, the loveliest of them
    all;
His dark, dark eyes are closed, his rosy lip is pale,
The crust of blood lies black and dim upon his bur-
    nished mail ;
And evermore the hoarse tambour breaks in upon their
    wailing,
Its sound is like no earthly sound — " Alas! alas for
    Celin !"

The Moorish maid at the lattice stands, the Moor
    stands at his door;
One maid is wringing of her hands, and one is weep-
    ing sore;
Down to the dust men bow their heads, and ashes
    black they strew
Upon their broidered garments, of crimson, green, and
    blue;

Before each gate the bier stands still, — then bursts
    the loud bewailing,
From door and lattice, high and low — " Alas! alas
    for Celin!"

An old, old woman cometh forth, when she hears the
    people cry, —
Her hair is white as silver, like horn her glazèd eye:
'T was she that nursed him at her breast, that nursed
    him long ago;
She knows not whom they all lament, but soon she
    well shall know!
With one deep shriek, she thro' doth break, when her
    ears receive their wailing —
" Let me kiss my Celin ere I die — Alas! alas for
    Celin!"

J. G. LOCKHART.[1]
Spanish Ballads.

[1] JOHN GIBSON LOCKHART, born in 1794, in Lanarkshire, Scotland, was educated at Glasgow, and admitted to the Scotch bar in 1816. He contributed to the magazines of the day, and his literary propensities were confirmed by his marriage, in 1820, with Sophia, the eldest daughter of Sir Walter Scott. In 1826 he removed to London and accepted the editorship of the *London Quarterly Review*, a position which he retained until 1853. He wrote many essays, and some biographical and historical works as well as romances. His best works are his life of Scott and his translations of the ancient Spanish ballads. He died in 1854.

THE PRIDE OF YOUTH.

PROUD Maisie is in the wood,
　　Walking so early;
Sweet Robin sits on the bush,
　　Singing so rarely.

" Tell me, thou bonny bird,
　　When shall I marry me ? "
" When six braw gentlemen
　　Kirkward shall carry ye."

" Who makes the bridal bed,
　　Birdie, say truly ? "
" The gray-headed sexton
　　That delves the grave duly.

" The glow-worm o'er grave and stone
　　Shall light thee steady ;
The owl from the steeple sing,
　　Welcome, proud lady."

SIR WALTER SCOTT.
Heart of Mid-Lothian.

SHE WALKS IN BEAUTY.

SHE walks in beauty, like the night
　　Of cloudless climes and starry skies;
And all that's best of dark and bright
　　Meets in her aspect and her eyes:
Thus mellow'd to that tender light
　　Which heaven to gaudy day denies.

One shade the more, one ray the less,
  Had half impair'd the nameless grace
Which waves in every raven tress,
  Or softly lightens o'er her face;
Where thoughts serenely sweet express
  How pure, how dear their dwelling-place.

And on that cheek, and o'er that brow,
  So soft, so calm, yet eloquent,
The smiles that win, the tints that glow,
  But tell of days in goodness spent,
A mind at peace with all below,
  A heart whose love is innocent!

LORD BYRON.[1]

SHE WAS A PHANTOM OF DELIGHT.

SHE was a phantom of delight
When first she gleam'd upon my sight;

[1] GEORGE GORDON, LORD BYRON, the descendant of a very old, noble, and distinguished family, of which he was the last representative, was born in 1788, and educated at Harrow and at Trinity College, Cambridge. He had a head and face of great beauty, and an athletic frame, but he was deformed and incurably lame. His first verses were a failure; but on his return from travelling in the East, in 1811, he published the first two cantos of *Childe Harold*, and sprang at once into world-wide reputation. He married Miss Millbanke in 1815, and in the following year they separated. Lord Byron returned to voluntary exile on the Continent, and never came back to England. He headed an expedition for the liberation of Greece in 1823, and died at Missolonghi in 1824. He wrote many poems, and both the longer ones, like *Childe Harold*, and the short lyrics and songs, are among the greatest works of English poetry. His career was tarnished and his great genius sullied by reckless dissipation, by a bitter temper, and by an arrogant and vain disposition.

A lovely apparition, sent
To be a moment's ornament;
Her eyes as stars of twilight fair;
Like Twilight's, too, her dusky hair;
But all things else about her drawn
From May-time and the cheerful dawn;
A dancing shape, an image gay,
To haunt, to startle, and waylay.

I saw her upon nearer view,
A spirit, yet a woman too!
Her household motions, light and free,
And steps of virgin liberty;
A countenance in which did meet
Sweet records, promises as sweet;
A creature not too bright or good
For human nature's daily food,
For transient sorrows, simple wiles,
Praise, blame, love, kisses, tears, and smiles.

And now I see with eye serene
The very pulse of the machine;
A being breathing thoughtful breath,
A traveller between life and death;
The reason firm, the temperate will,
Endurance, foresight, strength, and skill;
A perfect woman, nobly plann'd
To warn, to comfort, and command;
And yet a spirit still, and bright
With something of an angel-light.

WILLIAM WORDSWORTH.[1]

[1] WILLIAM WORDSWORTH was born in Cumberland in 1770, and was educated at St. John's College, Cambridge. He inherited sufficient property to render him independent, and after living for a time in Dorsetshire, he finally established himself at

HYMN FOR THE DEAD.[1]

THAT day of wrath, that dreadful day,
When heaven and earth shall pass away,
What power shall be the sinner's stay?
How shall he meet that dreadful day?

When, shrivelling like a parchèd scroll,
The flaming heavens together roll;
When louder yet, and yet more dread,
Swells the high trump that wakes the dead!

O! on that day, that wrathful day,
When man to judgment wakes from clay,
Be *Thou* the trembling sinner's stay,
Though heaven and earth shall pass away!

SIR WALTER SCOTT.

Rydal Mount, among the English Lakes, where he remained
until his death. He had a sinecure position under government,
and subsequently a pension, and in 1843 he was made poet-
laureate, on the death of Southey. He died in 1850. He was
a prolific writer of verse, much of which is esteemed of great
beauty, and he is considered by his admirers to hold the next
place to Shakespeare and Milton, an opinion from which many
persons dissent. He was the most famous of the " Lake School "
of poets, and represented, perhaps, better than any one else, the
reaction of the nineteenth century against the school of Pope,
and the change from the highly artificial to the simple and
natural in poetry.

[1] This is a translation of a portion of the *Dies Iræ*, the most
famous hymn of the early church. Macaulay has translated the
whole hymn, and other versions, including an excellent one by
the late General Dix, are to be found in a little volume entitled
The Seven Great Hymns of the Mediæval Church.

THE DESTRUCTION OF SENNACHERIB.

THE Assyrian came down like the wolf on the fold,
And his cohorts were gleaming in purple and gold ;
And the sheen of their spears was like stars on the sea,
When the blue wave rolls nightly on deep Galilee.

Like the leaves of the forest when Summer is green,
That host with their banners at sunset were seen :
Like the leaves of the forest when Autumn hath blown,
That host on the morrow lay wither'd and strown.

For the Angel of Death spread his wings on the blast,
And breath'd in the face of the foe as he pass'd,
And the eyes of the sleepers wax'd deadly and chill,
And their hearts but once heav'd, and forever grew still !

And there lay the steed with his nostril all wide,
But through it there rolled not the breath of his pride :
And the foam of his gasping lay white on the turf,
And cold as the spray of the rock-beating surf.

And there lay the rider, distorted and pale,
With the dew on his brow, and the rust on his mail;
And the tents were all silent, the banners alone,
The lances unlifted, the trumpet unblown.

And the widows of Ashur are loud in their wail,
And the idols are broke in the temple of Baal ;
And the might of the Gentile, unsmote by the sword,
Hath melted like snow in the glance of the Lord !

LORD BYRON.

REBECCA'S HYMN.

When Israel, of the Lord beloved,
   Out from the land of bondage came,
Her fathers' God before her moved,
   An awful guide in smoke and flame.
By day, along the astonished lands,
   The cloudy pillar glided slow;
By night, Arabia's crimsoned sands
   Returned the fiery column's glow.

There rose the choral hymn of praise,
   And trump and timbrel answered keen,
And Zion's daughters poured their lays,
   With priest's and warrior's voice between.
No portents now our foes amaze,
   Forsaken Israel wanders lone :
Our fathers would not know Thy ways,
   And Thou hast left them to their own.

But present still, though now unseen !
   When brightly shines the prosperous day,
Be thoughts of Thee a cloudy screen
   To temper the deceitful ray.
And O, when stoops on Judah's path
   In shade and storm the frequent night,
Be Thou, long-suffering, slow to wrath,
   A burning and a shining light !

Our harps we left by Babel's streams,
   The tyrant's jest, the Gentile's scorn ;
No censer round our altar beams,
   And mute are timbrel, harp, and horn.

But Thou hast said, " The blood of goat,
 The flesh of rams, I will not prize ;
A contrite heart, a humble thought,
 Are mine accepted sacrifice."
Sir Walter Scott.
Ivanhoe.

VISION OF BELSHAZZAR.

The King was on his throne,
 The satraps throng'd the hall;
A thousand bright lamps shone
 O'er that high festival.
A thousand cups of gold,
 In Judah deem'd divine, —
Jehovah's vessels hold
 The godless Heathen's wine!

In that same hour and hall,
 The fingers of a hand
Came forth against the wall,
 And wrote as if on sand:
The fingers of a man; —
 A solitary hand
Along the letters ran,
 And traced them like a wand.

The monarch saw and shook,
 And bade no more rejoice;
All bloodless wax'd his look,
 And tremulous his voice.
" Let the men of lore appear
 The wisest of the earth,

And expound the words of fear,
  Which mar our royal mirth.''

Chaldea's seers are good,
  But here they have no skill;
And the unknown letters stood
  Untold and awful still.
And Babel's men of age
  Are wise and deep in lore;
But now they were not sage,
  They saw — but knew no more.

A captive in the land,
  A stranger and a youth,
He heard the King's command,
  He saw that writing's truth.
The lamps around were bright,
  The prophecy in view;
He read it on that night, —
  The morrow proved it true.

" Belshazzar's grave is made,
  His kingdom pass'd away,
He, in the balance weigh'd,
  Is light and worthless clay.
The shroud his robe of state,
  His canopy the stone;
The Mede is at his gate!
  The Persian on his throne!''

LORD BYRON.

THE BRIDAL OF ANDALLA.

" RISE up, rise up, Xarifa ! lay the golden cushion
    down;
Rise up, come to the window, and gaze with all the
    town !
From gay guitar and violin the silver notes are flowing,
And the lovely lute doth speak between the trumpet's
    lordly blowing,
And banners bright from lattice light are waving every-
    where,
And the tall, tall plume of our cousin's bridegroom
    floats proudly in the air:
Rise up, rise up, Xarifa! lay the golden cushion down;
Rise up, come to the window, and gaze with all the
    town !

" Arise, arise, Xarifa! I see Andalla's face, —
He bends him to the people with a calm and princely
    grace;
Through all the land of Xeres and banks of Guadal-
    quiver
Rode forth bridegroom so brave as he, so brave and
    lovely, never.
Yon tall plume waving o'er his brow, of purple mixed
    with white,
I guess 't was wreathed by Zara, whom he will wed
    to-night!
Rise up, rise up, Xarifa! lay the golden cushion down;
Rise up, come to the window, and gaze with all the
    town !

" What aileth thee, Xarifa? what makes thine eyes
    look down?
11

Why stay ye from the window far, nor gaze with all
    the town?
I 've heard you say on many a day, and sure you said
    the truth,
Andalla rides without a peer, among all Granada's
    youth.
Without a peer he rideth, and yon milk-white horse
    doth go,
Beneath his stately master, with a stately step and
    slow:
Then rise — O! rise, Xarifa, lay the golden cushion
    down;
Unseen here through the lattice, you may gaze with
    all the town!"

The Zegri lady rose not, nor laid her cushion down,
Nor came she to the window to gaze with all the
    town;
But though her eyes dwelt on her knee, in vain her
    fingers strove,
And though her needle pressed the silk, no flower
    Xarifa wove;
One bonny rose-bud she had traced, before the noise
    drew nigh;
That bonny bud a tear effaced, slow drooping from her
    eye.
"No — no!" she sighs, "bid me not rise, nor lay my
    cushion down,
To gaze upon Andalla with all the gazing town!"

"Why rise ye not, Xarifa, — nor lay your cushion
    down?
Why gaze ye not, Xarifa, — with all the gazing town?
Hear, hear the trumpet, how it swells, and how the
    people cry!

He stops at Zara's palace-gate — why sit ye still — O,
    why?"
"At Zara's gate stops Zara's mate; in him shall I dis-
    cover
The dark-eyed youth pledged me his truth with tears,
    and was my lover?
I will not rise, with weary eyes, nor lay my cushion
    down,
To gaze on false Andalla with all the gazing town!"

J. G. LOCKHART.
Spanish Ballads.

CORONACH.

HE is gone on the mountain,
    He is lost to the forest,
Like a summer-dried fountain,
    When our need was the sorest.
The fount, reappearing,
    From the raindrops shall borrow,
But to us comes no cheering,
    To Duncan no morrow!

The hand of the reaper
    Takes the ears that are hoary;
But the voice of the weeper
    Wails manhood in glory.
The autumn winds rushing
    Waft the leaves that are searest;
But our flower was in flushing
    When blighting was nearest.

Fleet foot on the correi,
    Sage counsel in cumber,

Red hand in the foray,
    How sound is thy slumber!
Like the dew on the mountain,
    Like the foam on the river,
Like the bubble on the fountain,
    Thou art gone, and forever!
                    SIR WALTER SCOTT.

HELVELLYN.

I CLIMBED the dark brow of the mighty Helvellyn,
Lakes and mountains beneath me gleamed misty and
        wide;
All was still, save by fits, when the eagle was yelling,
And starting around me the echoes replied.
On the right, Striden-edge round the Red-tarn was
        bending,
And Catchedicam its left verge was defending,
One huge nameless rock in the front was ascending,
When I marked the sad spot where the wanderer had
        died.

Dark green was the spot 'mid the brown mountain-
        heather,
Where the Pilgrim of Nature lay stretched in decay,
Like the corpse of an outcast abandoned to weather,
Till the mountain winds wasted the tenantless clay.
Nor yet quite deserted, though lonely extended,
For, faithful in death, his mute favorite attended,
The much-loved remains of her master defended,
And chased the hill-fox and the raven away.

How long didst thou think that his silence was slum-
     ber?
When the wind waved his garment, how oft didst thou
     start?
How many long days and long weeks didst thou num-
     ber,
Ere he faded before thee, the friend of thy heart?
And O, was it meet, that — no requiem read o'er
     him,
No mother to weep, and no friend to deplore him,
And thou, little guardian, alone stretched before
     him —
Unhonored the Pilgrim from life should depart?

When a Prince to the fate of the Peasant has yielded,
The tapestry waves dark round the dim-lighted hall;
With scutcheons of silver the coffin is shielded,
And pages stand mute by the canopied pall:
Through the courts, at deep midnight, the torches are
     gleaming;
In the proudly-arched chapel the banners are beaming.
Far adown the long aisle sacred music is streaming,
Lamenting a chief of the people should fall.

But meeter for thee, gentle lover of nature,
To lay down thy head like the meek mountain lamb,
When, wildered, he drops from some cliff huge in
     stature,
And draws his last sob by the side of his dam.
And more stately thy couch by this desert lake lying,
Thy obsequies sung by the gray plover flying,
With one faithful friend but to witness thy dying,
In the arms of Helvellyn and Catchedicam.
SIR WALTER SCOTT.

THE LORD OF BUTRAGO.

" YOUR horse is faint, my King — my Lord! your gal-
    lant horse is sick;
His limbs are torn, his breast is gored, on his eye the
    film is thick;
Mount, mount on mine, O, mount apace, I pray thee,
    mount and fly!
Or in my arms I 'll lift your grace, — their trampling
    hoofs are nigh!

" My King — my King! you 're wounded sore, — the
    blood runs from your feet;
But only lay a hand before, and I 'll lift you to your
    seat:
Mount, Juan, for they gather fast! I hear their com-
    ing cry!
Mount, mount, and ride for jeopardy! I 'll save you
    though I die!

" Stand, noble steed! this hour of need — be gentle as
    a lamb:
I 'll kiss the foam from off thy mouth — thy master
    dear I am!
Mount, Juan, mount! whate'er betide, away the bridle
    fling,
And plunge the rowels in his side! — my horse shall
    save my King!

" Nay, never speak: my sires, Lord King, received
    their land from yours,
And joyfully their blood shall spring, so be it thine se-
    cures:

If I should fly, and thou, my King, be found among
　　the dead,
How could I stand 'mong gentlemen, such scorn on my
　　gray head?

" Castile's proud dames shall never point the finger of
　　disdain,
And say, There's one that ran away when our good
　　lords were slain!
I leave Diego in your care, — you 'll fill his father's
　　place :
Strike, strike the spur, and never spare — God's bless-
　　ing on your grace!"

So spake the brave Montanez, Butrago's lord was he;
And turned him to the coming host in steadfastness
　　and glee;
He flung himself among them, as they came down the
　　hill;
He died, God wot! but not before his sword had drunk
　　its fill!

J. G. LOCKHART.
Spanish Ballads.

KUBLA KHAN.

In Xanadu did Kubla Khan
　　A stately pleasure-dome decree:
Where Alph, the sacred river, ran
Through caverns measureless to man
　　Down to a sunless sea.
So twice five miles of fertile ground
With walls and towers were girdled round:

And there were gardens bright with sinuous rills,
Where blossomed many an incense-bearing tree ;
And here were forests ancient as the hills,
Enfolding sunny spots of greenery.

But O! that deep romantic chasm which slanted
Down the green hill athwart a cedarn cover!
A savage place! as holy and enchanted
As e'er beneath a waning moon was haunted
By woman wailing for her demon lover!
And from this chasm, with ceaseless turmoil seething,
As if this earth in fast thick pants were breathing,
A mighty fountain momently was forced :
Amid whose swift half-intermitted burst
Huge fragments vaulted like rebounding hail,
Or chaffy grain beneath the thresher's flail:
And 'mid these dancing rocks at once and ever
It flung up momently the sacred river.
Five miles meandering with a mazy motion
Through wood and dale the sacred river ran,
Then reached the caverns measureless to man,
And sank in tumult to a lifeless ocean:
And 'mid this tumult Kubla heard from far
Ancestral voices prophesying war!
    The shadow of the dome of pleasure
    Floated midway on the waves;
    Where was heard the mingled measure
    From the fountain and the caves.
It was a miracle of rare device,
A sunny pleasure-dome with caves of ice!
    A damsel with a dulcimer
    In a vision once I saw:
    It was an Abyssinian maid,
    And on her dulcimer she played,
    Singing of Mount Abora.

Could I revive within me
Her symphony and song,
To such a deep delight 't would win me
That with music loud and long,
I would build that dome in air,
That sunny dome! those caves of ice!
And all who heard should see them there,
And all should cry, Beware! Beware!
His flashing eyes, his floating hair!
Weave a circle round him thrice,
And close your eyes with holy dread,
For he on honey-dew hath fed,
And drunk the milk of Paradise.

SAMUEL TAYLOR COLERIDGE.[1]

BERNARDO AND ALPHONSO.

WITH some good ten of his chosen men, Bernardo hath
    appeared
Before them all in the palace hall, the lying King to
    beard ;

[1] SAMUEL TAYLOR COLERIDGE, son of Rev. John Coleridge,
born in 1772, was educated at Christ's Hospital, and afterwards
at Jesus College, Cambridge. He entered the light dragoons,
but soon escaped from this uncongenial pursuit, and devoted
himself to literature, in which he achieved celebrity as poet,
philosopher, and critic. His fame rests principally on his prose
writings, but much of his poetry is of a very high order, particu-
larly the famous *Rime of the Ancient Mariner* and *Genevieve.*
He died in 1834. His activity was impaired and his career marred
and broken by excessive indulgence in opium. The famous
poem in the text, a fragment only, was composed during sleep produced, probably, by opium.

With cap in hand and eye on ground, he came in rev-
        erend guise,
But ever and anon he frowned, and flame broke from
        his eyes.

" A curse upon thee," cries the King, " who comest
        unbid to me ;
But what from traitor's blood should spring, save trai-
        tors like to thee?
His sire, lords, had a traitor's heart; perchance our
        champion brave
May think it were a pious part to share Don Sancho's
        grave."

" Whoever told this tale the King hath rashness to re-
        peat,"
Cries Bernard, "here my gage I fling before the liar's
        feet!
No treason was in Sancho's blood, no stain in mine doth
        lie:
Below the throne what knight will own the coward
        calumny?

" The blood that I like water shed, when Roland did
        advance,
By secret traitors hired and led, to make us slaves of
        France;
The life of King Alphonso I saved at Roncesval, —
Your words, Lord King, are recompense abundant for
        it all.

" Your horse was down, — your hope was flown, — I
        saw the falchion shine,
That soon had drunk your royal blood, had I not vent-
        ured mine;

But memory soon of service done deserteth the in-
       grate;
You 've thanked the son for life and crown by the fa-
       ther's bloody fate.

" Ye swore upon your kingly faith, to set Don Sancho
       free;
But, curse upon your paltering breath, the light he
       ne'er did see;
He died in dungeon cold and dim, by Alphonso's base
       decree,
And visage blind, and stiffened limb, were all they gave
       to me.

" The King that swerveth from his word hath stained
       his purple black;
No Spanish lord will draw the sword behind a liar's
       back;
But noble vengeance shall be mine, an open hate I 'll
       show, —
The King hath injured Carpio's line, and Bernard is
       his foe."

" Seize, seize him! " loud the King doth scream; " there
       are a thousand here!
Let his foul blood this instant stream!   What! caitiffs,
       do ye fear?
Seize, seize the traitor! "   But not one to move a fin-
       ger dareth;
Bernardo standeth by the throne, and calm his sword
       he bareth.

He drew the falchion from the sheath, and held it up
       on high,
And all the hall was still as death: cries Bernard,
       " Here am I, —

And here is the sword that owns no lord, excepting
    Heaven and me;
Fain would I know who dares his point, — King, Condé,
    or Grandee."

Then to his mouth the horn he drew (it hung below
    his cloak);
His ten true men the signal knew, and through the ring
    they broke;
With helm on head, and blade in hand, the knights the
    circle brake,
And back the lordlings 'gan to stand, and the false
    King to quake.

" Ha! Bernard," quoth Alphonso, " what means this
    warlike guise?
Ye know full well I jested, — ye know your worth I
    prize."
But Bernard turned upon his heel, and smiling passed
    away:
Long rued Alphonso and his realm the jesting of that
    day.

J. G. LOCKHART.
Spanish Ballads.

BERNARDO DEL CARPIO.

THE warrior bowed his crested head, and tamed his
    heart of fire,
And sued the haughty King to free his long-imprisoned
    sire;

"I bring thee here my fortress-keys, I bring my captive train,
I pledge thee faith, my liege, my lord! O! break my
 father's chain!"

"Rise, rise! ev'n now thy father comes, a ransom'd
 man this day;
Mount thy good horse, and thou and I will meet him
 on his way."
Then lightly rose that loyal son, and bounded on his
 steed,
And urged, as if with lance in rest, the charger's
 foamy speed.

And lo! from far, as on they press'd, there came a
 glittering band,
With one that 'midst them stately rode, as a leader in
 the land;
"Now haste, Bernardo, haste! for there in very truth
 is he,
The father whom thy faithful heart hath yearn'd so
 long to see."

His dark eye flash'd, his proud breast heav'd, his
 cheek's hue came and went;
He reach'd that gray-haired chieftain's side, and there
 dismounting bent;
A lowly knee to earth he bent, his father's hand he
 took, —
What was there in its touch that all his fiery spirit
 shook?

That hand was cold, a frozen thing, it dropp'd from
 his like lead;
He looked up to the face above, — the face was of the
 dead!

A plume waved o'er the noble brow, — the brow was
    fixed and white;
He met at last his father's eyes, but in them was no
    sight!

Up from the ground he sprang, and gazed; but who
    could paint that gaze?
They hush'd their very hearts that saw its horror and
    amaze.
They might have chain'd him as before that stony
    form he stood,
For the power was stricken from his arm, and from
    his lip the blood.

"Father!" at length he murmur'd low, and wept like
    childhood then:
Talk not of grief till thou hast seen the tears of war-
    like men!
He thought on all his glorious hopes, and all his
    young renown,
He flung his falchion from his side, and in the dust sat
    down.

Then covering with his steel-gloved hands his darkly
    mournful brow,
"No more, there is no more," he said, "to lift the
    sword for now.
My King is false, my hope betray'd, my father — O!
    the worth,
The glory, and the loveliness are pass'd away from
    earth.

"I thought to stand where banners waved, my sire,
    beside thee yet;
I would that there our kindred blood on Spain's free
    soil had met;

Thou wouldst have known my spirit then : for thee
    my fields were won,
And thou hast perish'd in thy chains, as though thou
    hadst no son ! "

Then starting from the ground once more, he seized
    the monarch's rein,
Amidst the pale and wilder'd looks of all the courtier-
    train ;
And with a fierce, o'er-mastering grasp the rearing
    war-horse led,
And sternly set them face to face, — the King before
    the dead.

" Came I not forth upon thy pledge, my father's hand
    to kiss?
Be still, and gaze thou on, false King ! and tell me,
    what is this ?
The voice, the glance, the heart I sought, — give an-
    swer, where are they?
If thou wouldst clear thy perjured soul, send life
    through this cold clay.

" Into these glassy eyes put light, — be still ! keep down
    thine ire ! —
Bid these white lips a blessing speak — this earth is
    not my sire.
Give me back him for whom I strove, for whom my
    blood was shed :
Thou canst not? — and a king ! — his dust be moun-
    tains on thy head ! "

He loosed the steed, his slack hand fell ; upon the
    silent face
He cast one long, deep, troubled look, then turn'd
    from that sad place.

His hope was crush'd, his after-fate untold in martial
    strain,
His banner led the spears no more amidst the hills of
    Spain.

FELICIA HEMANS.[1]

TO THE POETS.

BARDS of Passion and of Mirth,
  Ye have left your souls on earth!
  Have ye souls in heaven too,
  Doubled-lived in regions new?
Yes, and those of heaven commune
With the spheres of sun and moon;
With the noise of fountains wondrous,
And the parle of voices thund'rous;
With the whisper of heaven's trees
And one another, in soft ease
Seated on Elysian lawns,
Browsed by none but Dian's fawns;
Underneath large blue-bells tented,
Where the daisies are rose-scented,
And the rose herself has got
Perfume which on earth is not;
Where the nightingale doth sing
Not a senseless, trancèd thing,

[1] FELICIA DOROTHEA HEMANS, born in Liverpool in 1794,
was the daughter of a merchant, and was married in 1812 to
Captain Hemans of the Fourth Regiment, who not long after
deserted her and their children. Mrs. Hemans then returned to
her family, and devoted herself to the education of her sons.
She died in 1835. Such time as she could spare from household cares was devoted to literature, and she published a number of works both in verse and in prose.

But divine melodious truth ;
Philosophic numbers smooth ;
Tales and golden histories
Of heaven and its mysteries.

Thus ye live on high, and then
On the earth ye live again ;
And the souls ye left behind you
Teach us here the way to find you,
Where your other souls are joying,
Never slumber'd, never cloying.
Here, your earth-born souls still speak
To mortals, of their little week ;
Of their sorrows and delights ;
Of their passions and their spites ;
Of their glory and their shame ;
What doth strengthen and what maim.
Thus ye teach us, every day,
Wisdom, though fled far away.

Bards of Passion and of Mirth,
Ye have left your souls on earth !
Ye have souls in heaven too,
Double-lived in regions new !

JOHN KEATS.[1]

[1] JOHN KEATS, the son of a stable-keeper, born in London
in 1796, was educated at a classical school in Enfield, and in his
fifteenth year apprenticed to a surgeon at Edmonton. He soon,
however, abandoned medicine for literature. His first volume
was treated by the critics with crushing severity, which preyed
upon his mind and injured his health. After the publication of
a second volume of poems, which fully redeemed the promise
of the first, he went abroad for his health, and died at Rome
in 1821. Much of the little poetry he left is of most exquisite
beauty, and entitles him to a high place among the group of

THE CLOUD.

I.

I BRING fresh showers for the thirsting flowers,
    From the seas and the streams;
I bear light shades for the leaves when laid
    In their noon-day dreams.
From my wings are shaken the dews that waken
    The sweet buds every one,
When rocked to rest on their mother's breast,
    As she dances about the sun.
I wield the flail of the lashing hail,
    And whiten the green plains under,
And then again I dissolve it in rain,
    And laugh as I pass in thunder.

II.

I sift the snow on the mountains below,
    And their great pines groan aghast;
And all the night 't is my pillow white,
    While I sleep in the arms of the blast.
Sublime on the towers of my skiey bowers,
    Lightning my pilot sits;
In a cavern under is fettered the thunder,
    It struggles and howls at fits ;
Over earth and ocean with gentle motion
    This pilot is guiding me,
Lured by the love of the genii that move
    In the depths of the purple sea ;
Over the rills, and the crags, and the hills,
    Over the lakes and the plains,

writers who made the beginning of the nineteenth century the
most brilliant period of English literature, with the exception of
that of Elizabeth.

Wherever he dream, under mountain or stream,
    The spirit he loves remains;
And I all the while bask in heaven's blue smile,
    Whilst he is dissolving in rains.

III.

The sanguine sunrise, with his meteor eyes,
    And his burning plumes outspread,
Leaps on the back of my sailing rack,
    When the morning star shines dead.
As on the jag of a mountain crag,
    Which an earthquake rocks and swings,
An eagle alit one moment may sit
    In the light of its golden wings.
And when sunset may breathe, from the lit sea beneath,
    Its ardors of rest and of love,
And the crimson pall of eve may fall
    From the depth of heaven above,
With wings folded I rest, on mine airy nest,
    As still as a brooding dove.

IV.

That orbèd maiden, with white fire laden,
    Whom mortals call the moon,
Glides glimmering o'er my fleece-like floor,
    By the midnight breezes strewn ;
And wherever the beat of her unseen feet,
    Which only the angels hear,
May have broken the woof of my tent's thin roof,
    The stars peep behind her and peer ;
And I laugh to see them whirl and flee,
    Like a swarm of golden bees,
When I widen the rent in my wind-built tent,
    Till the calm rivers, lakes, and seas,
Like strips of the sky fallen through me on high,
    Are each paved with the moon and these.

V.

I bind the sun's throne with the burning zone,
      And the moon's with a girdle of pearl ;
The volcanoes are dim, and the stars reel and swim,
      When the whirlwinds my banner unfurl.
From cape to cape, with a bridge-like shape,
      Over a torrent sea,
Sunbeam-proof, I hang like a roof,
      The mountains its columns be.
The triumphal arch through which I march,
      With hurricane, fire, and snow,
When the powers of the air are chained to my chair,
      Is the million-colored bow ;
The sphere-fire above its soft colors wove,
      While the moist earth was laughing below.

VI.

I am the daughter of earth and water,
      And the nursling of the sky :
I pass through the pores of the ocean and shores ;
      I change, but I cannot die.
For after the rain, when with never a stain
      The pavilion of heaven is bare,
And the winds and sunbeams, with their convex gleams,
      Build up the blue dome of air,
I silently laugh at my own cenotaph,
      And out of the caverns of rain,
Like a child from the womb, like a ghost from the tomb,
      I arise and unbuild it again.

                  PERCY BYSSHE SHELLEY.[1]

---

[1] PERCY BYSSHE SHELLEY, born in 1792, was the son of Sir
Timothy Shelley, and of ancient family. He was educated at
Eton and went thence to University College, Oxford, whence he
was expelled in 1811 for publishing a tract entitled *A Defence
of Atheism*. He then wrote his first important poem, *Queen*

PRO PATRIA MORI.

WHEN he who adores thee has left but the name
    Of his fault and his sorrows behind,
O ! say, wilt thou weep, when they darken the fame
    Of a life that for thee was resigned ?
Yes, weep, and however my foes may condemn,
    Thy tears shall efface their decree;
For, Heaven can witness, though guilty to them,
    I have been but too faithful to thee.

With thee were the dreams of my earliest love;
    Every thought of my reason was thine :
In my last humble prayer to the Spirit above
    Thy name shall be mingled with mine !
O ! blest are the lovers and friends who shall live
    The days of thy glory to see ;
But the next dearest blessing that Heaven can give
    Is the pride of thus dying for thee.

                      THOMAS MOORE.

Mab, and not long after married Miss Harriet Westbrooke. This marriage proved very unhappy, and Shelley and his wife soon separated. In 1816 Mrs. Shelley committed suicide, and Shelley then married Mary, the daughter of the celebrated William Godwin and his hardly less celebrated wife, Mary Wollstonecraft. This second marriage was a happy one. Shelley went to Italy, where he passed the rest of his life supported by an allowance from his father, and where he was constantly in the society of Lord Byron. In June, 1822, when he was out sailing, a squall came up, the boat capsized, and Shelley and his companions were drowned. His writings are almost wholly in verse, and many of his poems are of the most perfect and finished beauty. His mind, however, was morbid almost to the verge of disease, and this gives a peculiar tone to all his poetry.

THE LANDING OF THE PILGRIM FATHERS.

The breaking waves dashed high
  On a stern and rock-bound coast,
And the woods, against a stormy sky,
  Their giant branches tost ;

And the heavy night hung dark
  The hills and waters o'er,
When a band of exiles moored their bark
  On the wild New England shore.

Not as the conqueror comes,
  They, the true-hearted, came,
Not with the roll of the stirring drums,
  And the trumpet that sings of fame ;

Not as the flying come,
  In silence and in fear, —
They shook the depths of the desert gloom
  With their hymns of lofty cheer.

Amidst the storm they sang,
  And the stars heard, and the sea !
And the sounding aisles of the dim woods rang
  To the anthem of the free !

The ocean-eagle soared
  From his nest by the white wave's foam,
And the rocking pines of the forest roared, —
  This was their welcome home !

There were men with hoary hair
  Amidst that pilgrim band, —

Why had they come to wither there
　Away from their childhood's land?

There was woman's fearless eye,
　Lit by her deep love's truth ;
There was manhood's brow, serenely high,
　And the fiery heart of youth.

What sought they thus afar?
　Bright jewels of the mine?
The wealth of seas, the spoils of war?
　They sought a faith's pure shrine !

Ay, call it holy ground,
　The soil where first they trod !
They have left unstained what there they found —
　Freedom to worship God !

FELICIA HEMANS.

TO THE MEMORY OF EDWARD THE BLACK PRINCE.

O FOR the voice of that wild horn,
On Fontarabian echoes borne,
　　The dying hero's call,
That told imperial Charlemagne,
How Paynim sons of swarthy Spain
　　Had wrought his champion's fall.

Sad over earth and ocean sounding,
And England's distant cliffs astounding,
　　Such are the notes should say

How Britain's hope and France's fear,
Victor of Cressy and Poitier,
   In Bourdeaux dying lay.

" Raise my faint head, my squires," he said,
" And let the casement be displayed,
   That I may see once more
The splendor of the setting sun
Gleam on thy mirrored wave, Garonne,
   And Blaye's empurpled shore.

" Like me, he sinks to Glory's sleep,
His fall the dews of evening steep,
   As if in sorrow shed.
So soft shall fall the trickling tear,
When England's maids and matrons hear
   Of their Black Edward dead.

" And though my sun of glory set,
Nor France nor England shall forget
   The terror of my name ;
And oft shall Britain's heroes rise,
New planets in these southern skies,
   Through clouds of blood and flame."
               SIR WALTER SCOTT.
                   Rob Roy.

THE ISLES OF GREECE.

THE isles of Greece, the isles of Greece !
   Where burning Sappho loved and sung,
Where grew the arts of war and peace,
   Where Delos rose, and Phœbus sprung !

Eternal summer gilds them yet,
But all, except their sun, is set.

The Scian and the Teian muse,
  The hero's harp, the lover's lute,
Have found the fame your shores refuse;
  Their place of birth alone is mute
To sounds which echo further west
Than your sire's " Islands of the Blest."

The mountains look on Marathon, —
  And Marathon looks on the sea;
And musing there an hour alone,
  I dream'd that Greece might still be free;
For standing on the Persians' grave,
I could not deem myself a slave.

A King sate on the rocky brow
  Which looks o'er sea-born Salamis;
And ships, by thousands, lay below,
  And men in nations, — all were his!
He counted them at break of day, —
And when the sun set where were they?

And where are they? and where art thou,
  My country? On thy voiceless shore,
The heroic lay is tuneless now,
  The heroic bosom beats no more!
And must thy lyre, so long divine,
Degenerate into hands like mine?

'T is something, in the dearth of fame,
  Though link'd among a fetter'd race,
To feel at least a patriot's shame,
  Even as I sing, suffuse my face;

For what is left the poet here?
For Greeks a blush, — for Greece a tear.

Must *we* but weep o'er days more blest?
　Must *we* but blush?　Our fathers bled.
Earth! render back from out thy breast
　A remnant of our Spartan dead!
Of the three hundred grant but three,
To make a new Thermopylae!

What, silent still? and silent all?
　Ah! no ; the voices of the dead
Sound like a distant torrent's fall,
　And answer, " Let one living head,
But one, arise, — we come, we come ! "
'T is but the living who are dumb.

In vain — in vain ! strike other chords;
　Fill high the cup with Samian wine !
Leave battles to the Turkish hordes,
　And shed the blood of Scio's vine !
Hark ! rising to the ignoble call,
How answers each bold Bacchanal !

You have the Pyrrhic dance as yet,
　Where is the Pyrrhic phalanx gone?
Of two such lessons, why forget
　The nobler and the manlier one?
You have the letters Cadmus gave, —
Think ye he meant them for a slave ?

Fill high the bowl with Samian wine !
　We will not think of themes like these!
It made Anacreon's song divine :
　He served — but served Polycrates —

A tyrant; but our masters then
Were still, at least, our countrymen.

The tyrant of the Chersonese
　　Was freedom's best and bravest friend;
That tyrant was Miltiades!
　　O! that the present hour would lend
Another despot of the kind!
Such chains as his were sure to bind.

Fill high the bowl with Samian wine!
　　On Suli's rock and Parga's shore
Exists the remnant of a line
　　Such as the Doric mothers bore;
And there, perhaps, some seed is sown,
The Heracleidan blood might own.

Trust not for freedom to the Franks, —
　　They have a King who buys and sells:
In native swords and native ranks
　　The only hope of courage dwells;
But Turkish force and Latin fraud
Would break your shield, however broad.

Fill high the bowl with Samian wine!
　　Our virgins dance beneath the shade;
I see their glorious black eyes shine;
　　But gazing on each glowing maid,
My own the burning tear-drop laves,
To think such breasts must suckle slaves.

Place me on Sunium's marbled steep,
　　Where nothing, save the waves and I,
May hear our mutual murmurs sweep;
　　There, swan-like, let me sing and die:

A land of slaves shall ne'er be mine, —
Dash down yon cup of Samian wine!

LORD BYRON.

HESTER.

WHEN maidens such as Hester die,
Their place ye may not well supply,
Though ye among a thousand try
    With vain endeavor.
A month or more has she been dead,
Yet cannot I by force be led
To think upon the wormy bed
    And her together.

A springy motion in her gait,
A rising step, did indicate
Of pride and joy no common rate
    That flush'd her spirit:
I know not by what name beside
I shall it call: if 't was not pride,
It was a joy to that allied,
    She did inherit.

Her parents held the Quaker rule
Which doth the human feeling cool;
But she was train'd in Nature's school,
    Nature had blest her.
A waking eye, a prying mind,
A heart that stirs, is hard to bind;
A hawk's keen sight ye cannot blind,
    Ye could not Hester.

My sprightly neighbor! gone before
To that unknown and silent shore,
Shall we not meet, as heretofore
        Some summer morning, —
When from thy cheerful eyes a ray
Hath struck a bliss upon the day,
A bliss that would not go away,
        A sweet fore-warning?
                        CHARLES LAMB.[1]

WINTER.

A WIDOW bird sate mourning for her Love
        Upon a wintry bough;
The frozen wind crept on above,
        The freezing stream below.

There was no leaf upon the forest bare,
        No flower upon the ground,
And little motion in the air
        Except the mill-wheel's sound.
                        PERCY BYSSHE SHELLEY.

[1] CHARLES LAMB, born in London in 1775, was educated at Christ's Hospital, and in 1792 obtained a situation in the East India house, which he held until 1825, when he retired on a pension. His life was devoted to the guardianship of his sister, a woman of much talent, who assisted him in his literary work but who was subject to fits of insanity. The hard monotony of an accountant's life was varied and relieved by excursions into various fields of literature. The best of Lamb's works are the famous *Essays of Elia*, abounding in humor and clever criticism of character and manners. Lamb was also a most charming companion, very witty, and famous as a story teller. He died in 1834.

TO THOMAS MOORE.

My boat is on the shore,
   And my bark is on the sea;
But before I go, Tom Moore,
   Here's a double health to thee!

Here's a sigh to those who love me,
   And a smile to those who hate;
And, whatever sky's above me,
   Here's a heart for every fate.

Though the ocean roar around me,
   Yet it still shall bear me on;
Though a desert should surround me,
   It hath springs that may be won.

Were't the last drop in the well,
   As I gasp'd upon the brink,
Ere my fainting spirit fell,
   'T is to thee that I would drink.

With that water, as this wine,
   The libation I would pour
Should be — peace with thine and mine,
   And a health to thee, Tom Moore.
LORD BYRON.

BONNY DUNDEE.[1]

To the Lords of Convention 't was Claver'se who spoke,
" Ere the King's crown shall fall there are crowns to
     be broke ;
So let each Cavalier who loves honor and me
Come follow the bonnet of Bonny Dundee.
     Come fill up my cup, come fill up my can,
     Come saddle your horses, and call up your men ;
     Come open the West Port and let me gang free,
     And it 's room for the bonnets of Bonny Dundee."

Dundee he is mounted, he rides up the street,
The bells are rung backward, the drums they are
     beat ;
But the Provost, douce man, said, " Just e'en let him
     be,
The gude town is weel quit of that Deil of Dundee."

With sour - featured Whigs the Grassmarket was
     crammed,
As if half the West had set tryst to be hanged :
There was spite in each look, there was fear in each
     ee,
As they watched for the bonnets of Bonny Dundee.

[1] JOHN GRAHAM, of Claverhouse, Viscount Dundee, born
about 1650.   He was distinguished by his military talents
and dashing exploits, but was a man of hard and cruel temper.
He served in the Dutch army, and returned to Scotland in 1677,
where he engaged in the work of suppressing the Covenanters.
He espoused the cause of James II., when that monarch abdi-
cated, and raised a troop of horse.   He defeated the troops of
William III. at Killiecrankie, where he fell in the moment of
victory.   The next poem relates to the last scene of his life.

These cowls of Kilmarnock had spits and had spears,
And lang-hafted gullies to kill Cavaliers;
And they shrunk to close-heads, and the causeway was
        free,
At the toss of the bonnet of Bonny Dundee.

"Away to the hills, to the caves, to the rocks, —
Ere I own an usurper, I'll couch with the fox;
And tremble, false Whigs, in the midst of your glee,
You have not seen the last of my bonnets and me."

Sir Walter Scott.
The Doom of Devorgoil.

THE BURIAL–MARCH OF DUNDEE.

I.

Sound the fife, and cry the slogan;
    Let the pibroch shake the air
With its wild triumphal music,
    Worthy of the freight we bear.
Let the ancient hills of Scotland
    Hear once more the battle-song
Swell within their glens and valleys
    As the clansmen march along!
Never from the field of combat,
    Never from the deadly fray,
Was a nobler trophy carried
    Than we bring with us to-day;
Never, since the valiant Douglas
    On his dauntless bosom bore
Good King Robert's heart — the priceless —
    To our dear Redeemer's shore!

Lo! we bring with us the hero ;
  Lo! we bring the conquering Graeme,
Crowned as best beseems a victor
  From the altar of his fame;
Fresh and bleeding from the battle
  Whence his spirit took its flight,
Midst the crashing charge of squadrons,
  And the thunder of the fight !
Strike, I say, the notes of triumph,
  As we march o'er moor and lea!
Is there any here will venture
  To bewail our dead Dundee ?
Let the widows of the traitors
  Weep until their eyes are dim !
Wail ye may full well for Scotland, —
  Let none dare to mourn for him!
See ! above his glorious body
  Lies the royal banner's fold ;
See ! his valiant blood is mingled
  With its crimson and its gold ;
See how calm he looks, and stately,
  Like a warrior on his shield,
Waiting till the flush of morning
  Breaks along the battle-field!
See — O never more, my comrades,
  Shall we see that falcon eye
Redden with its inward lightning,
  As the hour of fight drew nigh!
Never shall we hear the voice that,
  Clearer than the trumpet's call,
Bade us strike for King and country,
  Bade us win the field, or fall!

13

II.

On the heights of Killiecrankie
    Yester-morn our army lay :
Slowly rose the mist in columns
    From the river's broken way;
Hoarsely roared the swollen torrent,
    And the pass was wrapt in gloom,
When the clansmen rose together
    From their lair amidst the broom.
Then we belted on our tartans,
    And our bonnets down we drew,
And we felt our broadswords' edges,
    And we proved them to be true ;
And we prayed the prayer of soldiers,
    And we cried the gathering-cry,
And we clasped the hands of kinsmen,
    And we swore to do or die!
Then our leader rose before us
    On his war-horse black as night, —
Well the Cameronian rebels
    Knew that charger in the fight! —
And a cry of exultation
    From the bearded warriors rose;
For we loved the house of Claver'se,
    And we thought of good Montrose.
But he raised his hand for silence :
    "Soldiers! I have sworn a vow :
Ere the evening star shall glisten
    On Schehallion's lofty brow,
Either we shall rest in triumph,
    Or another of the Graemes
Shall have died in battle-harness
    For his country and King James!
Think upon the Royal Martyr —
    Think of what his race endure —

Think of him whom butchers murdered
  On the field of Magus Muir:
By his sacred blood I charge ye,
  By the ruined hearth and shrine,
By the blighted hopes of Scotland,
  By your injuries and mine,
Strike this day as if the anvil
  Lay beneath your blows the while,
Be they covenanting traitors,
  Or the brood of false Argyle !
Strike ! and drive the trembling rebels
  Backwards o'er the stormy Forth ;
Let them tell their pale Convention
  How they fared within the North.
Let them tell that Highland honor
  Is not to be bought nor sold,
That we scorn their prince's anger
  As we loathe his foreign gold.
Strike ! and when the fight is over,
  If ye look in vain for me,
Where the dead are lying thickest,
  Search for him that was Dundee !"

III.

Loudly then the hills reëchoed
  With our answer to his call,
But a deeper echo sounded
  In the bosoms of us all.
For the lands of wild Breadalbane,
  Not a man who heard him speak
Would that day have left the battle.
  Burning eye and flushing cheek
Told the clansmen's fierce emotion,
  And they harder drew their breath ;
For their souls were strong within them,

Stronger than the grasp of death.
Soon we heard a challenge-trumpet
  Sounding in the pass below,
And the distant tramp of horses,
  And the voices of the foe:
Down we crouched amid the bracken,
  Till the Lowland ranks drew near,
Panting like the hounds in summer,
  When they scent the stately deer.
From the dark defile emerging,
  Next we saw the squadrons come,
Leslie's foot and Leven's troopers
  Marching to the tuck of drum;
Through the scattered wood of birches,
  O'er the broken ground and heath,
Wound the long battalion slowly,
  Till they gained the plain beneath;
Then we bounded from our covert.
  Judge how looked the Saxons then,
When they saw the rugged mountain
  Start to life with armèd men!
Like a tempest down the ridges
  Swept the hurricane of steel,
Rose the slogan of Macdonald,
  Flashed the broadsword of Lochiell!
Vainly sped the withering volley
  'Mongst the foremost of our band;
On we poured until we met them,
  Foot to foot, and hand to hand.
Horse and man went down like drift-wood
  When the floods are black at Yule,
And their carcasses are whirling
  In the Garry's deepest pool.
Horse and man went down before us, —
  Living foe there tarried none

On the field of Killiecrankie,
  When that stubborn fight was done !

IV.

And the evening star was shining
  On Schehallion's distant head,
When we wiped our bloody broadswords,
  And returned to count the dead.
There we found him gashed and gory,
  Stretched upon the cumbered plain,
As he told us where to seek him,
  In the thickest of the slain.
And a smile was on his visage,
  For within his dying ear
Pealed the joyful note of triumph,
  And the clansmen's clamorous cheer :
So, amidst the battle's thunder,
  Shot, and steel, and scorching flame,
In the glory of his manhood
  Passed the spirit of the Graeme !

V.

Open wide the vaults of Atholl,
  Where the bones of heroes rest;
Open wide the hallowed portals
  To receive another guest!
Last of Scots, and last of freemen,
  Last of all that dauntless race
Who would rather die unsullied
  Than outlive the land's disgrace!
O thou lion-hearted warrior!
  Reck not of the after-time:
Honor may be deemed dishonor,
  Loyalty be called a crime.
Sleep in peace with kindred ashes

Of the noble and the true,
Hands that never failed their country,
    Hearts that never baseness knew.
Sleep! — and till the latest trumpet
    Wakes the dead-from earth and sea,
Scotland shall not boast a braver
    Chieftain than our own Dundee!

WILLIAM EDMONDSTOUNE AYTOUN.[1]

PAST AND PRESENT.

I REMEMBER, I remember
    The house where I was born,
The little window where the sun
    Came peeping in at morn;
He never came a wink too soon,
    Nor brought too long a day;
But now, I often wish the night
    Had borne my breath away.

I remember, I remember
    The roses, red and white,
The violets, and the lily-cups —
    Those flowers made of light!

[1] WILLIAM EDMONDSTOUNE AYTOUN, born in 1813, was a
member of the Edinburgh bar. He became professor of literature and belles-lettres in the University of Edinburgh, and
editor of *Blackwood's Magazine.* Besides his fine *Lays of the
Scottish Cavaliers,* from which the two poems given in this collection are taken, he wrote a number of clever parodies under
the name of "Bon Gaultier." He has also written on history
and literature. He died in 1865.

The lilacs where the robin built,
  And where my brother set
The laburnum on his birthday,—
  The tree is living yet !

I remember, I remember
  Where I was used to swing,
And thought the air must rush as fresh
  To swallows on the wing;
My spirit flew in feathers then
  That is so heavy now,
And summer pools could hardly cool
  The fever on my brow.

I remember, I remember
  The fir trees dark and high;
I used to think their slender tops
  Were close against the sky:
It was a childish ignorance,
  But now 't is little joy
To know I 'm farther off from Heaven
  Than when I was a boy.

THOMAS HOOD.[1]

[1] THOMAS HOOD, the famous humorist, was born in 1798.
He was placed at an early age in a merchant's counting-house,
but soon abandoned it for literature. He wrote for and edited
magazines, and was an early contributor to *Punch.* His life
was a hard struggle with poverty and ill-health. He wrote
much both in verse and in prose. His writings are chiefly humorous, but he had a strong pathetic vein, and some of his serious poems have attained an almost unbounded popularity. He
died in 1845.

THE LOST LEADER.

Just for a handful of silver he left us,
   Just for a riband to stick in his coat, —
Found the one gift of which fortune bereft us,
   Lost all the others she lets us devote;
They, with the gold to give, doled him out silver,
   So much was theirs who so little allowed:
How all our copper had gone for his service!
   Rags — were they purple, his heart had been proud.
We that had loved him so, followed him, honored him,
   Lived in his mild and magnificent eye,
Learned his great language, caught his clear accents,
   Made him our pattern to live and to die!
Shakespeare was of us, Milton was for us,
   Burns, Shelley, were with us, — they watch from
         their graves!
He alone breaks from the van and the freemen,
   He alone sinks to the rear and the slaves!

We shall march prospering, — not thro' his presence;
   Songs may inspirit us, — not from his lyre;
Deeds will be done, — while he boasts his quiescence,
   Still bidding crouch whom the rest bade aspire:
Blot out his name, then, record one lost soul more,
   One task more declined, one more footpath untrod,
One more devils'-triumph and sorrow for angels,
   One wrong more to man, one more insult to God!
Life's night begins! let him never come back to us!
   There would be doubt, hesitation, and pain,
Forced praise on our part, — the glimmer of twilight,
   Never glad, confident morning again!
Best fight on well, for we taught him, — strike gallantly,
   Menace our heart ere we master his own;

Then let him receive the new knowledge, and wait us,
Pardoned in heaven, the first by the throne!
ROBERT BROWNING.[1]

HOME-THOUGHTS, FROM THE SEA.

NOBLY, nobly Cape Saint Vincent to the northwest
    died away;
Sunset ran, one glorious blood-red, reeking into Cadiz
    Bay;
Bluish 'mid the burning water, full in face Trafalgar
    lay;
In the dimmest northeast distance dawned Gibraltar,
    grand and gray;
"Here and here did England help me: how can I help
    England?" say,
Whoso turns as I, this evening, turn to God to praise
    and pray,
While Jove's planet rises yonder, silent over Africa.
ROBERT BROWNING.

[1] ROBERT BROWNING, with the exception of Tennyson the most famous of living English poets, was born in Camberwell, near London, in 1812. He was educated at the University of London, and published his first important poem, *Paracelsus*, in 1835. In 1840 he married the poetess Elizabeth Barrett. This poem of *The Lost Leader* refers to William Wordsworth, who changed his politics from the Liberal to the Tory side.

OLD IRONSIDES.[1]

AY, tear her tattered ensign down !
　Long has it waved on high,
And many an eye has danced to see
　That banner in the sky;
Beneath it rung the battle shout,
　And burst the cannon's roar;
The meteor of the ocean air
　Shall sweep the clouds no more!

Her deck, once red with heroes' blood,
　Where knelt the vanquished foe,
When winds were hurrying o'er the flood,
　And waves were white below,
No more shall feel the victor's tread,
　Or know the conquered knee, —
The harpies of the shore shall pluck
　The eagle of the sea!

O better that her shattered hulk
　Should sink beneath the wave;
Her thunders shook the mighty deep,
　And there should be her grave;
Nail to the mast her holy flag,
　Set every threadbare sail,
And give her to the god of storms,
　The lightning and the gale.

OLIVER WENDELL HOLMES.[2]

[1] The famous American ship of war, the Constitution, was called Old Ironsides in allusion to her victories over the English in the war of 1812, and this poem was called forth by a proposal which was made to break her up and sell the iron and timber.

[2] OLIVER WENDELL HOLMES, son of the Rev. Abiel Holmes,

THE WRECK OF THE HESPERUS.

IT was the schooner Hesperus,
　That sailed the wintry sea,
And the skipper had taken his little daughter,
　To bear him company.

Blue were her eyes as the fairy-flax,
　Her cheeks like the dawn of day,
And her bosom white as the hawthorn buds,
　That ope in the month of May.

The skipper he stood beside the helm,
　His pipe was in his mouth,
And he watched how the veering flaw did blow
　The smoke now west, now south.

Then up and spake an old sailor,
　Had sailed to the Spanish Main,
" I pray thee, put into yonder port,
　For I fear a hurricane.

" Last night the moon had a golden ring,
　And to-night no moon we see ! "
The skipper, he blew a whiff from his pipe,
　And a scornful laugh laughed he.

was born in Cambridge, Mass., in 1809, and graduated at Harvard
College in 1829. He studied medicine in Europe, returned to
the United States, and accepted the professorship of anatomy
in Dartmouth College in 1838. In 1847 he became professor of
anatomy in the Harvard Medical School, a position he still
holds, and has, since his acceptance of that post, lived in Boston. His name, one of the most distinguished in our literature,
is familiar to all Americans as that of a poet, critic, novelist,
and humorist.

Colder and louder blew the wind,
  A gale from the northeast;
The snow fell hissing in the brine,
  And the billows frothed like yeast.

Down came the storm, and smote amain
  The vessel in its strength;
She shuddered and paused, like a frighted steed,
  Then leaped her cable's length.

" Come hither! come hither ! my little daughter,
  And do not tremble so;
For I can weather the roughest gale
  That ever wind did blow."

He wrapped her warm in his seaman's coat
  Against the stinging blast ;
He cut a rope from a broken spar,
  And bound her to the mast.

" O father ! I hear the church-bells ring,
  O say, what may it be ?"
" 'T is a fog-bell on a rock-bound coast ! " —
  And he steered for the open sea.

" O father ! I hear the sound of guns,
  O say, what may it be ?"
" Some ship in distress, that cannot live
  In such an angry sea ! "

" O father! I see a gleaming light,
  O say, what may it be ? "
But the father answered never a word,
  A frozen corpse was he.

Lashed to the helm, all stiff and stark,
  With his face turned to the skies,
The lantern gleamed through the gleaming snow
  On his fixed and glassy eyes.

Then the maiden clasped her hands and prayed
  That savèd she might be;
And she thought of Christ, who stilled the wave,
  On the Lake of Galilee.

And fast through the midnight dark and drear,
  Through the whistling sleet and snow,
Like a sheeted ghost, the vessel swept
  Tow'rds the reef of Norman's Woe.

And ever the fitful gusts between
  A sound came from the land;
It was the sound of the trampling surf
  On the rocks and the hard sea-sand.

The breakers were right beneath her bows,
  She drifted a dreary wreck,
And a whooping billow swept the crew
  Like icicles from her deck.

She struck where the white and fleecy waves
  Looked soft as carded wool,
But the cruel rocks, they gored her side
  Like the horns of an angry bull.

Her rattling shrouds, all sheathed in ice,
  With the masts went by the board;
Like a vessel of glass, she stove and sank,
  Ho! ho! the breakers roared!

At daybreak, on the bleak sea-beach,
  A fisherman 'stood aghast,
To see the form of a maiden fair,
  Lashed close to a drifting mast.

The salt sea was frozen on her breast,
  The salt tears in her eyes ;
And he saw her hair, like the brown sea-weed,
  On the billows fall and rise.

Such was the wreck of the Hesperus,
  In the midnight and the snow!
Christ save us all from a death like this,
  On the reef of Norman's Woe.
            HENRY WADSWORTH LONGFELLOW.[1]

THE SKELETON IN ARMOR.

" SPEAK! speak! thou fearful guest!
  Who, with thy hollow breast
  Still in rude armor drest,
    Comest to daunt me!

[1] HENRY WADSWORTH LONGFELLOW, son of the Hon.
Stephen Longfellow, was born in Portland, Maine, in 1807, and
graduated at Bowdoin College in 1825. He studied law for a
short time and was soon after appointed professor of modern
languages at Bowdoin. He then travelled abroad for three
years, returning in 1829. In 1835 he was appointed professor
of belles-lettres at Harvard College, a position which he re-
signed in 1854. On his appointment he came to Cambridge,
where he still lives. He is deservedly among the best known
and most popular of modern poets, both in England and in this
country, and the selections in this volume are abundant evidence
of the skill, grace, and artistic form of his narrative poems.

Wrapt not in Eastern balms,
But with thy fleshless palms
Stretched, as if asking alms,
    Why dost thou haunt me?"

Then, from those cavernous eyes
Pale flashes seemed to rise,
As when the Northern skies
    Gleam in December;
And, like the water's flow
Under December's snow,
Came a dull voice of woe
    From the heart's chamber.

"I was a Viking old!
My deeds, though manifold,
No Skald in song has told,
    No Saga taught thee!
Take heed, that in thy verse
Thou dost the tale rehearse,
Else dread a dead man's curse;
    For this I sought thee.

"Far in the Northern Land,
By the wild Baltic's strand,
I, with my childish hand,
    Tamed the gerfalcon;
And, with my skates fast-bound,
Skimmed the half-frozen Sound,
That the poor whimpering hound
    Trembled to walk on.

' Oft to his frozen lair
Tracked I the grisly bear,
While from my path the hare

Fled like a shadow;
Oft through the forest dark
Followed the were-wolf's bark,
Until the soaring lark
　　Sang from the meadow.

" But when I older grew,
Joining a corsair's crew,
O'er the dark sea I flew
　　With the marauders.
Wild was the life we led;
Many the souls that sped,
Many the hearts that bled,
　　By our stern orders.

" Many a wassail-bout
Wore the long winter out ;
Often our midnight shout
　　Set the cocks crowing,
As we the Berserk's tale
Measured in cups of ale,
Draining the oaken pail,
　　Filled to o'erflowing.

" Once as I told in glee
Tales of the stormy sea,
Soft eyes did gaze on me,
　　Burning yet tender;
And as the white stars shine
On the dark Norway pine,
On that dark heart of mine
　　Fell their soft splendor.

" I wooed the blue-eyed maid,
Yielding, yet half afraid,

And in the forest's shade
　　Our vows were plighted.
Under its loosened vest
Fluttered her little breast,
Like birds within their nest
　　By the hawk frighted.

" Bright in her father's hall
Shields gleamed upon the wall,
Loud sang the minstrels all,
　　Chanting his glory;
When of old Hildebrand
I asked his daughter's hand,
Mute did the minstrels stand
　　To hear my story.

" While the brown ale he quaffed
Loud then the champion laughed,
And as the wind-gusts waft
　　The sea-foam brightly,
So the loud laugh of scorn,
Out of those lips unshorn,
From the deep drinking-horn
　　Blew the foam lightly.

" She was a Prince's child,
I but a Viking wild,
And though she blushed and smiled,
　　I was discarded!
Should not the dove so white
Follow the sea-mew's flight,
Why did they leave that night
　　Her nest unguarded?

14

" Scarce had I put to sea,
　Bearing the maid with me,
　Fairest of all was she
　　　Among the Norsemen !
　When on the white sea-strand,
　Waving his armèd hand,
　Saw we old Hildebrand,
　　　With twenty horsemen.

" Then launched they to the blast,
　Bent like a reed each mast,
　Yet we were gaining fast,
　　　When the wind failed us ;
　And with a sudden flaw
　Came round the gusty Skaw,
　So that our foe we saw
　　　Laugh as he hailed us.

" And as to catch the gale
　Round veered the flapping sail,
　Death ! was the helmsman's hail,
　　　Death without quarter !
　Mid-ships with iron keel
　Struck we her ribs of steel ;
　Down her black hulk did reel
　　　Through the black water !

" As with his wings aslant,
　Sails the fierce cormorant,
　Seeking some rocky haunt,
　　　With his prey laden,
　So toward the open main,
　Beating to sea again,

Through the wild hurricane,
    Bore I the maiden.

" Three weeks we westward bore,
And when the storm was o'er,
Cloudlike we saw the shore
    Stretching to lee-ward ;
There for my lady's bower
Built I the lofty tower,
Which, to this very hour,
    Stands looking sea-ward.

" There lived we many years ;
Time dried the maiden's tears ;
She had forgot her fears,
    She was a mother ;
Death closed her mild blue eyes,
Under that tower she lies ;
Ne'er shall the sun arise
    On such another !

" Still grew my bosom then,
Still as a stagnant fen !
Hateful to me were men,
    The sun-light hateful !
In the vast forest here,
Clad in my warlike gear,
Fell I upon my spear,
    O, death was grateful!

" Thus, seamed with many scars,
Bursting these prison bars,
Up to its native stars
    My soul ascended !
There from the flowing bowl

Deep drinks the warrior's soul,
Skoal! to the Northland ! *skoal!* "
Thus the tale ended.[1]
Henry Wadsworth Longfellow.

THE ARMADA.

A FRAGMENT.

Attend, all ye who list to hear our noble England's
    praise ;
I tell of the thrice famous deeds she wrought in an-
    cient days,
When that great fleet invincible against her bore in
    vain
The richest spoils of Mexico, the stoutest hearts of Spain.

It was about the lovely close of a warm summer day,
There came a gallant merchant-ship full sail to Plym-
    outh Bay ;
Her crew hath seen Castile's black fleet, beyond Au-
    rigny's isle,
At earliest twilight, on the waves lie heaving many a
    mile.
At sunrise she escaped their van, by God's especial
    grace ;

---

[1] This fine poem was suggested by the discovery in a sand-bank, near Fall River, Mass., of a skeleton with some remains of armor clinging to it. The early visits of the Norsemen to New England gave support to the theory that this was one of that race. It is more probable, however, that the skeleton was that of an Indian of the tribes which were found in Central America, as the armor corresponded to that worn by the aboriginal inhabitants of those regions.

And the tall Pinta, till the noon, had held her close in
    chase.
Forthwith a guard at every gun was placed along the
    wall ;
The beacon blazed upon the roof of Edgecumbe's lofty
    hall ;
Many a light fishing-bark put out to pry along the
    coast,
And with loose rein and bloody spur rode inland many
    a post.
With his white hair unbonneted, the stout old sheriff
    comes ;
Behind him march the halberdiers ; before him sound
    the drums ;
His yeomen round the market cross make clear an
    ample space ;
For there behoves him to set up the standard of Her
    Grace.
And haughtily the trumpets peal, and gayly dance the
    bells,
As slow upon the laboring wind the royal blazon swells.
Look how the Lion of the sea lifts up his ancient crown,
And underneath his deadly paw treads the gay lilies
    down.
So stalked he when he turned to flight, on that famed
    Picard field,
Bohemia's plume, and Genoa's bow, and Cæsar's eagle
    shield.
So glared he when at Agincourt in wrath he turned to
    bay,
And crushed and torn beneath his claws the princely
    hunters lay.
Ho ! strike the flagstaff deep, Sir Knight; ho ! scatter
    flowers, fair maids ;
Ho ! gunners, fire a loud salute ; ho ! gallants, draw
    your blades ;

Thou sun, shine on her joyously ; ye breezes, waft
    her wide, —
Our glorious Semper Eadem, the banner of our pride.
The freshening breeze of eve unfurled that banner's
    massive fold ;
The parting gleam of sunshine kissed that haughty
    scroll of gold ;
Night sank upon the dusky beach, and on the purple
    sea,
Such night in England ne'er had been, nor e'er again
    shall be.
From Eddystone to Berwick bounds, from Lynn to
    Milford Bay,
That time of slumber was as bright and busy as the
    day ;
For swift to east and swift to west the ghastly war-
    flame spread,
High on St. Michael's Mount it shone : it shone on
    Beachy Head.
Far on the deep the Spaniard saw, along each southern
    shire,
Cape beyond cape, in endless range, those twinkling
    points of fire.
The fisher left his skiff to rock on Tamar's glittering
    waves :
The rugged miners poured to war from Mendip's sun-
    less caves :
O'er Longleat's towers, o'er Cranbourne's oaks, the
    fiery herald flew :
He roused the shepherds of Stonehenge, the rangers
    of Beaulieu.
Right sharp and quick the bells all night rang out from
    Bristol town,
And ere the day three hundred horse had met on Clif-
    ton down ;

The sentinel on Whitehall gate looked forth into the
    night,
And saw o'erhanging Richmond Hill the streak of
    blood-red light.
Then bugle's note and cannon's roar the death-like si-
    lence broke,
And with one start, and with one cry, the royal city
    woke.
At once on all her stately.gates arose the answering
    fires ;
At once the wild alarum clashed from all her reeling
    spires;
From all the batteries of the Tower pealed loud the
    voice of fear ;
And all the thousand masts of Thames sent back a
    louder cheer :
And from the furthest wards was heard the rush of
    hurrying feet,
And the broad streams of pikes and flags rushed down
    each roaring street ;
And broader still became the blaze, and louder still the
    din,
As fast from every village round the horse came spur-
    ring in :
And eastward straight from wild Blackheath the war-
    like errand went,
And roused in many an ancient hall the gallant squires
    of Kent.
Southward from Surrey's pleasant hills flew those bright
    couriers forth;
High on bleak Hampstead's swarthy moor they started
    for the north;
And on, and on, without a pause untired they bounded
    still :
All night from tower to tower they sprang ; they sprang
    from hill to hill :

Till the proud peak unfurled the flag o'er Darwin's
　　rocky dales,
Till like volcanoes flared to heaven the stormy hills of
　　Wales,
Till twelve fair counties saw the blaze on Malvern's
　　lonely height,
Till streamed in crimson on the wind the Wrekin's
　　crest of light,
Till broad and fierce the star came forth on Ely's
　　stately fane,
And tower and hamlet rose in arms o'er all the bound-
　　less plain ;
Till Belvoir's lordly terraces the sign to Lincoln sent,
And Lincoln sped the message on o'er the wide vale of
　　Trent ;
Till Skiddaw saw the fire that burnt on Gaunt's em-
　　battled pile,
And the red glare on Skiddaw roused the burghers of
　　Carlisle.

LORD MACAULAY.[1]

[1] THOMAS BABINGTON MACAULAY, born in 1800, was a son
of Zachary Macaulay, an eminent philanthropist. He was educated at Trinity College, Cambridge, and in boyhood and
youth gave ample promise of his extraordinary mental powers.
In 1825 he published his essay on Milton, which at once made
him famous, and in 1826 he was called to the bar. He entered
Parliament as a Whig in 1830, and rose rapidly in politics by
his strong intellect and great oratorical powers. In 1834 he was
sent to India as one of the Supreme Council, and on his return
was elected to Parliament from Edinburgh, in 1840. In 1846,
when the Whig party returned to power, he was made Pay-
master General of the Forces, with a seat in the cabinet. He
was defeated for Parliament in 1847, but again elected from
Edinburgh in 1852, resigning his seat in 1856, in order to devote
himself to literature. In 1857 he was raised to the peerage as
Baron Macaulay of Rothley. He died in 1859. He was eminent both as a statesman and as a writer. His poems were few

SIR NICHOLAS AT MARSTON MOOR.[1]

To horse, to horse, Sir Nicholas ! the clarion's note is
    high ;
To horse, to horse, Sir Nicholas ! the huge drum makes
    reply :
Ere this hath Lucas marched with his gallant cavaliers,
And the bray of Rupert's trumpets grows fainter on
    our ears.
To horse, to horse, Sir Nicholas ! White Guy is at the
    door,
And the vulture whets his beak o'er the field of Mars-
    ton Moor.

Up rose the Lady Alice from her brief and broken
    prayer,
And she brought a silken standard down the narrow
    turret stair.
O, many were the tears that those radiant eyes had
    shed,
As she worked the bright word " Glory " in the gay
    and glancing thread;
And mournful was the smile that o'er those beauteous
    features ran,
As she said, " It is your lady's gift, unfurl it in the
    van."

in number, and although not the highest kind, have very great
merit combined with force of expression and thought. His
fame rests on his essays and his history of England.

1 The battle of Marston Moor was fought July 2, 1644, between the Scotch and Parliamentary forces and those of King
Charles. The battle was doubtful for a time, but was finally de-
cided by the attack of Cromwell, and the Royalists were utterly
routed.

"It shall flutter, noble wench, where the best and
    boldest ride,
Through the steel-clad files of Skippon and the black
    dragoons of Pride;
The recreant soul of Fairfax will feel a sicklier qualm,
And the rebel lips of Oliver give out a louder psalm,
When they see my lady's gew-gaw flaunt bravely on
    their wing,
And hear her loyal soldiers' shout, for God and for the
    King!"

'T is noon; the ranks are broken along the royal line:
They fly, the braggarts of the court, the bullies of the
    Rhine:
Stout Langley's cheer is heard no more, and Astley's
    helm is down,
And Rupert sheaths his rapier with a curse and with a
    frown;
And cold Newcastle mutters, as he follows in the
    flight,
"The German boar had better far have supped in
    York to-night."

The Knight is all alone, his steel cap cleft in twain,
His good buff jerkin crimsoned o'er with many a gory
    stain;
But still he waves the standard, and cries amid the
    rout:
"For Church and King, fair gentlemen, spur on and
    fight it out!"
And now he wards a Roundhead's pike, and now he
    hums a stave,
And here he quotes a stage-play, and there he fells a
    knave.

Good speed to thee, Sir Nicholas! thou hast no thought
    of fear;
Good speed to thee, Sir Nicholas! but fearful odds are
    here.
The traitors ring thee round, and with every blow and
    thrust,
"Down, down," they cry, "with Belial, down with
    him to the dust!"
"I would," quoth grim old Oliver, "that Belial's
    trusty sword
This day were doing battle for the Saints and for the
    Lord!"

The Lady Alice sits with her maidens in her bower;
The gray-haired warden watches on the castle's high-
    est tower.
"What news, what news, old Anthony?" "The field
    is lost and won;
The ranks of war are melting as the mists beneath the
    sun;
And a wounded man speeds hither,—I am old and
    cannot see,
Or sure I am that sturdy step my master's step should
    be."

"I bring thee back the standard from as rude and
    rough a fray,
As e'er was proof of soldier's thews, or theme for
    minstrel's lay.
Bid Hubert fetch the silver bowl, and liquor *quantum
    suff;*
I'll make a shift to drain it, ere I part with boot and
    buff;

Though Guy through many a gaping wound is breathing out his life,
And I come to thee a landless man, my fond and faithful wife!

" Sweet, we will fill our money-bags and freight a ship
 for France,
And mourn in merry Paris for this poor realm's mis-
 chance;
Or, if the worst betide me, why, better axe or rope,
Than life with Lenthal for a king, and Peters for a
 pope!
Alas, alas, my gallant Guy!—out on the crop-eared
 boor,
That sent me with my standard on foot from Marston
 Moor!"

WINTHROP MACKWORTH PRAED.[1]

THE EXECUTION OF MONTROSE.[2]

COME hither, Evan Cameron!
 Come, stand beside my knee;
I hear the river roaring down
 Towards the wintry sea.
There 's shouting on the mountain side,
 There 's war within the blast;

[1] WINTHROP MACKWORTH PRAED, born in London in 1802, was educated at Eton and Cambridge, where he was distinguished as a scholar and orator. He was called to the bar in 1829, and entered Parliament in the following year. He rose rapidly both in politics and in literature, but died, while still very young, in 1839. His poems are light and graceful.

[2] JAMES GRAHAM, Marquis of Montrose. See page 44.

Old faces look upon me,
  Old forms go trooping past:
I hear the pibroch wailing
  Amidst the din of fight,
And my dim spirit wakes again
  Upon the verge of night.

'T was I that led the Highland host
  Through wild Lochaber's snows
What time the plaided clans came down
  To battle with Montrose.
I 've told thee how the Southrons fell
  Beneath the broad claymore,
And how we smote the Campbell clan
  By Inverlochy's shore.
I 've told thee how we swept Dundee,
  And tamed the Lindsays' pride;
But never have I told thee yet
  How the Great Marquis died.

A traitor sold him to his foes;
  O deed of deathless shame!
I charge thee, boy, if e'er thou meet
  With one of Assynt's name, —
Be it upon the mountain's side,
  Or yet within the glen,
Stand he in martial gear alone,
  Or backed by armèd men, —
Face him, as thou wouldst face the man
  Who wronged thy sire's renown;
Remember of what blood thou art,
  And strike the caitiff down!

They brought him to the Watergate,
  Hard bound with hempen span,

As though they held a lion there,
  And not a fenceless man.
They set him high upon a cart, —
  The hangman rode below, —
They drew his hands behind his back,
  And bared his noble brow.
Then, as a hound is slipped from leash,
  They cheered, the common throng,
And blew the note with yell and shout,
  And bade him pass along.

It would have made a brave man's heart
  Grow sad and sick that day,
To watch the keen malignant eyes
  Bent down on that array.
There stood the Whig west-country lords
  In balcony and bow;
There sat their gaunt and withered dames,
  And their daughters all a-row.
And every open window
  Was full as full might be
With black-robed Covenanting carles,
  That goodly sport to see!

But when he came, though pale and wan,
  He looked so great and high,
So noble was his manly front,
  So calm his steadfast eye,
The rabble rout forbore to shout,
  And each man held his breath,
For well they knew the hero's soul
  Was face to face with death.
And then a mournful shudder
  Through all the people crept,
And some that came to scoff at him
  Now turned aside and wept.

Had I been there with sword in hand,
  And fifty Camerons by,
That day through high Dunedin's streets
  Had pealed the slogan-cry.
Not all their troops of trampling horse,
  Nor might of mailèd men, —
Not all the rebels in the south
  Had borne us backwards then!
Once more his foot on Highland heath
  Had trod as free as air,
Or I, and all who bore my name,
  Been laid around him there!

It might not be.   They placed him next
  Within the solemn hall,
Where once the Scottish kings were throned
  Amidst their nobles all.
But there was dust of vulgar feet
  On that polluted floor,
And perjured traitors filled the place
  Where good men sate before.
With savage glee came Warristoun
  To read the murderous doom;
And then uprose the great Montrose
  In the middle of the room.

" Now, by my faith as belted knight,
  And by the name I bear,
And by the bright Saint Andrew's cross
  That waves above us there,
Yea, by a greater, mightier oath, —
  And O, that such should be! —
By that dark stream of royal blood.
  That lies 'twixt you and me,
I have not sought in battle-field

A wreath of such renown,
Nor dared I hope on my dying day
To win the martyr's crown!

" There is a chamber far away
  Where sleep the good and brave,
But a better place ye have named for me
  Than by my father's grave.
For truth and right, 'gainst treason's might,
  This hand hath always striven,
And ye raise it up for a witness still
  In the eye of earth and heaven.
Then nail my head on yonder tower —
  Give every town a limb —
And God who made shall gather them :
  I go from you to Him! "

The morning dawned full darkly,
  The rain came flashing down,
And the jagged streak of the levin-bolt
  Lit up the gloomy town :
The thunder crashed across the heaven,
  The fatal hour was come;
Yet aye broke in with muffled beat
  The 'larum of the drum.
There was madness on the earth below,
  And anger in the sky,
And young and old, and rich and poor,
  Came forth to see him die.

Ah, God! that ghastly gibbet!
  How dismal 't is to see
The great tall spectral skeleton,
  The ladder and the tree!
Hark! hark! it is the clash of arms —

The bells begin to toll —
" He is coming! he is coming!
    God's mercy on his soul! "
One last long peal of thunder —
    The clouds are cleared away,
And the glorious sun once more looks down
    Amidst the dazzling day.

" He is coming! he is coming! "
    Like a bridegroom from his room,
Came the hero from his prison
    To the scaffold and the doom.
There was glory on his forehead,
    There was lustre in his eye,
And he never walked to battle
    More proudly than to die:
There was color in his visage,
    Though the cheeks of all were wan,
And they marvelled as they saw him pass,
    That great and goodly man !

He mounted up the scaffold,
    And he turned him to the crowd;
But they dared not trust the people,
    So he might not speak aloud.
But he looked upon the heavens,
    And they were clear and blue,
And in the liquid ether
    The eye of God shone through !
Yet a black and murky battlement
    Lay resting on the hill,
As though the thunder slept within, —
    All else was calm and still.
15

The grim Geneva ministers
 With anxious scowl drew near,
As you have seen the ravens flock
 Around the dying deer.
He would not deign them word nor sign,
 But alone he bent the knee;
And veiled his face for Christ's dear grace,
 Beneath the gallows-tree.
Then radiant and serene he rose,
 And cast his cloak away:
For he had ta'en his latest look
 Of earth and sun and day.

A beam of light fell o'er him,
 Like a glory round the shriven,
And he climbed the lofty ladder
 As it were the path to heaven,
Then came a flash from out the cloud,
 And a stunning thunder-roll;
And no man dared to look aloft,
 For fear was on every soul.
There was another heavy sound,
 A hush and then a groan;
And darkness swept across the sky, —
 The work of death was done.

    William Edmondstoune Aytoun.

THE DREAM OF ARGYLE.[1]

EARTHLY arms no more uphold him,
  On his prison's stony floor,
Waiting death in his last slumber,
  Lies the doomed MacCallum More.

And he dreams a dream of boyhood;
  Rise again his heathery hills,
Sound again the hound's long baying,
  Cry of moor-fowl, laugh of rills.

Now he stands amidst his clansmen
  In the low, long banquet-hall,
Over grim, ancestral armor
  Sees the ruddy firelight fall.

Once again, with pulses beating,
  Hears the wandering minstrel tell
How Montrose on Inverary
  Thief-like from his mountains fell.

Down the glen, beyond the castle,
  Where the linn's swift waters shine,
Round the youthful heir of Argyle
  Shy feet glide and white arms twine.

---

[1] Archibald Campbell, ninth Earl of Argyle. He fought for
the royal cause at Dunbar in 1650, and in 1663 was restored to
his earldom and estates. Being required to take the "Test" in
1681 he declined unless he could make a reservation in favor of
the Protestant faith. For this he was condemned to death and
obliged to flee the country. He returned in 1685, was taken
prisoner and executed, as his father had been before him. He
is said to have slept soundly a few hours before his execution.

Fairest of the rustic dancers,
  Blue-eyed Effie smiles once more,
Bends to him her snooded tresses,
  Treads with him the grassy floor.

Now he hears the pipes lamenting,
  Harpers for his mother mourn,
Slow, with sable plume and pennon,
  To her cairn of burial borne.

Then anon his dreams are darker,
  Sounds of battle fill his ears,
And the pibroch's mournful wailing
  For his father's fall he hears.

Wild Lochaber's mountain echoes
  Wail in concert for the dead,
And Loch Awe's deep waters murmur
  For the Campbell's glory fled!

Fierce and strong the godless tyrants
  Trample the apostate land,
While her poor and faithful remnant
  Wait for the avenger's hand.

Once again at Inverary,
  Years of weary exile o'er,
Armed to lead his scattered clansmen,
  Stands the bold MacCallum More.

Once again to battle calling
  Sound the war-pipes through the glen;
And the court-yard of Dunstaffnage
  Rings with tread of armèd men.

All is lost! the godless triumph,
  And the faithful ones and true
From the scaffold and the prison
  Covenant with God anew.

On the darkness of his dreaming
  Great and sudden glory shone;
Over bonds and death victorious
  Stands he by the Father's throne!

From the radiant ranks of martyrs
  Notes of joy and praise he hears,
Songs of his poor land's deliverance
  Sounding from the future years.

Lo, he wakes! but airs celestial
  Bathe him in immortal rest,
And he sees with unsealed vision
  Scotland's cause with victory blest.

Shining hosts attend and guard him
  As he leaves his prison door;
And to death as to a triumph
  Walks the great MacCallum More!
          ELIZABETH H. WHITTIER.[1]

BOOT AND SADDLE.

BOOT, saddle, to horse, and away!
Rescue my castle before the hot day
Brightens to blue from its silvery gray,
  Chorus. Boot, saddle, to horse, and away!

[1] ELIZABETH H. WHITTIER, sister of the poet, John G.
Whittier. See page 322.

Ride past the suburbs, asleep as you 'd say;
Many 's the friend there will listen and pray,
" 'God's luck to gallants that strike up the lay, —
   Chorus.   " Boot, saddle, to horse, and away ! "

Forty miles off, like a roebuck at bay,
Flouts castle Brancepeth the Roundheads' array:
Who laughs, " Good fellows ere this, by my fay,
   Chorus.   " Boot, saddle, to horse, and away ? "

Who? my wife Gertrude; that, honest and gay,
Laughs when you talk of surrendering, " Nay! "
" I 've better counsellors; what counsel they?
   Chorus.   " Boot, saddle, to horse, and away! "
ROBERT BROWNING.

THE NORMAN BARON.

In his chamber, weak and dying,
Was the Norman baron lying;
Loud, without, the tempest thundered,
   And the castle-turret shook.

In this fight was Death the gainer,
Spite of vassal and retainer,
And the lands his sires had plundered,
   Written in the Doomsday Book.

By his bed a monk was seated,
Who in humble voice repeated
Many a prayer and pater-noster,
   From the missal on his knee;

And, amid the tempest pealing,
Sounds of bells came faintly stealing,
Bells, that from the neighboring kloster
    Rang for the Nativity.

In the hall, the serf and vassal
Held, that night, their Christmas wassail;
Many a carol, old and saintly,
    Sang the minstrels and the waits;

And so loud these Saxon gleemen
Sang to slaves the songs of freemen,
That the storm was heard but faintly,
    Knocking at the castle-gates.

Till at length the lays they chanted
Reached the chamber terror-haunted,
Where the monk, with accents holy,
    Whispered at the baron's ear.

Tears upon his eyelids glistened,
As he paused a while and listened,
And the dying baron slowly
    Turned his weary head to hear.

"Wassail for the kingly stranger
Born and cradled in a manger!
King, like David, priest, like Aaron,
    Christ is born to set us free!"

And the lightning showed the sainted
Figures on the casement painted,
And exclaimed the shuddering baron,
    "Miserere, Domine!"

In that hour of deep contrition
He beheld, with clearer vision,
Through all outward show and fashion,
   Justice, the Avenger, rise.

All the pomp of earth had vanished,
Falsehood and deceit were banished,
Reason spake more loud than passion,
   And the truth wore no disguise.

Every vassal of his banner,
Every serf born to his manor,
All those wronged and wretched creatures,
   By his hand were freed again.

And, as on the sacred missal
He recorded their dismissal,
Death relaxed his iron features,
   And the monk replied, "Amen!"

Many centuries have been numbered
Since in death the baron slumbered
By the convent's sculptured portal,
   Mingling with the common dust :

But the good deed, through the ages,
Living in historic pages,
Brighter grows, and gleams immortal,
   Unconsumed by moth or rust.
       HENRY WADSWORTH LONGFELLOW.

THE WARDEN OF THE CINQUE PORTS.

A MIST was driving down the British Channel,
 The day was just begun,
And through the window-panes, on floor and panel,
 Streamed the red autumn sun.

It glanced on flowing flag and rippling pennon,
 And the white sails of ships;
And, from the frowning rampart, the black cannon
 Hailed it with feverish lips.

Sandwich and Romney, Hastings, Hithe, and Dover
 Were all alert that day,
To see the French war-steamers speeding over,
 When the fog cleared away.

Sullen and silent, and like couchant lions,
 Their cannon, through the night,
Holding their breath, had watched, in grim defiance,
 The sea-coast opposite.

And now they roared at drum-beat from their stations,
 On every citadel;
Each answering each, with morning salutations,
 That all was well.

And down the coast, all taking up the burden,
 Replied the distant forts,
As if to summon from his sleep the Warden
 And Lord of the Cinque Ports.

Him shall no sunshine from the fields of azure,
 No drum-beat from the wall,

No morning-gun from the black fort's embrasure,
    Awaken with its call!

No more, surveying with an eye impartial
    The long line of the coast,
Shall the gaunt figure of the old Field Marshal
    Be seen upon his post!

For in the night, unseen, a single warrior,
    In sombre harness mailed,
Dreaded of man, and surnamed the Destroyer,
    The rampart wall had scaled.

He passed into the chamber of the sleeper,
    The dark and silent room,
And as he entered, darker grew, and deeper,
    The silence and the gloom.

He did not pause to parley or dissemble,
    But smote the Warden hoar;
Ah! what a blow! that made all England tremble
    And groan from shore to shore.

Meanwhile, without, the surly cannon waited,
    The sun rose bright o'erhead;
Nothing in Nature's aspect intimated
    That a great man was dead.
                HENRY WADSWORTH LONGFELLOW.

HOW THEY BROUGHT THE GOOD NEWS
FROM GHENT TO AIX.

[16—.]

I SPRANG to the stirrup, and Joris, and he;
I galloped, Dirck galloped, we galloped all three;
"Good speed!" cried the watch, as the gate-bolts
    undrew;
"Speed!" echoed the wall to us galloping through;
Behind shut the postern, the lights sank to rest,
And into the midnight we galloped abreast.

Not a word to each other; we kept the great pace
Neck by neck, stride by stride, never changing our
    place;
I turned in my saddle and made its girths tight,
Then shortened each stirrup, and set the pique right,
Rebuckled the cheek-strap, chained slacker the bit,
Nor galloped less steadily Roland a whit.

'T was moonset at starting; but while we drew near
Lokeren, the cocks crew and twilight dawned clear;
At Boom, a great yellow star came out to see;
At Düffield, 't was morning as plain as could be;
And from Mecheln church-steeple we heard the half-
    chime,
So Joris broke silence with, "Yet there is time!"

At Aershot, up leaped of a sudden the sun,
And against him the cattle stood black every one,
To stare thro' the mist at us galloping past,
And I saw my stout galloper Roland at last,
With resolute shoulders each butting away
The haze, as some bluff river headland its spray :

And his low head and crest, just one sharp ear bent
    back
For my voice, and the other pricked out on his track ;
And one eye's black intelligence, — ever that glance
O'er its white edge at me, his own master, askance!
And the thick heavy spume-flakes which aye and
    anon
His fierce lips shook upwards in galloping on.

By Hasselt, Dirck groaned; and cried Joris, "Stay
    spur!
Your Roos galloped bravely, the fault 's not in her,
We 'll remember at Aix " — for one heard the quick
    wheeze
Of her chest, saw the stretched neck and staggering
    knees,
And sunk tail, and horrible heave of the flank,
As down on her haunches she shuddered and sank.

So we were left galloping, Joris and I,
Past Looz and past Tongres, no cloud in the sky ;
The broad sun above laughed a pitiless laugh,
'Neath our feet broke the brittle bright stubble like
    chaff:
Till over by Dalhem a dome-spire sprung white,
And " Gallop," gasped Joris, " for Aix is in sight! "

" How they 'll greet us! " — and all in a moment his
    roan
Rolled neck and croup over, lay dead as a stone ;
And there was my Roland, to bear the whole weight
Of the news which alone could save Aix from her
    fate,
With his nostrils like pits full of blood to the brim,
And with circles of red for his eye-sockets' rim.

Then I cast loose my buffcoat, each holster let fall,
Shook off both my jack-boots, let go belt and all,
Stood up in the stirrup, leaned, patted his ear,
Called my Roland his pet name, my horse without
     peer;
Clapped my hands, laughed and sang, any noise, bad
     or good,
Till at length into Aix Roland galloped and stood.

And all I remember is, friends flocking round
As I sat with his head 'twixt my knees on the ground
And no voice but was praising this Roland of mine,
As I poured down his throat our last measure of wine,
Which (the burgesses voted by common consent)
Was no more than his due who brought good news
     from Ghent.

ROBERT BROWNING.

THE BELFRY OF BRUGES.

IN the market-place of Bruges stands the belfry old
    and brown;
Thrice consumed and thrice rebuilded, still it watches
    o'er the town.

As the summer morn was breaking, on that lofty tower
    I stood,
And the world threw off the darkness, like the weeds
    of widowhood.

Thick with towns and hamlets studded, and with
    streams and vapors gray,
Like a shield embossed with silver, round and vast the
    landscape lay.

At my feet the city slumbered.   From its chimneys,
      here and there,
Wreaths of snow-white smoke, ascending, vanished,
      ghost-like, into air.

Not a sound rose from the city at that early morning
      hour,
But I heard a heart of iron beating in the ancient
      tower.

From their nests beneath the rafters sang the swallows
      wild and high;
And the world, beneath me sleeping, seemed more dis-
      tant than the sky.

Then most musical and solemn, bringing back the
      olden times,
With their strange, unearthly changes rang the
      melancholy chimes,

Like the psalms from some old cloister, when the nuns
      sing in the choir;
And the great bell tolled among them, like the chant-
      ing of a friar.

Visions of the days departed, shadowy phantoms
      filled my brain;
They who live in history only seemed to walk the
      earth again;

All the Foresters of Flanders, — mighty Baldwin Bras
      de Fer,
Lyderick du Bucq and Cressy, Philip, Guy de Dam-
      pierre.

I beheld the pageants splendid that adorned those days
　　　of old;
Stately dames, like queens attended, knights who
　　　bore the Fleece of Gold.

Lombard and Venetian merchants with deep-laden ar-
　　　gosies;
Ministers from twenty nations; more than royal pomp
　　　and case.

I beheld proud Maximilian, kneeling humbly on the
　　　ground;
I beheld the gentle Mary, hunting with her hawk and
　　　hound;

And her lighted bridal-chamber, where a duke slept
　　　with the queen,
And the armèd guard around them, and the sword un-
　　　sheathed between.

I beheld the Flemish weavers, with Namur and Juliers
　　　bold,
Marching homeward from the bloody battle of the
　　　Spurs of Gold.

Saw the fight at Minnewater, saw the White Hoods
　　　moving west,
Saw great Artevelde victorious scale the Golden
　　　Dragon's nest.

And again the whiskered Spaniard all the land with
　　　terror smote;
And again the wild alarum sounded from the tocsin's
　　　throat.

Till the bell of Ghent responded o'er lagoon and dike
    of sand,
" I am Roland! I am Roland! there is victory in the
    land!"

Then the sound of drums aroused me. The awakened
    city's roar
Chased the phantoms I had summoned back into their
    graves once more.

Hours had passed away like minutes; and, before I
    was aware,
Lo! the shadow of the belfry crossed the sun-illumined
    square.

HENRY WADSWORTH LONGFELLOW.

HORATIUS.

LARS PORSENA of Clusium
  By the Nine Gods he swore
That the great house of Tarquin
  Should suffer wrong no more.
By the Nine Gods he swore it
  And named a trysting day,
And bade his messengers ride forth,
East and west and south and north,
  To summon his array.

East and west and south and north
  The messengers ride fast,
And tower and town and cottage
  Have heard the trumpet's blast.
Shame on the false Etruscan
  Who lingers in his home,

When Porsena of Clusium
  Is on the march for Rome.

And now hath every city
  Sent up her tale of men;
The foot are fourscore thousand,
  The horse are thousands ten.
Before the gates of Sutrium
  Is met the great array.
A proud man was Lars Porsena
  Upon the trysting day.

For all the Etruscan armies
  Were ranged beneath his eye,
And many a banished Roman,
  And many a stout ally;
And with a mighty following
  To join the muster came
The Tusculan Mamilius,
  Prince of the Latian name.

But by the yellow Tiber
  Was tumult and affright:
From all the spacious champaign
  To Rome men took their flight.
A mile around the city
  The throng stopped up the ways;
A fearful sight it was to see
  Through two long nights and days.

To eastward and to westward
  Have spread the Tuscan bands;
Nor house, nor fence, nor dove-cote
  In Crustumerium stands.
Verbenna down to Ostia

Hath wasted all the plain;
Astur hath stormed Janiculum,
    And the stout guards are slain.

I wis, in all the Senate,
    There was no heart so bold,
But sore it ached and fast it beat,
    When that ill news was told.
Forthwith up rose the Consul,
    Up rose the Fathers all;
In haste they girded up their gowns,
    And hied them to the wall.

They held a council standing
    Before the River-Gate;
Short time was there, ye well may guess,
    For musing or debate.
Out spake the Consul roundly:
    " The bridge must straight go down ;
For, since Janiculum is lost,
    Nought else can save the town."

Just then a scout came flying,
    All wild with haste and fear:
" To arms! to arms! Sir Consul:
    Lars Porsena is here!"
On the low hills to westward
    The Consul fixed his eye,
And saw the swarthy storm of dust
    Rise fast along the sky.

And nearer fast and nearer
    Doth the red whirlwind come;
And louder still and still more loud,
From underneath that rolling cloud,

Is heard the trumpet's war-note proud,
    The trampling and the hum.
And plainly and more plainly
    Now through the gloom appears,
Far to left and far to right,
In broken gleams of dark-blue light,
The long array of helmets bright,
    The long array of spears.

Fast by the royal standard,
    O'erlooking all the war,
Lars Porsena of Clusium
    Sat in his ivory car.
By the right wheel rode Mamilius,
    Prince of the Latian name;
And by the left false Sextus,
    That wrought the deed of shame.

But when the face of Sextus
    Was seen among the foes,
A yell that rent the firmament
    From all the town arose.
On the house-tops was no woman
    But spat towards him and hissed,
No child but screamed out curses,
    And shook its little fist.

But the Consul's brow was sad,
    And the Consul's speech was low,
And darkly looked he at the wall,
    And darkly at the foe.
" Their van will be upon us
    Before the bridge goes down;
And if they once may win the bridge,
    What hope to save the town? "

Then out spake brave Horatius,
   The Captain of the Gate:
" To every man upon this earth
   Death cometh soon or late.
And how can man die better
   Than facing fearful odds,
For the ashes of his fathers,
   And the temples of his Gods,

" And for the tender mother
   Who dandled him to rest,
And for the wife who nurses
   His baby at her breast,
And for the holy maidens
   Who feed the eternal flame,
To save them from false Sextus
   That wrought the deed of shame ?

" Hew down the bridge, Sir Consul,
   With all the speed ye may;
I, with two more to help me,
   Will hold the foe in play.
In yon strait path a thousand
   May well be stopped by three.
Now who will stand on either hand,
   And keep the bridge with me ? "

Then out spake Spurius Lartius;
   A Ramnian proud was he:
" Lo, I will stand at thy right hand,
   And keep the bridge with thee."
And out spake strong Herminius;
   Of Titian blood was he:
" I will abide on thy left side,
   And keep the bridge with thee."

" Horatius," quoth the Consul,
  " As thou sayest, so let it be."
And straight against that great array
  Forth went the dauntless Three.
For Romans in Rome's quarrels
  Spared neither land nor gold,
Nor son nor wife, nor limb nor life,
  In the brave days of old.

Then none was for a party;
  Then all were for the state;
Then the great man helped the poor,
  And the poor man loved the great;
Then lands were fairly portioned;
  Then spoils were fairly sold:
The Romans were like brothers
  In the brave days of old.

Now Roman is to Roman
  More hateful than a foe,
And the Tribunes beard the high,
  And the Fathers grind the low.
As we wax hot in faction,
  In battle we wax cold:
Wherefore men fight not as they fought
  In the brave days of old.

Now while the Three were tightening
  Their harness on their backs,
The Consul was the foremost man
  To take in hand an axe:
And Fathers mixed with Commons
  Seized hatchet, bar, and crow,
And smote upon the planks above,
  And loosed the props below.

Meanwhile the Tuscan army,
  Right glorious to behold,
Come flashing back the noonday light,
Rank behind rank, like surges bright
  Of a broad sea of gold.
Four hundred trumpets sounded
  A peal of warlike glee,
As that great host with measured tread,
And spears advanced, and ensigns spread,
Rolled slowly towards the bridge's head,
  Where stood the dauntless Three.

The Three stood calm and silent,
  And looked upon the foes,
And a great shout of laughter
  From all the vanguard rose:
And forth three chiefs came spurring
  Before that deep array;
To earth they sprang, their swords they drew,
And lifted high their shields, and flew
  To win the narrow way;

Aunus from green Tifernum,
  Lord of the Hill of Vines;
And Seius, whose eight hundred slaves
  Sicken in Ilva's mines;
And Picus, long to Clusium
  Vassal in peace and war,
Who led to fight his Umbrian powers
From that gray crag where, girt with towers,
The fortress of Nequinum lowers
  O'er the pale waves of Nar.

Stout Lartius hurled down Aunus
  Into the stream beneath;

Herminius struck at Seius
　And clove him to the teeth;
At Picus brave Horatius
　Darted one fiery thrust;
And the proud Umbrian's gilded arms
　Clashed in the bloody dust.

Then Ocnus of Falerii
　Rushed on the Roman Three;
And Lausulus of Urgo,
　The rover of the sea;
And Aruns of Volsinium,
　Who slew the great wild boar, —
The great wild boar that had his den
Amidst the reeds of Cosa's fen,
And wasted fields, and slaughtered men,
　Along Albinia's shore.

Herminius smote down Aruns;
　Lartius laid Ocnus low;
Right to the heart of Lausulus
　Horatius sent a blow.
" Lie there," he cried, " fell pirate!
　No more, aghast and pale,
From Ostia's walls the crowd shall mark
The track of thy destroying bark.
No more Campania's hinds shall fly
To woods and caverns when they spy
　Thy thrice accursèd sail."

But now no sound of laughter
　Was heard among the foes.
A wild and wrathful clamor
　From all the vanguard rose.
Six spears' length from the entrance

Halted that deep array,
And for a space no man came forth
　　To win the narrow way.

But hark! the cry is Astur:
　　And lo! the ranks divide;
And the great Lord of Luna
　　Comes with his stately stride.
Upon his ample shoulders
　　Clangs loud the four-fold shield,
And in his hand he shakes the brand
　　Which none but he can wield.

He smiled on those bold Romans
　　A smile serene and high ;
He eyed the flinching Tuscans,
　　And scorn was in his eye.
Quoth he, " The she-wolf's litter
　　Stand savagely at bay :
But will ye dare to follow,
　　If Astur clears the way?"

Then, whirling up his broadsword
　　With both hands to the height,
He rushed against Horatius,
　　And smote with all his might.
With shield and blade Horatius
　　Right deftly turned the blow.
The blow, though turned, came yet too nigh ;
It missed his helm, but gashed his thigh :
The Tuscans raised a joyful cry
　　To see the red blood flow.

He reeled, and on Herminius
　　He leaned one breathing-space ;

Then, like a wild-cat mad with wounds,
  Sprang right at Astur's face.
Through teeth, and skull, and helmet,
  So fierce a thrust he sped,
The good sword stood a hand-breadth out
  Behind the Tuscan's head.

And the great Lord of Luna
  Fell at that deadly stroke,
As falls on Mount Alvernus
  A thunder-smitten oak.
Far o'er the crashing forest
  The giant arms lie spread;
And the pale augurs, muttering low,
  Gaze on the blasted head.

On Astur's throat Horatius
  Right firmly pressed his heel,
And thrice and four times tugged amain,
  Ere he wrenched out the steel.
" And see," he cried, " the welcome,
  Fair guests, that waits you here !
What noble Lucumo comes next
  To taste our Roman cheer ? "

But at his haughty challenge
  A sullen murmur ran,
Mingled of wrath, and shame, and dread,
  Along that glittering van.
There lacked not men of prowess,
  Nor men of lordly race;
For all Etruria's noblest
  Were round the fatal place.

But all Etruria's noblest
  Felt their hearts sink to see

On the earth the bloody corpses,
  In the path the dauntless Three :
And, from the ghostly entrance
  Where those bold Romans stood,
All shrank, like boys who unaware,
Ranging the woods to start a hare,
Come to the mouth of the dark lair
Where, growling low, a fierce old bear
  Lies amidst bones and blood.

Was none who would be foremost
  To lead such dire attack;
But those behind cried " Forward ! "
  And those before cried " Back ! "
And backward now and forward
  Wavers the deep array;
And on the tossing sea of steel,
To and fro the standards reel;
And the victorious trumpet-peal
  Dies fitfully away.

Yet one man for one moment
  Strode out before the crowd ;
Well known was he to all the Three,
  And they gave him greeting loud.
" Now welcome, welcome, Sextus !
  Now welcome to thy home !
Why dost thou stay, and turn away ?
  Here lies the road to Rome."

Thrice looked he at the city;
  Thrice looked he at the dead ;
And thrice came on in fury,
  And thrice turned back in dread ;
And, white with fear and hatred,
  Scowled at the narrow way

Where, wallowing in a pool of blood,
  The bravest Tuscans lay.

But meanwhile axe and lever
  Have manfully been plied ;
And now the bridge hangs tottering
  Above the boiling tide.
" Come back, come back, Horatius ! "
  Loud cried the Fathers all.
" Back, Lartius ! Back, Herminius !
  Back, ere the ruin fall ! "

Back darted Spurius Lartius ;
  Herminius darted back :
And, as they passed, beneath their feet
  They felt the timbers crack.
But when they turned their faces,
  And on the farther shore
Saw brave Horatius stand alone,
  They would have crossed once more.

But with a crash like thunder
  Fell every loosened beam,
And, like a dam, the mighty wreck
  Lay right athwart the stream ;
And a long shout of triumph
  Rose from the walls of Rome,
As to the highest turret-tops
  Was splashed the yellow foam.

And, like a horse unbroken
  When first he feels the rein,
The furious river struggled hard,
  And tossed his tawny mane,
And burst the curb, and bounded,

Rejoicing to be free,
And, whirling down, in fierce career,
Battlement, and plank, and pier,
Rushed headlong to the sea.

Alone stood brave Horatius,
But constant still in mind;
Thrice thirty thousand foes before,
And the broad flood behind.
" Down with him ! " cried false Sextus,
With a smile on his pale face.
" Now yield thee," cried Lars Porsena,
" Now yield thee to our grace."

Round turned he, as not deigning
Those craven ranks to see ;
Nought spake he to Lars Porsena,
To Sextus nought spake he ;
But he saw on Palatinus
The white porch of his home ;
And he spake to the noble river
That rolls by the towers of Rome.

" O Tiber ! father Tiber !
To whom the Romans pray,
A Roman's life, a Roman's arms,
Take thou in charge this day ! "
So he spake, and speaking sheathed
The good sword by his side,
And, with his harness on his back,
Plunged headlong in the tide.

No sound of joy or sorrow
Was heard from either bank;
But friends and foes in dumb surprise,

With parted lips and straining eyes,
   Stood gazing where he sank;
And when above the surges
   They saw his crest appear,
All Rome sent forth a rapturous cry,
And even the ranks of Tuscany
   Could scarce forbear to cheer.

But fiercely ran the current,
   Swollen high by months of rain,
And fast his blood was flowing,
   And he was sore in pain,
And heavy with his armor,
   And spent with changing blows:
And oft they thought him sinking,
   But still again he rose.

Never, I ween, did swimmer,
   In such an evil case,
Struggle through such a raging flood
   Safe to the landing place:
But his limbs were borne up bravely
   By the brave heart within,
And our good father Tiber
   Bare bravely up his chin.

"Curse on him!" quoth false Sextus;
   "Will not the villain drown?
But for this stay, ere close of day
   We should have sacked the town!"
"Heaven help him!" quoth Lars Porsena,
   "And bring him safe to shore;
For such a gallant feat of arms
   Was never seen before."

And now he feels the bottom;
 Now on dry earth he stands;
Now round him 'throng the Fathers,
 To press his gory hands;
And now, with shouts and clapping,
 And noise of weeping loud,
He enters through the River-Gate,
 Borne by the joyous crowd.

They gave him of the corn-land,
 That was of public right,
As much as two strong oxen
 Could plough from morn till night;
And they made a molten image,
 And set it up on high,
And there it stands unto this day
 To witness if I lie.

It stands in the Comitium,
 Plain for all folk to see:
Horatius in his harness,
 Halting upon one knee:
And underneath is written,
 In letters all of gold,
How valiantly he kept the bridge
 In the brave days of old.

And still his name sounds stirring
 Unto the men of Rome,
As the trumpet-blast that cries to them
 To charge the Volscian home ;
And wives still pray to Juno
 For boys with hearts as bold
As his who kept the bridge so well
 In the brave days of old.

LORD MACAULAY.

BURIAL OF THE MINNISINK.

On sunny slope and beechen swell,
The shadowed light of evening fell;
And, where the maple's leaf was brown,
With soft and silent lapse came down
The glory that the wood receives,
At sunset, in its golden leaves.

Far upward in the mellow light
Rose the blue hills.   One cloud of white,
Around a far uplifted cone,
In the warm blush of evening shone;
An image of the silver lakes,
By which the Indian's soul awakes.

But soon a funeral hymn was heard
Where the soft breath of evening stirred
The tall, gray forest; and a band
Of stern in heart, and strong in hand,
Came winding down beside the wave,
To lay the red chief in his grave.

They sang, that by his native bowers
He stood, in the last moon of flowers,
And thirty snows had not yet shed
Their glory on the warrior's head;
But, as the summer fruit decays,
So died he in those naked days.

A dark cloak of the roebuck's skin
Covered the warrior, and within
Its heavy folds the weapons, made
For the hard toils of war, were laid;

The cuirass, woven of plaited reeds,
And the broad belt of shells and beads.

Before, a dark-haired virgin train
Chanted the death-dirge of the slain;
Behind, the long procession came
Of hoary men and chiefs of fame,
With heavy hearts, and eyes of grief,
Leading the war-horse of their chief.

Stripped of his proud and martial dress,
Uncurbed, unreined, and riderless,
With darting eye, and nostril spread,
And heavy and impatient tread,
He came; and oft that eye so proud
Asked for his rider in the crowd.

They buried the dark chief; they freed
Beside the grave his battle-steed;
And swift an arrow cleaved its way
To his stern heart!   One piercing neigh
Arose, and, on the dead man's plain,
The rider grasps his steed again.

HENRY WADSWORTH LONGFELLOW.

THE PILGRIM'S VISION.

In the hour of twilight shadows
　　The Pilgrim sire looked out;
He thought of the " bloudy Salvages "
　　That lurked all round about,
Of Wituwamet's pictured knife
　　And Pecksuot's whooping shout;

For the baby's limbs were feeble,
  Though his father's arms were stout.

His home was a freezing cabin,
  Too bare for the hungry rat,
Its roof was thatched with ragged grass,
  And bald enough of that;
The hole that served for casement
  Was glazed with an ancient hat;
And the ice was gently thawing
  From the log whereon he sat.

Along the dreary landscape
  His eyes went to and fro,
The trees all clad in icicles,
  The streams that did not flow;
A sudden thought flashed o'er him, —
  A dream of long ago, —
He smote his leathern jerkin,
  And murmured, "Even so!"

"Come hither, God-be-Glorified,
  And sit upon my knee,
Behold the dream unfolding,
  Whereof I spake to thee
By the winter's hearth in Leyden
  And on the stormy sea;
True is the dream's beginning, —
  So may its ending be!

"I saw in the naked forest
  Our scattered remnant cast,
A screen of shivering branches
  Between them and the blast;
The snow was falling round them,
17

The dying fell as fast;
I looked to see them perish,
When lo, the vision passed.

" Again mine eyes were opened, —
The feeble had waxed strong,
The babes had grown to sturdy men,
The remnant was a throng;
By shadowed lake and winding stream,
And all the shores along,
The howling demons quaked to hear
The Christian's godly song.

" They slept, — the village fathers, —
By river, lake, and shore,
When far adown the steep of Time
The vision rose once more;
I saw along the winter snow
A spectral column pour,
And high above their broken ranks
A tattered flag they bore.

" Their Leader rode before them,
Of bearing calm and high,
The light of Heaven's own kindling
Throned in his awful eye,
These were a Nation's champions
Her dread appeal to try;
God for the right! I faltered,
And lo, the train passed by.

" Once more, — the strife is ended,
The solemn issue tried,
The Lord of Hosts, his mighty arm
Has helped our Israel's side;

Gray stone and grassy hillock
  Tell where our martyrs died,
But peaceful smiles the harvest,
  And stainless flows the tide.

" A crash, — as when some swollen cloud
  Cracks o'er the tangled trees!
With side to side, and spar to spar,
  Whose smoking decks are these?
I know Saint George's blood-red cross,
  Thou Mistress of the Seas, —
But what is she, whose streaming bars
  Roll out before the breeze?

" Ah, well her iron ribs are knit,
  Whose thunders strive to quell
The bellowing throats, the blazing lips,
  That pealed the Armada's knell!
The mist was cleared, a wreath of stars
  Rose o'er the crimsoned swell,
And, wavering from its haughty peak,
  The cross of England fell!

" O trembling Faith! though dark the morn,
  A heavenly torch is thine;
While feebler races melt away,
  And paler orbs decline,
Still shall the fiery pillar's ray
  Along thy pathway shine,
To light the chosen tribe that sought
  This Western Palestine!

" I see the living tide roll on;
  It crowns with flaming towers
The icy capes of Labrador,

The Spaniard's 'land of flowers'!
It streams beyond the splintered ridge
    That parts the northern showers;
From eastern rock to sunset wave
    The continent is ours!"

He ceased, — the grim old soldier-saint, —
    Then softly bent to cheer
The pilgrim-child, whose wasting face
    Was meekly turned to hear;
And drew his toil-worn sleeve across,
    To brush the manly tear
From cheeks that never changed in woe,
    And never blanched in fear.

The weary pilgrim slumbers,
    His resting-place unknown;
His hands were crossed, his lids were closed,
    The dust was o'er him strown;
The drifting soil, the mouldering leaf,
    Along the sod were blown;
His mound has melted into earth,
    His memory lives alone.

So let it live unfading,
    The memory of the dead,
Long as the pale anemone
    Springs where their tears were shed,
Or, raining in the summer's wind
    In flakes of burning red,
The wild rose sprinkles with its leaves
    The turf where once they bled!

Yea, when the frowning bulwarks
    That guard this holy strand

Have sunk beneath the trampling surge
  In beds of sparkling sand,
While in the waste of ocean
  One hoary rock shall stand,
Be this its latest legend,
  Here was the Pilgrim's land!
            OLIVER WENDELL HOLMES.

PAUL REVERE'S RIDE.

LISTEN, my children, and you shall hear
Of the midnight ride of Paul Revere,
On the eighteenth of April, in Seventy-five;
Hardly a man is now alive
Who remembers that famous day and year.

He said to his friend, "If the British march
By land or sea from the town to-night,
Hang a lantern aloft in the belfry arch
Of the North Church tower as a signal light, —
One, if by land, and two, if by sea;
And I on the opposite shore will be,
Ready to ride and spread the alarm
Through every Middlesex village and farm,
For the country-folk to be up and to arm."

Then he said, "Good-night!" and with muffled oar
Silently rowed to the Charlestown shore,
Just as the moon rose over the bay,
Where swinging wide at her moorings lay
The Somerset, British man-of-war;
A phantom ship, with each mast and spar
Across the moon like a prison bar,

And a huge black hulk, that was magnified
By its own reflection in the tide.

Meanwhile, his friend, through alley and street,
Wanders and watches with eager ears,
Till in the silence around him he hears
The muster of men at the barrack door,
The sound of arms, and the tramp of feet,
And the measured tread of the grenadiers,
Marching down to their boats on the shore.

Then he climbed the tower of the Old North Church,
By the wooden stairs, with stealthy tread,
To the belfry-chamber overhead,
And startled the pigeons from their perch
On the sombre rafters, that round him made
Masses and moving shapes of shade, —
By the trembling ladder steep and tall,
To the highest window in the wall,
Where he paused to listen and look down
A moment on the roofs of the town,
And the moonlight flowing over all.

Beneath, in the churchyard, lay the dead,
In their night encampment on the hill,
Wrapped in silence so deep and still
That he could hear, like a sentinel's tread,
The watchful night-wind, as it went
Creeping along from tent to tent,
And seeming to whisper, " All is well! "
A moment only he feels the spell
Of the place and the hour, and the secret dread
Of the lonely belfry and the dead;
For suddenly all his thoughts are bent
On a shadowy something far away,

Where the river widens to meet the bay, —
A line of black that bends and floats
On the rising tide, like a bridge of boats.

Meanwhile, impatient to mount and ride,
Booted and spurred, with a heavy stride
On the opposite shore walked Paul Revere.
Now he patted his horse's side,
Now gazed at the landscape far and near,
Then, impetuous, stamped the earth,
And turned and tightened his saddle-girth;
But mostly he watched with eager search
The belfry-tower of the Old North Church,
As it rose above the graves on the hill,
Lonely and spectral and sombre and still.
And lo ! as he looks, on the belfry's height
A glimmer, and then a gleam of light !
He springs to the saddle, the bridle he turns,
But lingers and gazes, till full on his sight
A second lamp in the belfry burns !

A hurry of hoofs in a village street,
A shape in the moonlight, a bulk in the dark,
And beneath, from the pebbles, in passing, a spark
Struck out by a steed flying fearless and fleet :
That was all ! And yet, through the gloom and the
        light,
The fate of a nation was riding that night;
And the spark struck out by that steed, in his flight,
Kindled the land into flame with its heat.

He has left the village and mounted the steep,
And beneath him, tranquil and broad and deep,
Is the Mystic, meeting the ocean tides;
And under the alders, that skirt its edge,

Now soft on the sand, now loud on the ledge,
Is heard the tramp of his steed as he rides.

It was twelve by the village clock
When he crossed the bridge into Medford town.
He heard the crowing of the cock,
And the barking of the farmer's dog,
And felt the damp of the river fog,
That rises after the sun goes down.

It was one by the village clock
When he galloped into Lexington.
He saw the gilded weathercock
Swim in the moonlight as he passed,
And the meeting-house windows, blank and bare,
Gaze at him with a spectral glare,
As if they already stood aghast
At the bloody work they would look upon.

It was two by the village clock
When he came to the bridge in Concord town.
He heard the bleating of the flock,
And the twitter of birds among the trees,
And felt the breath of the morning breeze
Blowing over the meadows brown.
And one was safe and asleep in his bed
Who at the bridge would be first to fall,
Who that day would be lying dead,
Pierced by a British musket-ball.

You know the rest.   In the books you have read,
How the British Regulars fired and fled, —
How the farmers gave them ball for ball,
From behind each fence and farm-yard wall,
Chasing the red-coats down the lane,

Then crossing the fields to emerge again
Under the trees at the turn of the road,
And only pausing to fire and load.

So through the night rode Paul Revere;
And so through the night went his cry of alarm
To every Middlesex village and farm, —
A cry of defiance and not of fear,
A voice in the darkness, a knock at the door,
And a word that shall echo forevermore !
For, borne on the night-wind of the Past,
Through all our history, to the last,
In the hour of darkness and peril and need,
The people will waken and listen to hear
The hurrying hoof-beats of that steed,
And the midnight message of Paul Revere.
HENRY WADSWORTH LONGFELLOW.

LEXINGTON.

SLOWLY the mist o'er the meadow was creeping,
Bright on the dewy buds glistened the sun,
When from his couch, while his children were sleeping,
Rose the bold rebel and shouldered his gun.
    Waving her golden veil
    Over the silent dale,
Blithe looked the morning on cottage and spire ;
    Hushed was his parting sigh,
    While from his noble eye
Flashed the last sparkle of liberty's fire.

On the smooth green where the fresh leaf is springing,
Calmly the first-born of glory have met ;

Hark! the death-volley around them is ringing!
Look! with their life-blood the young grass is wet!
    Faint is the feeble breath,
    Murmuring low in death,
"Tell to our sons how their fathers have died;"
    Nerveless the iron hand,
    Raised for its native land,
Lies by the weapon that gleams at its side.

Over the hillsides the wild knell is tolling,
From their far hamlets the yeomanry come;
As through the storm-clouds the thunder burst rolling,
Circles the beat of the mustering drum.
    Fast on the soldier's path
    Darken the waves of wrath,
Long have they gathered and loud shall they fall;
    Red glares the musket's flash,
    Sharp rings the rifle's crash,
Blazing and clanging from thicket and wall.

Gayly the plume of the horseman was dancing,
Never to shadow his cold brow again;
Proudly at morning the war-steed was prancing,
Reeking and panting he droops on the rein;
    Pale is the lip of scorn,
    Voiceless the trumpet horn,
Torn is the silken-fringed red cross on high;
    Many a belted breast
    Low on the turf shall rest,
Ere the dark hunters the herd have passed by.

Snow-girdled crags where the hoarse wind is raving,
Rocks where the weary floods murmur and wail,
Wilds where the fern by the furrow is waving,
Reeled with the echoes that rode on the gale;

Far as the tempest thrills
Over the darkened hills,
Far as the sunshine streams over the plain,
Roused by the tyrant band,
Woke all the mighty land,
Girded for battle, from mountain to main.

Green be the graves where her martyrs are lying!
Shroudless and tombless they sunk to their rest, —
While o'er their ashes the starry fold flying
Wraps the proud eagle they roused from his nest.
Borne on her Northern pine,
Long o'er the foaming brine
Spread her broad banner to storm and to sun;
Heaven keep her ever free,
Wide as o'er land and sea
Floats the fair emblem her heroes have won!

OLIVER WENDELL HOLMES.

GRANDMOTHER'S STORY OF BUNKER HILL BATTLE.

AS SHE SAW IT FROM THE BELFRY.

'T is like stirring living embers when, at eighty, one remembers
All the achings and the quakings of " the times that tried men's souls;"
When I talk of *Whig* and *Tory*, when I tell the *Rebel* story,
To you the words are ashes, but to me they 're burning coals.

I had heard the muskets' rattle of the April running
    battle;
Lord Percy's hunted soldiers, I can see their red coats
    still;
But a deadly chill comes o'er me, as the day looms up
    before me,
When a thousand men lay bleeding on the slopes of
    Bunker's Hill.

'T was a peaceful summer's morning, when the first
    thing gave us warning
Was the booming of the cannon from the river and the
    shore.
" Child," says grandma, " what 's the matter, what is
    all this noise and clatter?
Have those scalping Indian devils come to murder us
    once more? "

Poor old soul! my sides were shaking in the midst of
    all my quaking,
To hear her talk of Indians when the guns began to
    roar :
She had seen the burning village, and the slaughter
    and the pillage,
When the Mohawks killed her father with their bullets
    through his door.

Then I said, " Now, dear old granny, don't you fret
    and worry any,
For I 'll soon come back and tell you whether this is
    work or play;
There can't be mischief in it, so I won't be gone a
    minute " —
For a minute then I started. I was gone the livelong
    day.

No time for bodice-lacing or for looking-glass grimac-
     ing,
Down my hair went as I hurried, tumbling half-way to
     my heels;
God forbid your ever knowing, when there's blood
     around her flowing,
How the lonely, helpless daughter of a quiet household
     feels!

In the street I heard a thumping, and I knew it was
     the stumping
Of the Corporal, our old neighbor, on that wooden leg
     he wore,
With a knot of women round him, — it was lucky I
     had found him,
So I followed with the others, and the Corporal marched
     before.

They were making for the steeple, — the old soldier
     and his people;
The pigeons circled round us as we climbed the creak-
     ing stair,
Just across the narrow river — O, so close it made me
     shiver ! —
Stood a fortress on the hill-top that but yesterday was
     bare.

Not slow our eyes to find it; well we knew who stood
     behind it,
Though the earthwork hid them from us, and the stub-
     born walls were dumb:
Here were sister, wife, and mother, looking wild upon
     each other,
And their lips were white with terror as they said,
     The hour has come !

The morning slowly wasted, not a morsel had we
    tasted,
And our heads were almost splitting with the cannon's
    deafening thrill,
When a figure tall and stately round the rampart strode
    sedately,
It was *Prescott*, one since told me ; he commanded on
    the hill.

Every woman's heart grew bigger when we saw his
    manly figure,
With the banyan buckled round it, standing up so
    straight and tall;
Like a gentleman of leisure who is strolling out for
    pleasure,
Through the storm of shells and cannon-shot he walked
    around the wall.

At eleven the streets were swarming, for the red-coats'
    ranks were forming,
At noon in marching order they were moving to the
    piers;
How the bayonets gleamed and glistened, as we looked
    far down and listened
To the trampling and the drum-beat of the belted gren-
    adiers!

At length the men have started, with a cheer (it seemed
    faint-hearted),
In their scarlet regimentals, with their knapsacks on
    their backs,
And the reddening, rippling water, as after a sea-fight's
    slaughter,
Round the barges gliding onward blushed like blood
    along their tracks.

So they crossed to the other border, and again they
    formed in order ;
And the boats came back for soldiers, came for sol-
    diers, soldiers still :
The time seemed everlasting to us women faint and
    fasting, —
At last they 're moving, marching, marching proudly
    up the hill.

We can see the bright steel glancing all along the lines
    advancing;
Now the front rank fires a volley, — they have thrown
    away their shot;
For behind their earthwork lying, all the balls above
    them flying,
Our people need not hurry, so they wait and answer
    not.

Then the Corporal, our old cripple (he would swear
    sometimes and tipple), —
He had heard the bullets whistle (in the old French
    war) before, —
Calls out in words of jeering, just as if they all were
    hearing, —
And his wooden leg thumps fiercely on the dusty belfry
    floor: —

"O! fire away, ye villains, and earn King George's
    shillin's,
But ye 'll waste a ton of powder afore a ' rebel '
    falls;
You may bang the dirt and welcome, they 're as safe
    as Dan'l Malcolm
Ten foot beneath the gravestone that you 've splintered
    with your balls!"

In the hush of expectation, in the awe and trepida-
 tion
Of the dread approaching moment, we are well-nigh
 breathless all;
Though the rotten bars are failing on the rickety belfry railing,
We are crowding up against them like the waves
 against a wall.

Just a glimpse (the air is clearer), they are nearer, —
 nearer, — nearer,
When a flash — a curling smoke-wreath — then a
 crash — the steeple shakes —
The deadly truce is ended; the tempest's shroud is
 rended ;
Like a morning mist it gathered, like a thunder-cloud
 it breaks!

O the sight our eyes discover as the blue-black smoke
 blows over !
The red-coats stretched in windrows as a mower rakes
 his hay;
Here a scarlet heap is lying, there a headlong crowd
 is flying
Like a billow that has broken and is shivered into
 spray.

Then we cried, " The troops are routed! they are
 beat — it can't be doubted !
God be thanked, the fight is over ! " — Ah! the grim
 old soldier's smile !
" Tell us, tell us why you look so? " (we could
 hardly speak, we shook so), —
" Are they beaten? *Are* they beaten? ARE they
 beaten? " — " Wait awhile."

O the trembling and the terror! for too soon we saw
    our error:
They are baffled, not defeated; we have driven them
    back in vain;
And the columns that were scattered, round the colors
    that were tattered,
Toward the sullen silent fortress turn their belted
    breasts again.

All at once, as we are gazing, lo, the roofs of Charles-
    town blazing!
They have fired the harmless village; in an hour it
    will be down!
The Lord in heaven confound them, rain his fire and
    brimstone round them, —
The robbing, murdering red-coats, that would burn a
    peaceful town!

They are marching, stern and solemn; we can see each
    massive column
As they near the naked earth-mound with the slanting
    walls so steep.
Have our soldiers got faint-hearted, and in noiseless
    haste departed?
Are they panic-struck and helpless?   Are they palsied
    or asleep?

Now! the walls they 're almost under! scarce a rod the
    foes asunder!
Not a firelock flashed against them! up the earthwork
    they will swarm!
But the words have scarce been spoken, when the omi-
    nous calm is broken,
And a bellowing crash has emptied all the vengeance
    of the storm!

So again, with murderous slaughter, pelted backwards
    to the water,
Fly Pigot's running heroes and the frightened braves
    of Howe;
And we shout, " At last they 're done for, it 's their
    barges they have run for:
They are beaten, beaten, beaten; and the battle 's over
    now ! "

And we looked, poor timid creatures, on the rough old
    soldier's features,
Our lips afraid to question, but he knew what we would
    ask:
" Not sure," he said, " keep quiet, — once more, I
    guess, they 'll try it, —
Here 's damnation to the cut-throats ! " — then he
    handed me his flask,

Saying, " Gal, you 're looking shaky; have a drop of
    old Jamaiky;
I 'm afeared there 'll be more trouble afore the job is
    done; "
So I took one scorching swallow; dreadful faint I felt,
    and hollow,
Standing there from early morning when the firing was
    begun.

All through those hours of trial I had watched a calm
    clock dial,
As the hands kept creeping, creeping, — they were
    creeping round to four,
When the old man said, " They 're forming with their
    bagonets fixed for storming,
It 's the death-grip that 's a coming, — they will try the
    works once more."

With brazen trumpets blaring, the flames behind them
    glaring,
The deadly wall before them, in close array they
    come;
Still onward, upward toiling, like a dragon's fold un-
    coiling, —
Like the rattlesnake's shrill warning the reverberating
    drum !

Over heaps all torn and gory — shall I tell the fearful
    story,
How they surged above the breastwork, as a sea breaks
    over a deck;
How, driven, yet scarce defeated, our worn-out men
    retreated,
With their powder horns all emptied, like the swim-
    mers from a wreck?

It has all been told and painted; as for me, they say I
    fainted,
And the wooden-legged old Corporal stumped with me
    down the stair:
When I woke from dreams affrighted the evening
    lamps were lighted, —
On the floor a youth was lying; his bleeding breast
    was bare.

And I heard through all the flurry, " Send for Warren!
    hurry! hurry!
Tell him here 's a soldier bleeding, and he 'll come and
    dress his wound ! "
Ah, we knew not till the morrow told its tale of death
    and sorrow,
How the starlight found him stiffened on the dark and
    bloody ground.

Who the youth was, what his name was, where the
    place from which he came was,
Who had brought him from the battle, and had left
    him at our door,
He could not speak to tell us; but 't was one of our
    brave fellows,
As the homespun plainly showed us which the dying
    soldier wore.

For they all thought he was dying, as they gathered
    round him crying,
And they said, "O, how they 'll miss him!" and,
    "What *will* his mother do?"
Then his eyelids just unclosing like a child's that has
    been dozing,
He faintly murmured, "Mother!"—and—I saw his
    eyes were blue.

"Why, grandma, how you 're winking!"—Ah, my
    child, it sets me thinking
Of a story not like this one. Well, he somehow lived
    along;
So we came to know each other, and I nursed him like
    a—mother,
Till at last he stood before me, tall, and rosy-cheeked,
    and strong.

And we sometimes walked together in the pleasant
    summer weather—
"Please to tell us what his name was?"—Just your
    own, my little dear,—
There 's his picture Copley painted: we became so
    well acquainted,
That—in short, that 's why I 'm grandma, and you
    children all are here!

OLIVER WENDELL HOLMES.

HYMN OF THE MORAVIAN NUNS OF BETHLEHEM,

AT THE CONSECRATION OF PULASKI'S BANNER.

When the dying flame of day
Through the chancel shot its ray,
Far the glimmering tapers shed
Faint light on the cowlèd head;
And the censer burning swung,
Where, before the altar, hung
The crimson banner, that with prayer
Had been consecrated there.
And the nuns' sweet hymn was heard the while,
Sung low, in the dim, mysterious aisle.

" Take thy banner!   May it wave
Proudly o'er the good and brave;
When the battle's distant wail
Breaks the Sabbath of our vale,
When the clarion's music thrills
To the hearts of these lone hills,
When the spear in conflict shakes,
And the strong lance shivering breaks.

" Take thy banner! and, beneath
The battle-cloud's encircling wreath,
Guard it, till our homes are free!
Guard it! God will prosper thee!
In the dark and trying hour,
In the breaking forth of power,
In the rush of steeds and men,
His right hand will shield thee then.

"Take thy banner!   But when night
   Closes round the ghastly fight,
   If the vanquished warrior bow,
   Spare him!   By our holy vow,
   By our prayers and many tears,
   By the mercy that endears,
   Spare him! he our love hath shared!
   Spare him! as thou wouldst be spared!

"Take thy banner! and if e'er
   Thou shouldst press the soldier's bier,
   And the muffled drum should beat
   To the tread of mournful feet,
   Then this crimson flag shall be
   Martial cloak and shroud for thee."

The warrior took that banner proud,
And it was his martial cloak and shroud!
          HENRY WADSWORTH LONGFELLOW.

INCIDENT OF THE FRENCH CAMP.

I.

You know, we French stormed Ratisbon;
   A mile or so away,
On a little mound, Napoleon
   Stood on our storming-day;
With neck out-thrust, you fancy how,
   Legs wide, arms locked behind,
As if to balance the prone brow
   Oppressive with its mind.

II.

Just as perhaps he mused, "My plans,
   That soar, to earth may fall,
Let once my army-leader Lannes
   Waver at yonder wall," —
Out-'twixt the battery-smokes there flew
   A rider, bound on bound
Full-galloping; nor bridle drew
   Until he reached the mound.

III.

Then off there flung in smiling joy,
   And held himself erect
By just his horse's mane, a boy:
   You hardly could suspect —
(So tight he kept his lips compressed
   Scarce any blood came through)
You looked twice ere you saw his breast
   Was all but shot in two.

IV.

"Well," cried he, "Emperor, by God's grace
   We 've got you Ratisbon!
The marshal 's in the market-place,
   And you 'll be there anon
To see your flag-bird flap his vans
   Where I, to heart's desire,
Perched him!" The chief's eye flashed; his plans
   Soared up again like fire.

V.

The chief's eye flashed; but presently
   Softened itself, as sheathes
A film the mother-eagle's eye
   When her bruised eaglet breathes :

"You 're wounded!" "Nay," the soldier's pride
    Touched to the quick, he said:
"I 'm killed, Sire!" And his chief beside,
    Smiling, the boy fell dead.

ROBERT BROWNING.

THE CHARGE OF THE LIGHT BRIGADE.[1]

I.

HALF a league, half a league,
    Half a league onward,
All in the valley of Death
    Rode the six hundred.
"Forward, the Light Brigade!
Charge for the guns!" he said:
Into the valley of Death
    Rode the six hundred.

II.

"Forward, the Light Brigade!"
Was there a man dismay'd?
Not tho' the soldiers knew
    Some one had blunder'd;
Theirs not to make reply,
Theirs not to reason why,

[1] October 28, 1854, the battle of Balaklava, in the Crimea, was fought between the Russian and the allied French and English forces. By a misconception of Lord Raglan's order the light cavalry, six hundred and seventy strong, under Lord Cardigan, charged the main body of the Russian army of twelve thousand. They inflicted great loss upon the enemy, but only one hundred and ninety-eight men returned from the charge.

Theirs but to do and die:
Into the valley of Death
   Rode the six hundred.

III.

Cannon to right of them,
Cannon to left of them,
Cannon in front of them
   Volley'd and thunder'd;
Stormed at with shot and shell,
Boldly they rode and well,
Into the jaws of Death,
Into the mouth of Hell
   Rode the six hundred.

IV.

Flash'd all their sabres bare,
Flash'd as they turn'd in air,
Sabring the gunners there,
   Charging an army, while
All the world wonder'd:
Plunged in the battery-smoke
Right thro' the line they broke;
Cossack and Russian
Reel'd from the sabre-stroke
Shatter'd and sunder'd.
Then they rode back, but not,
   Not the six hundred.

V.

Cannon to right of them,
Cannon to left of them,
Cannon behind them
   Volley'd and thunder'd;
Stormed at with shot and shell,

While horse and hero fell,
They that had fought so well
Came thro' the jaws of Death,
Back from the mouth of Hell,
All that was left of them,
  Left of six hundred.

VI.

When can their glory fade?
O the wild charge they made!
  All the world wonder'd.
Honor the charge they made!
Honor the Light Brigade,
  Noble six hundred!

            ALFRED TENNYSON.[1]

VICTOR GALBRAITH.

UNDER the walls of Monterey [2]
At daybreak the bugles began to play,
  Victor Galbraith!

[1] ALFRED TENNYSON, the laureate of England, and, with the exception of Robert Browning, the greatest of living English poets, was born in 1810 at Somersby, Lincolnshire. He is of an ancient family and was educated at Trinity College, Cambridge, and published his first poems while still in college. He was made poet-laureate in 1850, on the death of Wordsworth. He has led a retired life at his home in the Isle of Wight, and has written and published many poems. His longest and most important poems are the *Idyls of the King* and *In Memoriam*, and his lyrics and songs are many of them of great beauty.

[2] This refers to the period of the war between Mexico and the United States. The battle of Monterey was fought September 24, 1846.

In the mist of the morning damp and gray,
These were the words they seemed to say:
      " Come forth to thy death,
        Victor Galbraith!"

Forth he came, with a martial tread;
Firm was his step, erect his head;
        Victor Galbraith,
He who so well the bugle played,
Could not mistake the words it said:
      " Come forth to thy death,
        Victor Galbraith!"

He looked at the earth, he looked at the sky,
He looked at the files of musketry,
        Victor Galbraith!
And he said, with a steady voice and eye,
" Take good aim; I am ready to die!"
        Thus challenges death
        Victor Galbraith.

Twelve fiery tongues flashed straight and red,
Six leaden balls on their errand sped;
        Victor Galbraith
Falls to the ground, but he is not dead;
His name was not stamped on those balls of lead,
        And they only scath
        Victor Galbraith.

Three balls are in his breast and brain,
But he rises out of the dust again,
        Victor Galbraith !
The water he drinks has a bloody stain ;
" O kill me, and put me out of my pain!"
        In his agony prayeth
        Victor Galbraith.

Forth dart once more those tongues of flame,
And the bugler has died a death of shame,
    Victor Galbraith !
His soul has gone back to whence it came,
And no one answers to the name,
    When the sergeant saith,
    " Victor Galbraith ! "

Under the walls of Monterey
By night a bugle is heard to play,
    Victor Galbraith !
Through the mist of the valley damp and gray,
The sentinels hear the sound, and say,
    " That is the wraith
    Of Victor Galbraith ! "
    Henry Wadsworth Longfellow.

THE SOLDIER FROM BINGEN.

A soldier of the Legion lay dying in Algiers;
There was lack of woman's nursing, there was dearth
    of woman's tears;
But a comrade stood beside him, while the life-blood
    ebbed away,
And bent with pitying glance to hear each word he
    had to say.
The dying soldier faltered, as he took that comrade's
    hand,
And he said : " I never more shall see my own — my
    native land !

Take a message and a token to the distant friends of
    mine,
For I was born at Bingen — at Bingen on the Rhine !

" Tell my brothers and companions, when they meet
    and crowd around,
To hear my mournful story, in the pleasant vineyard
    ground,
That we fought the battle bravely, and when the day
    was done,
Full many a corse lay ghastly pale, beneath the setting
    sun;
And midst the dead and dying were some grown old in
    wars,
The death-wound on their gallant breasts, — the last
    of many scars !
But some were young, and suddenly beheld Life's
    morn decline, —
And *one* had come from Bingen — fair Bingen on the
    Rhine !

" Tell my mother that her other sons shall comfort her
    old age,
For I was still a truant bird, that thought his home a
    cage ;
For my father was a soldier, and, even when a child,
My heart leaped forth to hear him tell of struggles
    fierce and wild ;
And when he died, and left us to divide his scanty
    hoard,
I let them take whate'er they would, but kept my
    father's sword !
And with boyish love I hung it where the bright light
    used to shine,
On the cottage wall at Bingen — calm Bingen on the
    Rhine !

" Tell my sisters not to weep for me, and sob with
      drooping head,
When the troops come marching home again, with
      glad and gallant tread;
But to look upon them proudly, with a calm and stead-
      fast eye,
For their brother was a soldier, too, and not afraid to
      die !
And if a comrade seek her love, I ask her in my name
To listen to him kindly, without regret and shame ;
And to hang the old sword in its place (my father's
      sword and mine),
For the honor of old Bingen — dear Bingen on the
      Rhine !

" There 's another, — not a sister, — in happy days
      gone by,
You 'd have known her by the merriment that spar-
      kled in her eye ;
Too innocent for coquetry, too fond for idle scorn-
      ing, —
O ! friend, I fear the lightest heart makes sometimes
      heaviest mourning !
Tell her the last night of my life — for ere the morn
      be risen,
My body will be out of pain, my soul be out of
      prison —
I dreamed I stood with her, and saw the yellow sun-
      light shine
On the vine-clad hills of Bingen — fair Bingen on the
      Rhine !

" I saw the blue Rhine sweep along; I heard, or seemed
      to hear,
The German songs we used to sing, in chorus sweet
      and clear ;

And down the pleasant river, and up the slanting hill,
The echoing chorus sounded, through the evening calm
    and still;
And her glad blue eyes were on me, as we passed,
    with friendly talk,
Down many a path beloved of yore, and well remem-
    bered walk;
And her little hand lay lightly, confidingly, in mine, —
But we 'll meet no more at Bingen — loved Bingen on
    the Rhine ! "

His trembling voice grew faint and hoarse, his gasp
    was childish weak,
His eyes put on a dying look, — he sighed, and ceased
    to speak;
His comrade bent to lift him, but the spark of life had
    fled, —
The soldier of the Legion in a foreign land was dead!
And the soft moon rose up slowly, and calmly she
    looked down
On the red sand of the battle-field, with bloody corses
    strown!
Yes, calmly on that dreadful scene her pale light
    seemed to shine,
As it shone on distant Bingen — fair Bingen on the
    Rhine!

CAROLINE E. S. NORTON.[1]

[1] CAROLINE ELIZABETH SARAH NORTON, granddaughter of Richard Brinsley Sheridan, was born in 1808, and married in 1827 to the Hon. George Chapple Norton, from whom she was divorced in 1836. Late in life she made a second marriage with Sir William Stirling Maxwell. She died in 1878. She was a woman of great beauty, very accomplished, and possessed brilliant talents. She wrote much both in prose and in verse.

THE OLD CLOCK ON THE STAIRS.

SOMEWHAT back from the village street
Stands the old-fashioned country-seat.
Across its antique portico
Tall poplar-trees their shadows throw;
And from its station in the hall
An ancient time-piece says to all, —
  " Forever — never!
  Never — forever! "

Half-way up the stairs it stands,
And points and beckons with its hands
From its case of massive oak,
Like a monk, who, under his cloak,
Crosses himself, and sighs, alas!
With sorrowful voice to all who pass, —
  " Forever — never!
  Never — forever! "

By day its voice is low and light;
But in the silent dead of night,
Distinct as a passing footstep's fall,
It echoes along the vacant hall,
Along the ceiling, along the floor,
And seems to say, at each chamber-door, —
  " Forever — never!
  Never — forever! "

Through days of sorrow and of mirth,
Through days of death and days of birth,
Through every swift vicissitude
Of changeful time, unchanged it has stood,

And as if, like God, it all things saw,
It calmly repeats those words of awe, —
    " Forever -— never!
    Never — forever! "

In that mansion used to be
Free-hearted Hospitality;
His great fires up the chimney roared;
The stranger feasted at his board;
But, like the skeleton at the feast,
That warning timepiece never ceased, —
    " Forever — never!
    Never — forever! "

There groups of merry children played ;
There youths and maidens dreaming strayed;
O precious hours! O golden prime,
And affluence of love and time!
Even as a miser counts his gold,
Those hours the ancient timepiece told, —
    " Forever — never!
    Never — forever! "

From that chamber, clothed in white,
The bride came forth on her wedding-night;
There, in that silent room below,
The dead lay in his shroud of snow ;
And in the hush that followed the prayer,
Was heard the old clock on the stair, —
    " Forever — never!
    Never — forever! "

All are scattered now, and fled ;
Some are married, some are dead;
And when I ask, with throbs of pain,

"Ah! when shall they all meet again?"
As in the days long since gone by,
The ancient timepiece makes reply, —
        "Forever — never!
        Never — forever!"

Never here, forever there,
Where all parting, pain, and care,
And death, and time shall disappear, —
Forever there, but never here!
The horologe of Eternity
Sayeth this incessantly, —
        "Forever — never!
        Never — forever!"
                HENRY WADSWORTH LONGFELLOW.

THE DEACON'S MASTERPIECE; OR, THE WONDERFUL "ONE-HOSS SHAY."

A LOGICAL STORY.

HAVE you heard of the wonderful one-hoss shay,
That was built in such a logical way
It ran a hundred years to a day,
And then, of a sudden, it — ah, but stay,
I 'll tell you what happened without delay,
Scaring the parson into fits,
Frightening people out of their wits, —
Have you ever heard of that, I say?

Seventeen hundred and fifty-five.
Georgius Secundus was then alive, —
Snuffy old drone from the German hive.

That was the year when Lisbon-town
Saw the earth open and gulp her down,
And Braddock's army was done so brown,
Left without a scalp to its crown.
It was on the terrible Earthquake-day
That the Deacon finished the one-hoss shay.

Now in building of chaises, I tell you what,
There is always *somewhere* a weakest spot, —
In hub, tire, felloe, in spring or thill,
In panel, or crossbar, or floor, or sill,
In screw, bolt, thoroughbrace, lurking still,
Find it somewhere you must and will,
Above or below, or within or without,
And that's the reason, beyond a doubt,
That a chaise *breaks down*, but does n't *wear out*.

But the Deacon swore (as Deacons do,
With an " I dew vum," or an " I tell *yeou* ")
He would build one shay to beat the taown
'n' the keounty 'n' all the kentry raoun' ;
It should be so built that it *couldn'* break daown :
" Fur," said the Deacon, " 't 's mighty plain
Thut the weakes' place mus' stan' the strain;
'n' the way t' fix it, uz I maintain,
          Is only jest
T' make that place uz strong uz the rest."

So the Deacon inquired of the village folk
Where he could find the strongest oak,
That could n't be split nor bent nor broke, —
That was for spokes and floor and sills ;
He sent for lancewood to make the thills;
The crossbars were ash, from the straightest trees,
The panels of white-wood, that cuts like cheese,

But lasts like iron for things like these;
The hubs of logs from the " Settler's ellum," —
Last of its timber, — they could n't sell 'em,
Never an axe had seen their chips,
And the wedges flew from between their lips,
Their blunt ends frizzled like celery-tips;
Step and prop-iron, bolt and screw,
Spring, tire, axle, and linchpin too,
Steel of the finest, bright and blue;
Thoroughbrace bison-skin, thick and wide;
Boot, top, dasher, from tough old hide
Found in the pit when the tanner died.
That was the way he " put her through." —
" There! " said the Deacon, " naow she 'll dew! "

Do! I tell you, I rather guess
She was a wonder, and nothing less !
Colts grew horses, beards turned gray,
Deacon and deaconess dropped away,
Children and grandchildren — where were they?
But there stood the stout old one-hoss shay
As fresh as on Lisbon-earthquake-day!

EIGHTEEN HUNDRED ; — it came and found
The Deacon's masterpiece strong and sound.
Eighteen hundred increased by ten ; —
" Hahnsum kerridge " they called it then.
Eighteen hundred and twenty came ; —
Running as usual; much the same.
Thirty and forty at last arrive,
And then come fifty, and FIFTY-FIVE.

Little of all we value here
Wakes on the morn of its hundredth year
Without both feeling and looking queer.

In fact, there's nothing that keeps its youth,
So far as I know, but a tree and truth.
(This is a moral that runs at large;
Take it. — You 're welcome. — No extra charge.)

First of November, — the Earthquake-day, —
There are traces of age in the one-hoss shay,
A general flavor of mild decay,
But nothing local, as one may say.
There could n't be, — for the Deacon's art
Had made it so like in every part
That there was n't a chance for one to start.
For the wheels were just as strong as the thills,
And the floor was just as strong as the sills,
And the panels just as strong as the floor,
And the whipple-tree neither less nor more,
And the back-crossbar as strong as the fore,
And spring and axle and hub *encore*.
And yet, *as a whole*, it is past a doubt
In another hour it will be *worn out!*

First of November, 'Fifty-five!
This morning the parson takes a drive.
Now, small boys, get out of the way!
Here comes the wonderful one-hoss shay,
Drawn by a rat-tailed, ewe-necked bay.
" Huddup! " said the parson. — Off went they.
The parson was working his Sunday's text, —
Had got to *fifthly*, and stopped perplexed
At what the — Moses — was coming next.
All at once the horse stood still,
Close by the meet'n'-house on the hill.
— First a shiver, and then a thrill,
Then something decidedly like a spill, —
And the parson was sitting upon a rock,

At half past nine by the meet'n'-house clock, —
Just the hour of the earthquake shock!
— What do you think the parson found,
When he got up and stared around?
The poor old chaise in a heap or mound,
As if it had been to the mill and ground!
You see, of course, if you 're not a dunce,
How it went to pieces all at once, —
All at once, and nothing first, —
Just as bubbles do when they burst.

End of the wonderful one-hoss shay.
Logic is logic.   That 's all I say.
OLIVER WENDELL HOLMES.

VALENTINE.

TO THE HON. MARY C. STANHOPE (DAUGHTER OF LORD AND LADY MAHON).

HAIL, day of Music, day of Love,
On earth below, in air above.
In air the turtle fondly moans,
The linnet pipes in joyous tones;
On earth the postman toils along,
Bent double by huge bales of song,
Where, rich with many a gorgeous die,
Blazes all Cupid's heraldry, —
Myrtles and roses, doves and sparrows,
Love-knots and altars, lamps and arrows.
What nymph without wild hopes and fears
The double rap this morning hears?
Unnumbered lasses, young and fair,

From Bethnal Green to Belgrave Square,
With cheeks high flushed, and hearts loud beating,
Await the tender annual greeting.
The loveliest lass of all is mine, —
Good morrow to my Valentine !

Good morrow, gentle Child! and then
Again good morrow, and again,
Good morrow following still good morrow,
Without one cloud of strife or sorrow.
And when the God to whom we pay
In jest our homages to-day
Shall come to claim, no more in jest,
His rightful empire o'er thy breast,
Benignant may his aspect be,
His yoke the truest liberty:
And if a tear his power confess,
Be it a tear of happiness.
It shall be so.   The Muse displays
The future to her votary's gaze ;
Prophetic rage my bosom swells —
I taste the cake — I hear the bells!
From Conduit Street the close array
Of chariots barricades the way
To where I see, with outstretched hand,
Majestic, thy great kinsman stand,[1]
And half unbend his brow of pride,
As welcoming so fair a bride.
Gay favors, thick as flakes of snow,
Brighten St. George's portico:
Within I see the chancel's pale,
The orange flowers, the Brussels veil,
The page on which those fingers white,
Still trembling from the awful rite,

[1] The statue of Mr. Pitt in Hanover Square.

For the last time shall faintly trace
The name of Stanhope's noble race.
I see kind faces round thee pressing,
I hear kind voices whisper blessing;
And with those voices mingles mine, —
All good attend my Valentine!

LORD MACAULAY.

ST. VALENTINE'S DAY, 1851.

AUF WIEDERSEHEN!

SUMMER.

THE little gate was reached at last,
　Half hid in lilacs down the lane;
She pushed it wide, and, as she past,
A wistful look she backward cast,
　And said, "*Auf Wiedersehen!*"

With hand on latch, a vision white
　Lingered reluctant, and again
Half doubting if she did aright,
Soft as the dews that fell that night,
　She said, "*Auf Wiedersehen!*"

The lamp's clear gleam flits up the stair;
　I linger in delicious pain;
Ah, in that chamber, whose rich air
To breathe in thought I scarcely dare,
　Thinks she, "*Auf Wiedersehen!*"

'T is thirteen years; once more I press
　The turf that silences the lane;

I hear the rustle of her dress,
I smell the lilacs, and — ah, yes,
I hear "*Auf Wiedersehen!*"

Sweet piece of bashful maiden art!
The English words had seemed too fain,
But these — they drew us heart to heart,
Yet held us tenderly apart;
She said, "*Auf Wiedersehen!*"
JAMES RUSSELL LOWELL.[1]

DOROTHY Q.[2]

A FAMILY PORTRAIT.

GRANDMOTHER'S mother: her age, I guess,
Thirteen summers, or something less;
Girlish bust, but womanly air;
Smooth, square forehead with uprolled hair,

[1] JAMES RUSSELL LOWELL, the son of the Rev. Charles Lowell, and descended from an old and distinguished New England family, was born in Cambridge, Massachusetts, in 1819. He graduated from Harvard College in 1838, studied law and was admitted to the bar, which he soon deserted for literature. In 1855 he was appointed to succeed Mr. Longfellow as professor of belles-lettres in Harvard College, a position which he still retains. He has taken the highest rank in American literature as critic, essayist, satirist, and poet. He was appointed United States minister to Spain in 1877, and in 1880 was removed to the higher position of United States minister at London, a post which he now holds.

[2] Dorothy Quincy married Edward Wendell and thus became the ancestress of the poet. The portrait which is the subject of the poem is in the possession of Dr. Holmes.

Lips that lover has never kissed;
Taper fingers and slender wrist:
Hanging sleeves of stiff brocade;
So they painted the little maid.

On her hand a parrot green
Sits unmoving and broods serene.
Hold up the canvas full in view, —
Look! there 's a rent the light shines through,
Dark with a century's fringe of dust, —
That was a Red-Coat's rapier-thrust!
Such is the tale the lady old,
Dorothy's daughter's daughter, told.

Who the painter was none may tell, —
One whose best was not over well;
Hard and dry, it must be confessed,
Flat as a rose that has long been pressed;
Yet in her cheek the hues are bright,
Dainty colors of red and white,
And in her slender shape are seen
Hint and promise of stately mien.

Look not on her with eyes of scorn, —
Dorothy Q. was a lady born!
Ay! since the galloping Normans came,
England's annals have known her name;
And still to the three-hilled rebel town
Dear is that ancient name's renown,
For many a civic wreath they won,
The youthful sire and the gray-haired son.

O Damsel Dorothy! Dorothy Q.!
Strange is the gift that I owe to you;
Such a gift as never a king

Save to daughter or son might bring, —
All my tenure of heart and hand ;
All my title to house and land ;
Mother and sister and child and wife
And joy and sorrow and death and life!

What if a hundred years ago
Those close-shut lips had answered No,
When forth the tremulous question came
That cost the maiden her Norman name,
And under the folds that look so still
The bodice swelled with the bosom's thrill?
Should I be I, or would it be
One tenth another, to nine tenths me?

Soft is the breath of a maiden's YES:
Not the light gossamer stirs with less;
But never a cable that holds so fast
Through all the battles of wave and blast,
And never an echo of speech or song
That lives in the babbling air so long!
There were tones in the voice that whispered then
You may hear to-day in a hundred men.

O lady and lover, how faint and far
Your images hover, — and here we are,
Solid and stirring in flesh and bone, —
Edward's and Dorothy's — all their own, —
A goodly record for Time to show
Of a syllable spoken so long ago! —
Shall I bless you, Dorothy, or forgive
For the tender whisper that bade me live?

It shall be a blessing, my little maid!
I will heal the stab of the Red-Coat's blade,

And freshen the gold of the tarnished frame,
And gild with a rhyme your household name;
So you shall smile on us brave and bright
As first you greeted the morning's light,
And live untroubled by woes and fears
Through a second youth of a hundred years.
     OLIVER WENDELL HOLMES.

WHAT MR. ROBINSON THINKS.[1]

GUVENER B. is a sensible man;
 He stays to his home an' looks arter his folks;
He draws his furrer ez straight ez he can,
 An' into nobody's tater-patch pokes;
    But John P.
    Robinson he
  Sez he wunt vote fer Guvener B.

My! ain't it terrible? Wut shall we du?
 We can't never choose him, o' course, — thet 's flat;
Guess we shall hev to come round, (don't you?)
 An' go in fer thunder an' guns, an' all that;
    Fer John P.
    Robinson he
  Sez he wunt vote fer Guvener B.

Gineral C. is a dreffle smart man:
 He 's ben on all sides thet give places or pelf;

---

[1] This satire was directed against the Mexican war, which was forced upon the country in 1845, by the South, in conformity with their policy of an extension of slave territory.

But consistency still wuz a part of his plan, —
  He 's ben true to *one* party, — an' thet is himself ;
      So John P.
      Robinson he
    Sez he shall vote fer Gineral C.

Gineral C. he goes in fer the war ;
  He don't vally principle more 'n an old cud ;
Wut did God make us raytional creeturs fer,
  But glory an' gunpowder, plunder an' blood ?
      So John P.
      Robinson he
    Sez he shall vote fer Gineral C.

We were gittin' on nicely up here to our village,
  With good old idees o' wut 's right an' wut ain't,
We kind o' thought Christ went agin war an' pillage,
  An' thet eppyletts worn't the best mark of a saint ;
      But John P.
      Robinson he
    Sez this kind o' thing 's an exploded idee.

The side of our country must ollers be took,
  An' Presidunt Polk, you know, *he* is our country, —
An' the angel thet writes all our sins in a book
  Puts the *debit* to him, an' to us the *per contry ;*
      An' John P.
      Robinson he
    Sez this is his view o' the thing to a T.

Parson Wilbur he calls all these argimunts lies ;
  Sez they 're nothin' on airth but jest *fee, faw, fum ;*
An' thet all this big talk of our destinies
  Is half on it ign'ance, an' t' other half rum ;

But John P.
Robinson he
Sez it ain't no sech thing ; an' of course so must we.

Parson Wilbur sez *he* never heerd in his life
  Thet th' Apostles rigged out in their swaller-tail coats,
An' marched round in front of a drum an' a fife,
  To git some on 'em office, an' some on 'em votes ;
But John P.
Robinson he
Sez they did n't know everythin' down in Judee.

Wal, it 's a marcy we 've gut folks to tell us
  The rights an' the wrongs o' these matters, I vow,
God sends country lawyers, an' other wise fellers,
  To start the world's team wen it gits in a slough ;
Fer John P.
Robinson he
Sez the world 'll go right, ef he hollers out Gee !
       JAMES RUSSELL LOWELL.

THE BALLAD OF THE OYSTERMAN.

IT was a tall young oysterman lived by the river-side ;
His shop was just upon the bank, his boat was on the
    tide ;
The daughter of a fisherman, that was so straight and
    slim,
Lived over on the other bank, right opposite to him.

It was the pensive oysterman that saw a lovely maid,
Upon a moonlight evening, a sitting in the shade;

He saw her wave her handkerchief, as much as if to say,
" I 'm wide awake, young oysterman, and all the folks
    away."

Then up arose the oysterman, and to himself said he,
" I guess I 'll leave the skiff at home, for fear that
    folks should see ;
I read it in the story-book, that, for to kiss his dear,
Leander swam the Hellespont, — and I will swim this
    here."

And he has leaped into the waves, and crossed the
    shining stream,
And he has clambered up the bank all in the moonlight
    gleam ;
O there were kisses sweet as dew, and words as soft as
    rain, —
But they have heard the father's step, and in he leaps
    again !

Out spoke the ancient fisherman, — " O what was that,
    my daughter ? "
" 'T was nothing but a pebble, sir, I threw into the
    water."
" And what is that, pray tell me, love, that paddles off
    so fast ? "
" It 's nothing but a porpoise, sir, that 's been a swim-
    ming past."

Out spoke the ancient fisherman, — " Now bring me
    my harpoon !
I 'll get into my fishing-boat, and fix the fellow soon."
Down fell that pretty innocent, as falls a snow-white
    lamb,
Her hair drooped round her pallid cheeks, like seaweed
    on a clam.

Alas for those two loving ones ! she waked not from
　　her swound,
And he was taken with the cramp, and in the waves
　　was drowned ;
But Fate has metamorphosed them, in pity of their woe,
And now they keep an oyster-shop for mermaids down
　　below.

OLIVER WENDELL HOLMES.

THE SPECTRE PIG.

A BALLAD.

IT was the stalwart butcher man,
　　That knit his swarthy brow,
And said the gentle Pig must die,
　　And sealed it with a vow.

And O! it was the gentle Pig
　　Lay stretched upon the ground,
And ah! it was the cruel knife
　　His little heart that found.

They took him then, those wicked men,
　　They trailed him all along;
They put a stick between his lips,
　　And through his heels a thong ;

And round and round an oaken beam
　　A hempen cord they flung,
And, like a mighty pendulum,
　　All solemnly he swung.

Now say thy prayers, thou sinful man,
  And think what thou hast done,
And read thy catechism well,
  Thou bloody-minded one;

For if his sprite should walk by night,
  It better were for thee,
That thou wert mouldering in the ground,
  Or bleaching in the sea.

It was the savage butcher then,
  That made a mock of sin,
And swore a very wicked oath,
  He did not care a pin.

It was the butcher's youngest son, —
  His voice was broke with sighs,
And with his pocket handkerchief
  He wiped his little eyes;

All young and ignorant was he,
  But innocent and mild,
And in his soft simplicity
  Out spoke the tender child:—

" O father, father, list to me;
  The Pig is deadly sick,
And men have hung him by his heels,
  And fed him with a stick."

It was the bloody butcher then,
  That laughed as he would die,
Yet did he soothe the sorrowing child,
  And bid him not to cry:—
20

"O Nathan, Nathan, what 's a Pig,
    That thou shouldst weep and wail!
Come, bear thee like a butcher's child,
    And thou shalt have his tail!"

It was the butcher's daughter then,
    So slender and so fair,
That sobbed as if her heart would break,
    And tore her yellow hair;

And thus she spoke in thrilling tone, —
    Fast fell the tear-drops big, —
"Ah! woe is me!   Alas! Alas!
    The Pig!   The Pig!   The Pig!"

Then did her wicked father's lips
    Make merry with her woe,
And call her many a naughty name,
    Because she whimpered so.

Ye need not weep, ye gentle ones,
    In vain your tears are shed,
Ye cannot wash his crimson hand,
    Ye cannot soothe the dead.

The bright sun folded on his breast
    His robes of rosy flame,
And softly over all the west
    The shades of evening came.

He slept, and troops of murdered Pigs
    Were busy with his dreams;
Loud rang their wild, unearthly shrieks,
    Wide yawned their mortal seams.

The clock struck twelve; the Dead hath heard;
  He opened both his eyes,
And sullenly he shook his tail
  To lash the feeding flies.

One quiver of the hempen cord, —
  One struggle and one bound, —
With stiffened limb and leaden eye,
  The Pig was on the ground!

And straight towards the sleeper's house
  His fearful way he wended;
And hooting owl, and hovering bat,
  On midnight wing attended.

Back flew the bolt, up rose the latch,
  And open swung the door,
And little mincing feet were heard
  Pat, pat along the floor.

Two hoofs upon the sanded floor,
  And two upon the bed;
And they are breathing side by side,
  The living and the dead!

" Now wake, now wake, thou butcher man!
  What makes thy cheek so pale ?
Take hold! take hold ! thou dost not fear
  To clasp a spectre's tail? "

Untwisted every winding coil;
  The shuddering wretch took hold,
All like an icicle it seemed,
  So tapering and so cold.

" Thou com'st with me, thou butcher man!"—
    He strives to loose his grasp,
But, faster than the clinging vine,
    Those twining spirals clasp.

And open, open swung the door,
    And, fleeter than the wind,
The shadowy spectre swept before,
    The butcher trailed behind.

Fast fled the darkness of the night,
    And morn rose faint and dim;
They called full loud, they knocked full long,
    They did not waken him.

Straight, straight towards that oaken beam,
    A trampled pathway ran;
A ghastly shape was swinging there, —
    It was the butcher man.

OLIVER WENDELL HOLMES.

A RHYMED LESSON.

SOME words on LANGUAGE may be well applied,
And take them kindly, though they touch your pride;
Words lead to things; a scale is more precise,—
Coarse speech, bad grammar, swearing, drinking, vice.
    Our cold Northeaster's icy fetter clips
The native freedom of the Saxon lips;
See the brown peasant of the plastic South,
How all his passions play about his mouth!
With us, the feature that transmits the soul,
A frozen, passive, palsied breathing-hole.

The crampy shackles of the ploughboy's walk
Tie the small muscles when he strives to talk;
Not all the pumice of the polished town
Can smooth this roughness of the barnyard down;
Rich, honored, titled, he betrays his race
By this one mark, — he 's awkward in the face;—
Nature's rude impress, long before he knew
The sunny street that holds the sifted few.
It can't be helped, though, if we 're taken young,
We gain some freedom of the lips and tongue;
But school and college often try in vain
To break the padlock of our boyhood's chain:
One stubborn word will prove this axiom true, —
No quondam rustic can enunciate *view*.
A few brief stanzas may be well employed
To speak of errors we can all avoid.

Learning condemns beyond the reach of hope
The careless lips that speak of sŏap for sōap;
Her edict exiles from her fair abode
The clownish voice that utters rŏad for rōad;
Less stern to him, who calls his cōat a cŏat,
And steers his bōat, believing it a bŏat,
She pardoned one, our classic city's boast,
Who said, at Cambridge, mŏst instead of mōst,
But knit her brows and stamped her angry foot
To hear a Teacher call a rōot a rŏot.

Once more; speak clearly, if you speak at all;
Carve every word before you let it fall;
Don't, like a lecturer or dramatic star,
Try over hard to roll the British R;
Do put your accents in the proper spot;
Don't, — let me beg you, — don't say " How? " for
    " What? "

And, when you stick on conversation's burrs,
Don't strew your pathway with those dreadful *urs*.
OLIVER WENDELL HOLMES.

THE ROSE UPON MY BALCONY.

THE rose upon my balcony, the morning air perfuming,
Was leafless all the winter time and pining for the
    spring;
You ask me why her breath is sweet, and why her
    cheek is blooming:
It is because the sun is out and birds begin to sing.

The nightingale, whose melody is through the green-
    wood ringing,
Was silent when the boughs were bare and winds were
    blowing keen.
And if, Mamma, you ask of me the reason of his sing-
    ing,
It is because the sun is out and all the leaves are
    green.

Thus each performs his part, Mamma: the birds have
    found their voices,
The blowing rose a flush, Mamma, her bonny cheek to
    dye;
And there's sunshine in my heart, Mamma, which
    wakens and rejoices,
And so I sing and blush, Mamma, and that's the rea-
    son why.
WILLIAM MAKEPEACE THACKERAY.[1]
Vanity Fair.

[1] WILLIAM MAKEPEACE THACKERAY, born at Calcutta, in
1811, was educated at the Charter House, and at Cambridge

GREEN FIELDS OF ENGLAND.

Green fields of England! wheresoe'er
Across this watery waste we fare,
Your image at our hearts we bear,
Green fields of England, everywhere.

Sweet eyes in England, I must flee
Past where the waves' last confines be,
Ere your loved smile I cease to see,
Sweet eyes in England, dear to me.

Dear home in England, safe and fast
If but in thee my lot be cast,
The past shall seem a nothing past
To thee, dear home, if won at last;
Dear home in England, won at last.

Arthur Hugh Clough.[1]

University. He inherited a handsome property, but lost it, studied law, and finally took to literature. He wrote many charming poems, but his fame rests upon his novels, which have placed him at the head of English novelists. He died in 1863.

[1] Arthur Hugh Clough was born at Liverpool in 1820. He was educated at Rugby and Oxford, and was then a tutor for some time in Oriel College. In 1852 he visited the United States, and passed some time in Cambridge, Massachusetts. He died at Florence, Italy, in 1861. Besides a volume of very remarkable poems, he published a translation of Plutarch, in 1859.

THE DEATH OF THE FLOWERS.

The, melancholy days are come, the saddest of the
    year,
Of wailing winds, and naked woods, and meadows
    brown and sear.
Heaped in the hollows of the grove, the withered leaves
    lie dead:
They rustle to the eddying gust, and to the rabbit's
    tread.
The robin and the wren are flown, and from the shrubs
    the jay;
And from the wood-top calls the crow, through all the
    gloomy day.

Where are the flowers, the fair young flowers, that
    lately sprang and stood,
In brighter light and softer airs, a beauteous sister-
    hood?
Alas! they all are in their graves: the gentle race of
    flowers
Are lying in their lowly beds, with the fair and good
    of ours.
The rain is falling where they lie; but the cold No-
    vember rain
Calls not, from out the gloomy earth, the lovely ones
    again.

The wind-flower and the violet, they perished long
    ago;
And the brier-rose and the orchis died amid the sum-
    mer glow;
But on the hill the golden-rod, and the aster in the
    wood,

And the yellow sunflower by the brook, in autumn
    beauty stood,
Till fell the frost from the clear, cold heaven, as falls
    the plague on men,
And the brightness of their smile was gone from up-
    land, glade, and glen.

And now when comes the calm, mild day, as still such
    days will come,
To call the squirrel and the bee from out their winter
    home ;
When the sound of dropping nuts is heard, though all
    the trees are still,
And twinkle in the smoky light the waters of the
    rill, —
The south wind searches for the flowers whose fra-
    grance late he bore,
And sighs to find them in the wood and by the stream
    no more;

And then I think of one who in her youthful beauty
    died,
The fair, meek blossom that grew up, and faded by my
    side:
In the cold moist earth we laid her when the forest cast
    the leaf,
And we wept that one so lovely should have a life so
    brief ;
Yet not unmeet it was, that one, like that young friend
    of ours,
So gentle and so beautiful, should perish with the
    flowers.

WILLIAM CULLEN BRYANT.[1]

[1] WILLIAM CULLEN BRYANT was born at Cummington,
Massachusetts, in 1794. At the age of thirteen he published two

THE RAVEN.

ONCE upon a midnight dreary, while I pondered, weak
    and weary,
Over many a quaint and curious volume of forgotten
    lore —
While I nodded, nearly napping, suddenly there came
    a tapping,
As of some one gently rapping, rapping at my chamber
    door.
" 'T is some visitor," I muttered, " tapping at my
    chamber door —
        Only this and nothing more."

Ah, distinctly I remember it was in the bleak Decem-
    ber,
And each separate dying ember wrought its ghost upon
    the floor.
Eagerly I wished the morrow; vainly I had sought to
    borrow
From my books surcease of sorrow — sorrow for the lost
    Lenore —
For the rare and radiant maiden whom the angels
    named Lenore —
        Nameless here forevermore.

poems entitled *The Embargo* and *The Spanish Revolution*, the
former a political satire. He studied at Williams College, and
then practised law for several years. In 1816 he published *Than-
atopsis*, a poem which gave him immediate reputation. In 1825
he removed to New York, and accepted the editorship of the
Evening Post, which he held until his death, in 1878. He made
several journeys in Europe, of which he published descriptions,
and translated Homer, besides writing a small number of short
poems.

And the silken, sad, uncertain rustling of each purple
    curtain
Thrilled me — filled me with fantastic terrors never felt
    before;
So that now, to still the beating of my heart, I stood
    repeating,
" 'Tis some visitor, entreating entrance at my chamber
    door —
Some late visitor, entreating entrance at my chamber
    door;
        This it is, and nothing more."

Presently my soul grew stronger; hesitating then no
    longer,
" Sir," said I, " or Madam, truly your forgiveness I
    implore;
But the fact is I was napping, and so gently you came
    rapping,
And so faintly you came tapping, tapping at my cham-
    ber door,
That I scarce was sure I heard you "— here I opened
    wide the door, —
        Darkness there, and nothing more.

Deep into that darkness peering, long I stood there,
    wondering, fearing,
Doubting, dreaming dreams no mortals ever dared to
    dream before;
But the silence was unbroken, and the stillness gave
    no token,
And the only word there spoken was the whispered
    word, " Lenore? "
This I whispered, and an echo murmured back the
    word " Lenore!"
        Merely this, and nothing more.

Back into the chamber turning, all my soul within me
   burning,
Soon again I heard a tapping something louder than
   before.
" Surely," said I, " surely that is something at my
   window lattice;
Let me see, then, what thereat is, and this mystery
   explore —
Let my heart be still a moment, and this mystery explore : —
     'T is the wind, and nothing more."

Open here I flung the shutter, when, with many a
   flirt and flutter,
In there stepped a stately Raven of the saintly days of
   yore.
Not the least obeisance made he ; not a minute stopped
   or stayed he,
But, with mien of lord or lady, perched above my
   chamber door —
Perched upon a bust of Pallas just above my chamber
   door —
     Perched, and sat, and nothing more.

Then this ebony bird beguiling my sad fancy into
   smiling,
By the grave and stern decorum of the countenance it
   wore,
" Though thy crest be shorn and shaven, thou," said
   I, " art sure no craven,
Ghastly grim and ancient Raven, wandering from the
   Nightly shore —
Tell me what thy lordly name is on the Night's Plu-
   tonian shore."
     Quoth the Raven, " Nevermore."

Much I marvelled this ungainly fowl to hear discourse
     so plainly,
Though its answer little meaning — little relevancy
     bore ;
For we cannot help agreeing that no living human be-
     ing
Ever yet was blessed with seeing bird above his
     chamber door —
Bird or beast upon the sculptured bust above his
     chamber door,
         With such name as " Nevermore."

But the Raven, sitting lonely on that placid bust,
     spoke only
That one word, as if his soul in that one word he did
     outpour;
Nothing farther then he uttered; not a feather then he
     fluttered —
Till I scarcely more than muttered, " Other friends
     have flown before —
On the morrow *he* will leave me, as my Hopes have
     flown before."
         Then the bird said, " Nevermore."

Startled at the stillness broken by reply so aptly
     spoken,
" Doubtless," said I, " what it utters is its only
     stock and store,
Caught from some unhappy master, whom unmerciful
     Disaster
Followed fast and followed faster till his songs one
     burden bore —
Till the dirges of his Hope that melancholy burden
     bore
         Of ' Never — Nevermore.' "

But the Raven still beguiling all my sad soul into
     smiling,
Straight I wheeled a cushioned seat in front of bird
     and bust and door;
Then, upon the velvet sinking, I betook myself to
     linking
Fancy unto fancy, thinking what this ominous bird of
     yore —
What this grim, ungainly, ghastly, gaunt, and ominous
     bird of yore —
         Meant in croaking " Nevermore."

This I sat engaged in guessing, but no syllable ex-
     pressing
To the fowl, whose fiery eyes now burned into my
     bosom's core;
This and more I sat divining, with my head at ease
     reclining
On the cushion's velvet lining that the lamp-light
     gloated o'er,
But whose velvet violet lining with the lamp-light
     gloating o'er
         She shall press, ah, nevermore!

Then, methought, the air grew denser, perfumed
     from an unseen censer
Swung by Seraphim whose foot-falls tinkled on the
     tufted floor.
" Wretch," I cried, " thy God hath lent thee — by
     these angels he hath sent thee
Respite — respite and nepenthe from thy memories of
     Lenore!
Quaff, O quaff this kind nepenthe, and forget this lost
     Lenore!"
         Quoth the Raven, " Nevermore."

"Prophet!" said I, "thing of evil!— prophet still, if
 bird or devil!
Whether Tempter sent, or whether tempest tossed thee
 here ashore,
Desolate yet all undaunted, on this desert land enchanted —
On this home by Horror haunted — tell me truly, I implore —
Is there — *is* there balm in Gilead?— tell me — tell
 me, I implore!"
   Quoth the Raven, "Nevermore."

"Prophet!" said I, "thing of evil — prophet still, if
 bird or devil!
By that Heaven that bends above us — by that God
 we both adore —
Tell this soul with sorrow laden, if, within the distant
 Aidenn,
It shall clasp a sainted maiden whom the angels name
 Lenore —
Clasp a rare and radiant maiden whom the angels
 name Lenore."
   Quoth the Raven, "Nevermore."

"Be that word our sign of parting, bird or fiend!" I
 shrieked, upstarting —
"Get thee back into the tempest and the Night's Plu-
 tonian shore!
Leave no black plume as a token of that lie thy soul
 hath spoken!
Leave my loneliness unbroken!— quit the bust above
 my door!
Take thy beak from out my heart, and take thy form
 from off my door!"
   Quoth the Raven, "Nevermore."

And the Raven, never flitting, still is sitting, still is
    sitting
On the pallid bust of Pallas just above my chamber
    door;
And his eyes have all the seeming of a demon's that is
    dreaming,
And the lamp-light o'er him streaming throws his
    shadow on the floor;
And my soul from out that shadow that lies floating on
    the floor
        Shall be lifted — Nevermore!
                EDGAR ALLAN POE.[1]

IN SCHOOL-DAYS.

STILL sits the school-house by the road,
    A ragged beggar sunning;
Around it still the sumachs grow,
    And blackberry-vines are running.

Within, the master's desk is seen,
    Deep scarred by raps official;
The warping floor, the battered seats,
    The jack-knife's carved initial;

[1] EDGAR ALLAN POE, born in Baltimore in 1811, was educated there and in England, and graduated at the University of
Virginia, after which he passed a year in Europe. He wrote for
and edited various magazines, and it was at this time he produced his extraordinary stories. *The Raven* is the one work,
however, which has attained world-wide popularity and given
Poe enduring fame. His mind was of a gloomy and morbid
cast, which was enhanced by a loose life and intemperate habits.
He died at Baltimore in 1849.

The charcoal frescos on its wall;
  Its door's worn sill, betraying
The feet that, creeping slow to school,
  Went storming out to playing!

Long years ago a winter sun
  Shone over it at setting;
Lit up its western window-panes,
  And low eaves' icy fretting.

It touched the tangled golden curls,
  And brown eyes full of grieving,
Of one who still her steps delayed
  When all the school were leaving.

For near her stood the little boy
  Her childish favor singled:
His cap pulled low upon a face
  Where pride and shame were mingled.

Pushing with restless feet the snow
  To right and left he lingered;
As restlessly her tiny hands
  The blue-checked apron fingered.

He saw her lift her eyes; he felt
  The soft hand's light caressing,
And heard the tremble of her voice,
  As if a fault confessing.

" I 'm sorry that I spelt the word:
  I hate to go above you,
Because," — the brown eyes lower fell, —
  "Because, you see, I love you!"
  21

Still memory to a gray-haired man
  That sweet child-face is showing.
Dear girl! the grasses on her grave
  Have forty years been growing !

He lives to learn, in life's hard school,
  How few who pass above him
Lament their triumph and his loss,
  Like her, — because they love him.
                    JOHN GREENLEAF WHITTIER.[1]

ALADDIN.

WHEN I was a beggarly boy,
  And lived in a cellar damp,
I had not a friend nor a toy,
  But I had Aladdin's lamp;
When I could not sleep for cold,
  I had fire enough in my brain,
And builded, with roofs of gold,
  My beautiful castles in Spain!

Since then I have toiled day and night,
  I have money and power good store,
But I 'd give all my lamps of silver bright,
  For the one that is mine no more;

---

[1] JOHN GREENLEAF WHITTIER was born at Haverhill, Massachusetts, in 1808. He was brought up by his parents in the principles of the Quaker belief, and never went to college. He edited the *New England Review*, and afterwards the *Pennsylvania Freeman*, an organ of the antislavery party, of which he was a prominent member. He still lives in quiet retirement at Amesbury, Massachusetts.

Take, Fortune, whatever you choose,
  You gave, and may snatch again;
I have nothing 't would pain me to lose,
  For I own no more castles in Spain !

JAMES RUSSELL LOWELL.

THE COURTIN'.

GOD makes sech nights, all white an' still,
  Fur 'z you can look or listen,
Moonshine an' snow on field an' hill,
  All silence an' all glisten.

Zekle crep' up quite unbeknown
  An' peeked in thru' the winder,
An' there sot Huldy all alone,
  'ith no one nigh to hender.

A fireplace filled the room's one side,
  With half a cord o' wood-in, —
There warn't no stoves (tell comfort died)
  To bake ye to a puddin'.

The wa'nut logs shot sparkles out
  Towards the pootiest, bless her,
An' leetle flames danced all about
  The chiny on the dresser.

Agin the chimbley crook-necks hung,
  An' in amongst 'em rusted
The ole queen's-arm thet gran'ther Young
  Fetched back from Concord busted.

The very room, coz she was in,
    Seemed warm from floor to ceilin',
An' she looked full ez rosy agin
    Ez the apples she was peelin'.

'T was kin' o' kingdom-come to look
    On sech a blessed cretur,
A dogrose blushin' to a brook
    Ain't modester nor sweeter.

He was six foot o' man, A 1,
    Clear grit an' human natur';
None could n't quicker pitch a ton
    Nor dror a furrer straighter.

He 'd sparked it with full twenty gals,
    Hed squired 'em, danced 'em, druv 'em,
Fust this one, an' then thet, by spells, —
    All is, he could n't love 'em.

But long o' her his veins 'ould run
    All crinkly like curled maple,
The side she breshed felt full o' sun
    Ez a south slope in Ap'il.

She thought no v'ice hed sech a swing
    Ez hisn in the choir;
My! when he made Ole Hunderd ring,
    She *knowed* the Lord was nigher.

An' she 'd blush scarlit, right in prayer,
    When her new meetin'-bunnet
Felt somehow thru' its crown a pair
    O' blue eyes sot upon it.

Thet night, I tell ye, she looked *some* !
   She seemed to 've gut a new soul,
For she felt sartin-sure he 'd come,
   Down to her very shoe-sole.

She heered a foot, an' knowed it tu,
   A-raspin' on the scraper, —
All ways to once her feelins flew
   Like sparks in burnt-up paper!

He kin' o' l'itered on the mat,
   Some doubtfle o' the sekle,
His heart kep' goin' pity-pat,
   But hern went pity Zekle.

An' yit she gin her cheer a jirk
   Ez though she wished him furder,
An' on her apples kep' to work,
   Parin' away like murder.

" You want to see my Pa, I s'pose? "
   " Wal . . . . no . . . . I come dasignin' " —
" To see my Ma? She 's sprinklin' clo'es
   Agin to-morrer's i'nin'."

To say why gals acts so or so,
   Or don't, 'ould be presumin';
Mebby to mean *yes* an' say *no*
   Comes nateral to women.

He stood a spell on one foot fust,
   Then stood a spell on t' other,
An' on which one he felt the wust
   He could n't ha' told ye nuther.

Says he, "I 'd better call agin;"
  Says she, "Think likely, Mister:"
Thet last word pricked him like a pin,
  An' . . . . Wal, he up an' kist her.

When Ma bimeby upon 'em slips,
  Huldy sot pale ez ashes,
All kin' o' smily roun' the lips
  An' teary roun' the lashes.

For she was jes' the quiet kind
  Whose naturs never vary,
Like streams that keep a summer mind
  Snowhid in Jenooary.

The blood clost roun' her heart felt glued
  Too tight for all expressin',
Tell mother see how metters stood,
  An' gin 'em both her blessin'.

Then her red come back like the tide
  Down to the Bay o' Fundy,
An' all I know is they was cried
  In meetin' come nex' Sunday.
JAMES RUSSELL LOWELL.

NUREMBERG.

IN the valley of the Pegnitz, where across broad mead-
    ow-lands
Rise the blue Franconian mountains, Nuremberg, the
    ancient, stands.

Quaint old town of toil and traffic, quaint old town of
    art and song,
Memories haunt thy pointed gables, like the rooks that
    round them throng:

Memories of the Middle Ages, when the Emperors,
    rough and bold,
Had their dwelling in thy castle, time-defying, centu-
    ries old;

And thy brave and thrifty burghers boasted, in their
    uncouth rhyme,
That their great imperial city stretched its hand through
    every clime.

In the court-yard of the castle, bound with many an
    iron band,
Stands the mighty linden planted by Queen Cuni-
    gunde's hand;

On the square the oriel window, where in old heroic
    days
Sat the poet Melchior, singing Kaiser Maximilian's
    praise.

Everywhere I see around me rise the wondrous world
    of Art:
Fountains wrought with richest sculpture standing in
    the common mart;

And above cathedral doorways saints and bishops
    carved in stone,
By a former age commissioned as apostles to our
    own.

In the church of sainted Sebald sleeps enshrined his
  holy dust,
And in bronze the Twelve Apostles guard from age to
  age their trust;

In the church of sainted Lawrence stands a pix of
  sculpture rare,
Like the foamy sheaf of fountains, rising through the
  painted air.

Here, when Art was still religion, with a simple, rev-
  erent heart,
Lived and labored Albrecht Dürer, the Evangelist of
  Art;

Hence in silence and in sorrow, toiling still with busy
  hand,
Like an emigrant he wandered, seeking for the Better
  Land.

Emigravit is the inscription on the tombstone where
  he lies;
Dead he is not, but departed, — for the artist never
  dies.

Fairer seems the ancient city, and the sunshine seems
  more fair,
That he once has trod its pavement, that he once has
  breathed its air.

Through these streets so broad and stately, these obscure and dismal lanes,
Walked of yore the Mastersingers, chanting rude po-
  etic strains.

From remote and sunless suburbs came they to the
         friendly guild,
Building nests in Fame's great temple, as in spouts
         the sparrows build.

As the weaver plied the shuttle, wove he too the mys-
         tic rhyme,
And the smith his iron measures hammered to the an-
         vil's chime;

Thanking God, whose boundless wisdom makes the
         flowers of poesy bloom
In the forge's dust and cinders, in the tissues of the
         loom.

Here Hans Sachs, the cobbler-poet, laureate of the
         gentle craft,
Wisest of the Twelve Wise Masters, in huge folios
         sang and laughed.

But his house is now an ale-house, with a nicely
         sanded floor,
And a garland in the window, and his face above the
         door;

Painted by some humble artist, as in Adam Pusch-
         man's song,
As the old man gray and dove-like, with his great
         beard white and long.

And at night the swart mechanic comes to drown his
         cark and care,
Quaffing ale from pewter tankards, in the master's an-
         tique chair.

Vanished is the ancient splendor, and before my
    dreamy eye
Wave these mingling shapes and figures, like a faded
    tapestry.

Not thy Councils, not thy Kaisers, win for thee the
    world's regard,
But thy painter, Albrecht Dürer, and Hans Sachs thy
    cobbler-bard.

Thus, O Nuremberg, a wanderer from a region far
    away,
As he paced thy streets and court-yards, sang in
    thought his careless lay:

Gathering from the pavement's crevice, as a floweret
    of the soil,
The nobility of labor, — the long pedigree of toil.
        HENRY WADSWORTH LONGFELLOW.

THE HIGH TIDE ON THE COAST OF LINCOLNSHIRE.

' THE old mayor climbed the belfry tower,
    The ringers ran by two, by three;
" Pull, if ye never pulled before;
    Good ringers, pull your best," quoth he.
" Play up, play up, O Boston bells!
    Ply all your changes, all your swells,
      Play up ' The Brides of Enderby ' ! "

Men say it was a stolen tide, —
    The Lord that sent it, He knows all;

But in mine ears doth still abide
　　The message that the bells let fall:
And there was nought of strange, beside
The flights of mews and peewits pied,
　　By millions crouched on the old sea-wall.

I sat and spun within the door,
　　My thread brake off, I raised mine eyes;
The level sun, like ruddy ore,
　　Lay sinking in the barren skies;
And dark against day's golden death
She moved where Lindis wandereth, —
My son's fair wife, Elizabeth.

" Cusha! Cusha! Cusha!" calling,
　　Ere the early dews were falling,
　　Far away I heard her song.
" Cusha! Cusha!" all along;
　　Where the reedy Lindis floweth,
　　　　Floweth, floweth,
　　From the meads where melick groweth
　　Faintly came her milking-song.

" Cusha! Cusha! Cusha!" calling,
" For the dews will soon be falling;
　　Leave your meadow grasses mellow,
　　　　Mellow, mellow;
　　Quit your cowslips, cowslips yellow;
　　Come up, Whitefoot, come up, Lightfoot,
　　Quit the stalks of parsley hollow,
　　　　Hollow, hollow;
　　Come up, Jetty, rise and follow,
　　From the clovers lift your head;
　　Come up, Whitefoot, come up, Lightfoot,
　　Come up, Jetty, rise and follow,
　　Jetty, to the milking-shed."

If it be long, aye, long ago,
  When I begin to think how long,
Again I hear the Lindis flow,
  Swift as an arrow, sharp and strong;
And all the air it seemeth me
Is full of floating bells (saith she),
That ring the tune of Enderby.

All fresh the level pasture lay,
  And not a shadow might be seen,
Save where full five good miles away
  The steeple towered from out the green;
And lo! the great bell far and wide
Was heard in all the country side
That Saturday at eventide.

The swannerds where their sedges are
  Moved on in sunset's golden breath,
The shepherd lads I heard afar,
  And my son's wife, Elizabeth;
Till floating o'er the grassy sea
Came down that kindly message free,
The " Brides of Mavis Enderby."

Then some looked up into the sky,
  And all along where Lindis flows
To where the goodly vessels lie,
  And where the lordly steeple shows.
They said, " And why should this thing be?
What danger lowers by land or sea?
They ring the tune of Enderby!

" For evil news from Mablethorpe,
  Of pirate galleys warping down;
For ships ashore beyond the scorpe,
  They have not spared to wake the town;

But while the west is red to see,
And storms be none, and pirates flee,
Why ring ' The Brides of Enderby '? ''

I looked without, and lo! my son
   Came riding down with might and main.
He raised a shout as he drew on,
   Till all the welkin rang again,
'' Elizabeth! Elizabeth!''
(A sweeter woman ne'er drew breath
Than my son's wife, Elizabeth.)

'' The old sea wall (he cried) is down,
   The rising tide comes on apace,
And boats adrift in yonder town
   Go sailing up the market-place.''
He shook as one that looks on death:
'' God save you, mother!'' straight he saith;
'' Where is my wife, Elizabeth? ''

'' Good son, where Lindis winds away
   With her two bairns I marked her long;
And ere yon bells began to play,
   Afar I heard her milking song.''
He looked across the grassy sea,
To right, to left, '' Ho Enderby! ''
They rang '' The Brides of Enderby! ''

With that he cried and beat his breast;
   For lo! along the river's bed
A mighty eygre reared his crest,
   And up the Lindis raging sped.
It swept with thunderous noises loud;
Shaped like a curling snow-white cloud,
Or like a demon in a shroud.

And rearing Lindis, backward pressed,
  Shook all her trembling banks amain;
Then madly at the eygre's breast
  Flung up her weltering walls again.
Then banks came down with ruin and rout, —
Then beaten foam flew round about, —
Then all the mighty floods were out.

So far, so fast the eygre drave,
  The heart had hardly time to beat,
Before a shallow seething wave
  Sobbed in the grasses at our feet:
The feet had hardly time to flee
Before it brake against the knee,
And all the world was in the sea.

Upon the roof we sat that night,
  The noise of bells went sweeping by:
I marked the lofty beacon light
  Stream from the church tower, red and high, —
A lurid mark and dread to see;
And awsome bells they were to me,
That in the dark rang " Enderby."

They rang the sailor lads to guide
  From roof to roof who fearless rowed;
And I, — my son was at my side,
  And yet the ruddy beacon glowed:
And yet he moaned beneath his breath,
" O come in life, or come in death!
O lost! my love, Elizabeth."

And didst thou visit him no more?
  Thou didst, thou didst, my daughter dear!
The waters laid thee at his door,

Ere yet the early dawn was clear.
Thy pretty bairns in fast embrace,
The lifted sun shone on thy face,
Down drifted to thy dwelling-place.

That flow strewed wrecks about the grass;
  That ebb swept out the flocks to sea;
A fatal ebb and flow, alas!
  To many more than mine and me:
But each will mourn his own (she saith).
And sweeter woman ne'er drew breath
Than my son's wife, Elizabeth.

I shall never hear her more
By the reedy Lindis' shore,
" Cusha, Cusha, Cusha ! " calling,
Ere the early dews be falling;
I shall never hear her song,
" Cusha! Cusha! " all along,
Where the sunny Lindis floweth,
     Goeth, floweth;
From the meads where melick groweth,
When the water, winding down,
Onward floweth to the town.

I shall never see her more
Where the reeds and rushes quiver,
    Shiver, quiver:
Stand beside the sobbing river,
Sobbing, throbbing, in its falling,
To the sandy lonesome shore;
I shall never hear her calling,
" Leave your meadow grasses mellow,
    Mellow, mellow;
Quit your cowslips, cowslips yellow;

Come up, Whitefoot, come up, Lightfoot;
Quit your pipes of parsley hollow,
    Hollow, hollow;
Come up, Lightfoot, rise and follow;
    Lightfoot, Whitefoot,
From your clovers lift the head;
Come up, Jetty, follow, follow,
Jetty, to the milking shed."

JEAN INGELOW.[1]

QUA CURSUM VENTUS.

As ships, becalmed at eve, that lay
  With canvas drooping, side by side,
Two towers of sail at dawn of day
  Are scarce, long leagues apart, descried;

When fell the night, upsprung the breeze,
  And all the darkling hours they plied,
Nor dreamt but each the self-same seas
  By each was cleaving, side by side :

E'en so — but why the tale reveal
  Of those whom, year by year unchanged,
Brief absence joined anew to feel,
  Astounded, soul from soul estranged ?

At dead of night their sails were filled,
  And onward each rejoicing steered :

[1] JEAN INGELOW was born in Ipswich, Suffolk, England, about 1830. She has written many poems, and some novels, which have attained popularity.

Ah, neither blame, for neither willed,
Or wist, what first with dawn appeared !

To veer, how vain ! On, onward strain,
Brave barks ! In light, in darkness too,
Through winds and tides one compass guides, —
To that, and your own selves, be true !

But O blithe breeze, and O great seas,
Though ne'er, that earliest parting past,
On your wide plain they join again,
Together lead them home at last.

One port, methought, alike they sought,
One purpose hold where'er they fare, —
O bounding breeze, O rushing seas !
At last, at last, unite them there !

ARTHUR HUGH CLOUGH.

THE FIFTIETH BIRTHDAY OF AGASSIZ.

MAY 28, 1857.

IT was fifty years ago
In the pleasant month of May,
In the beautiful Pays de Vaud,
A child in its cradle lay.

And Nature, the old nurse, took
The child upon her knee,
Saying : "Here is a story-book
Thy Father has written for thee."
22

"Come, wander with me," she said,
    "Into regions yet untrod;
And read what is still unread
    In the manuscripts of God."

And he wandered away and away
    With Nature, the dear old nurse,
Who sang to him night and day
    The rhymes of the universe.

And whenever the way seemed long,
    Or his heart began to fail,
She would sing a more wonderful song,
    Or tell a more marvellous tale.

So she keeps him still a child,
    And will not let him go,
Though at times his heart beats wild
    For the beautiful Pays de Vaud;

Though at times he hears in his dreams
    The Ranz des Vaches of old,
And the rush of mountain streams
    From glaciers clear and cold ;

And the mother at home says, "Hark !
    For his voice I listen and yearn ;
It is growing late and dark,
    And my boy does not return !"
        HENRY WADSWORTH LONGFELLOW.

NEW YEAR'S EVE.

CVI.

RING out, wild bells, to the wild sky,
  The flying cloud, the frosty light :
  The year is dying in the night ;
Ring out, wild bells, and let him die.

Ring out the old, ring in the new,
  Ring, happy bells, across the snow :
  The year is going, let him go ;
Ring out the false, ring in the true.

Ring out the grief that saps the mind,
  For those that here we see no more ;
  Ring out the feud of rich and poor,
Ring in redress to all mankind.

Ring out a slowly dying cause,
  And ancient forms of party strife ;
  Ring in the nobler modes of life,
With sweeter manners, purer laws.

Ring out the want, the care, the sin,
  The faithless coldness of the times ;
  Ring out, ring out my mournful rhymes,
But ring the fuller minstrel in.

Ring out false pride in place and blood,
  The civic slander and the spite;
  Ring in the love of truth and right,
Ring in the common love of good.

Ring out old shapes of foul disease;
  Ring out the harrowing lust of gold;

Ring out the thousand wars of old,
Ring in the thousand years of peace.

Ring in the valiant man and free,
  The larger heart, the kindlier hand;
Ring out the darkness of the land,
Ring in the Christ that is to be.
                          ALFRED TENNYSON.
                                In Memoriam.

BREAK, BREAK.

BREAK, break, break,
  On thy cold gray stones, O Sea!
And I would that my tongue could utter
  The thoughts that arise in me.

O well for the fisherman's boy,
  That he shouts with his sister at play!
O well for the sailor lad,
  That he sings in his boat on the bay!

And the stately ships go on
  To their haven under the hill;
But O for the touch of a vanish'd hand,
  And the sound of a voice that is still!

Break, break, break,
  At the foot of thy crags, O Sea!
But the tender grace of a day that is dead
  Will never come back to me.
                          ALFRED TENNYSON.

A PSALM OF LIFE.

TELL me not, in mournful numbers,
  Life is but an empty dream!
For the soul is dead that slumbers,
  And things are not what they seem.

Life is real!   Life is earnest!
  And the grave is not its goal;
Dust thou art, to dust returnest,
  Was not spoken of the soul.

Not enjoyment, and not sorrow,
  Is our destined end or way;
But to act, that each to-morrow
  Find us farther than to-day.

Art is long, and Time is fleeting,
  And our hearts, though stout and brave,
Still, like muffled drums, are beating
  Funeral marches to the grave.

In the world's broad field of battle,
  In the bivouac of Life,
Be not like dumb, driven cattle!
  Be a hero in the strife!

Trust no Future, howe'er pleasant!
  Let the dead Past bury its dead!
Act — act in the living Present!
  Heart within, and God o'erhead!

Lives of great men all remind us
  We can make our lives sublime,

And, departing, leave behind us
  Footprints on the sands of time, —

Footprints, that perhaps another,
  Sailing o'er life's solemn main,
A forlorn and shipwrecked brother,
  Seeing, shall take heart again.

Let us, then, be up and doing,
  With a heart for any fate ;
Still achieving, still pursuing,
  Learn to labor and to wait.
       HENRY WADSWORTH LONGFELLOW.

THE SHIP.

O SHIP, ship, ship,
  That travellest over the sea,
What are the tidings, I pray thee,
  Thou bearest hither to me?

Are they tidings of comfort and joy,
  That shall make me seem to see
The sweet lips softly moving
  And whispering love to me?

Or are they of trouble and grief,
  Estrangement, sorrow, and doubt,
To turn into torture my hopes,
  And drive me from Paradise out?

O ship, ship, ship,
  That comest over the sea,

Whatever it be thou bringest,
Come quickly with it to me.
ARTHUR HUGH CLOUGH.

SIR GALAHAD.

MY good blade carves the casques of men,
My tough lance thrusteth sure,
My strength is as the strength of ten,
Because my heart is pure.
The shattering trumpet shrilleth high,
The hard brands shiver on the steel,
The splinter'd spear-shafts crack and fly,
The horse and rider reel:
They reel, they roll in clanging lists,
And when the tide of combat stands,
Perfume and flowers fall in showers,
That lightly rain from ladies' hands.

How sweet are looks that ladies bend
On whom their favors fall!
For them I battle till the end,
To save from shame and thrall:
But all my heart is drawn above,
My knees are bow'd in crypt and shrine:
I never felt the kiss of love,
Nor maiden's hand in mine.
More bounteous aspects on me beam,
Me mightier transports move and thrill;
So keep I fair thro' faith and prayer
A virgin heart in work and will.

When down the stormy crescent goes,
   A light before me swims,
Between dark stems the forest glows,
   I hear a noise of hymns :
Then by some secret shrine I ride ;
   I hear a voice, but none are there ;
The stalls are void, the doors are wide,
   The tapers burning fair.
Fair gleams the snowy altar cloth,
   The silver vessels sparkle clean,
The shrill bell rings, the censer swings,
   And solemn chaunts resound between.

Sometimes on lonely mountain-meres
   I find a magic bark ;
I leap on board : no helmsman steers :
   I float till all is dark.
A gentle sound, an awful light !
   Three angels bear the holy Grail :
With folded feet, in stoles of white,
   On sleeping wings they sail.
Ah, blessed vision ! blood of God !
   My spirit beats her mortal bars,
As down dark tides the glory slides,
   And star-like mingles with the stars.

When on my goodly charger borne
   Thro' dreaming towns I go,
The cock crows ere the Christmas morn,
   The streets are dumb with snow.
The tempest crackles on the leads,
   And, ringing, springs from brand and mail ;
But o'er the dark a glory spreads,
   And gilds the driving hail.
I leave the plain, I climb the height ;

No branchy thicket shelter yields ;
But blessed forms in whistling storms
  Fly o'er waste fens and windy fields.

A maiden knight — to me is given
  Such hope, I know not fear ;
I yearn to breathe the airs of heaven
  That often meet me here.
I muse on joy that will not cease,
  Pure spaces clothed in living beams,
Pure lilies of eternal peace,
  Whose odors haunt my dreams ;
And, stricken by an angel's hand,
  This mortal armor that I wear,
This weight and size, this heart and eyes,
  Are touch'd, are turn'd to finest air.

The clouds are broken in the sky,
  And thro' the mountain-walls
A rolling organ-harmony
  Swells up, and shakes and falls.
Then move the trees, the copses nod,
  Wings flutter, voices hover clear :
" O just and faithful knight of God !
  Ride on ! the prize is near."
So pass I hostel, hall, and grange ;
  By bridge and ford, by park and pale,
All-arm'd I ride, whate'er betide,
  Until I find the holy Grail.

ALFRED TENNYSON.

THE HAPPIEST LAND.

FROM THE GERMAN.

THERE sat one day in quiet,
　By an alehouse on the Rhine,
Four hale and hearty fellows,
　And drank the precious wine.

The landlord's daughter filled their cups,
　Around the rustic board;
Then sat they all so calm and still,
　And spake not one rude word.

But when the maid departed,
　A Swabian raised his hand,
And cried, all hot and flushed with wine,
　" Long live the Swabian land!

" The greatest kingdom upon earth
　Cannot with that compare;
With all the stout and hardy men,
　And the nut-brown maidens there."

" Ha! " cried a Saxon, laughing,
　And dashed his beard with wine;
" I had rather live in Lapland,
　Than that Swabian land of thine!

" The goodliest land on all this earth,
　It is the Saxon land!
There have I as many maidens
　As fingers on this hand!"

" Hold your tongues! both Swabian and Saxon!"
    A bold Bohemian cries;
" If there 's a heaven upon this earth,
    In Bohemia it lies.

" There the tailor blows the flute,
    And the cobbler blows the horn,
And the miner blows the bugle,
    Over mountain gorge and bourn."

    .   .   .   .

And then the landlord's daughter
    Up to heaven raised her hand,
And said, " Ye may no more contend,
    There lies the happiest land! "
            HENRY WADSWORTH LONGFELLOW.

ST. AGNES' EVE.

DEEP on the convent-roof the snows
    Are sparkling to the moon:
My breath to heaven like vapor goes:
    May my soul follow soon!
The shadows of the convent-towers
    Slant down the snowy sward,
Still creeping with the creeping hours
    That lead me to my Lord:
Make Thou my spirit pure and clear
    As are the frosty skies,
Or this first snowdrop of the year
    That in my bosom lies.

As these white robes are soil'd and dark
    To yonder shining ground;

As this pale taper's earthly spark,
    To yonder argent round;
So shows my soul before the Lamb,
    My spirit before Thee;
So in my earthly house I am,
    To that I hope to be.
Break up the heavens, O Lord! and far,
    Thro' all yon starlight keen,
Draw me, thy bride, a glittering star,
    In raiment white and clean.

He lifts me to the golden doors;
    The flashes come and go;
All heaven bursts her starry floors,
    And strows her light below,
And deepens on and up! the gates
    Roll back, and far within
For me the Heavenly Bridegroom waits,
    To make me pure of sin.
The sabbaths of Eternity,
    One sabbath deep and wide —
A light upon the shining sea —
    The Bridegroom with his bride!

ALFRED TENNYSON.

THE ROPEWALK.

In that building, long and low,
With its windows all a-row,
    Like the port-holes of a hulk,
Human spiders spin and spin,
Backward down their threads so thin
    Dropping, each a hempen bulk.

At the end, an open door;
Squares of sunshine on the floor
  Light the long and dusky lane;
And the whirring of a wheel,
Dull and drowsy, makes me feel
  All its spokes are in my brain.

As the spinners to the end
Downward go and reascend,
  Gleam the long threads in the sun;
While within this brain of mine
Cobwebs brighter and more fine
  By the busy wheel are spun.

Two fair maidens in a swing,
Like white doves upon the wing,
  First before my vision pass;
Laughing, as their gentle hands
Closely clasp the twisted strands,
  At their shadow on the grass.

Then a booth of mountebanks,
With its smell of tan and planks,
  And a girl poised high in air
On a cord, in spangled dress,
With a faded loveliness,
  And a weary look of care.

Then a homestead among farms,
And a woman with bare arms
  Drawing water from a well;
As the bucket mounts apace,
With it mounts her own fair face,
  As at some magician's spell.

Then an old man in a tower,
Ringing loud the noontide hour,
  While the rope coils round and round
Like a serpent at his feet,
And again, in swift retreat,
  Nearly lifts him from the ground.

Then within a prison-yard,
Faces fixed, and stern, and hard,
  Laughter and indecent mirth;
Ah! it is the gallows-tree!
Breath of Christian charity,
  Blow, and sweep it from the earth!

Then a school-boy, with his kite
Gleaming in a sky of light,
  And an eager, upward look;
Steeds pursued through lane and field;
Fowlers with their snares concealed;
  And an angler by a brook.

Ships rejoicing in the breeze,
Wrecks that float o'er unknown seas,
  Anchors dragged through faithless sand;
Sea-fog drifting overhead,
And, with lessening line and lead,
  Sailors feeling for the land.

All these scenes do I behold,
These and many left untold,
  In that building long and low;
While the wheel goes round and round,
With a drowsy, dreamy sound,
  And the spinners backward go.
      HENRY WADSWORTH LONGFELLOW.

THE FORCED RECRUIT.

SOLFERINO, 1859.

In the ranks of the Austrian you found him,
  He died with his face to you all;
Yet bury him here where around him
  You honor your bravest that fall.

Venetian, fair-featured and slender,
  He lies shot to death in his youth,
With a smile on his lips over-tender
  For any mere soldier's dead mouth.

No stranger, and yet not a traitor,
  Though alien the cloth on his breast,
Underneath it how seldom a greater
  Young heart has a shot sent to rest!

By your enemy tortured and goaded
  To march with them, stand in their file,
His musket (see) never was loaded,
  He facing your guns with that smile!

As orphans yearn on to their mothers,
  He yearned to your patriot bands:
"Let me die for our Italy, brothers,
  If not in your ranks, by your hands!

"Aim straightly, fire steadily! spare me
  A ball in the body which may
Deliver my heart here, and tear me
  This badge of the Austrian away!"

So thought he, so died he this morning.
    What then? many others have died.
Ay, but easy for men to die scorning
    The death-stroke, who fought side by side,

One tricolor floating above them;
    Struck down by triumphant acclaims
Of an Italy rescued to love them
    And blazon the brass with their names.

But he, without witness or honor,
    Mixed, shamed in his country's regard,
With the tyrants who march in upon her,
    Died faithful and passive; 't was hard.

'T was sublime. In a cruel restriction
    Cut off from the guerdon of sons,
With most filial obedience, conviction,
    His soul kissed the lips of her guns.

That moves you? Nay, grudge not to show it,
    While digging a grave for him here :
The others who died, says your poet,
    Have glory, — let *him* have a tear.

Elizabeth Barrett Browning.[1]

[1] Elizabeth Barrett Browning, the daughter of Mr. Barrett, a wealthy London merchant, was born in Ledbury, about 1807. She began to write verses while still a child, and displayed strong literary tastes. She speedily acquired reputation both for her learning and for her writings. In 1846 she married Robert Browning. She wrote many poems, both long and short, of varying merit, some of a very high order, and published some translations from the Greek. She died in Florence, in 1861.

THE CUMBERLAND.

At anchor in Hampton Roads we lay,
  On board of the Cumberland, sloop-of-war;
And at times from the fortress across the bay
    The alarum of drums swept past,
    Or a bugle blast
From the camp on the shore.

Then far away to the south up rose
  A little feather of snow-white smoke,
And we knew that the iron ship of our foes
    Was steadily steering its course
    To try the force
Of our ribs of oak.

Down upon us heavily runs,
  Silent and sullen, the floating fort;
Then comes a puff of smoke from her guns,
    And leaps the terrible death,
    With fiery breath,
From each open port.

We are not idle, but send her straight
  Defiance back in a full broadside!
As hail rebounds from a roof of slate,
    Rebounds our heavier hail
    From each iron scale
Of the monster's hide.

" Strike your flag!" the rebel cries,
  In his arrogant old plantation strain.
" Never!" our gallant Morris replies;
    " It is better to sink than to yield!"
23

And the whole air pealed
With the cheers of our men.

Then, like a kraken huge and black,
    She crushed our ribs in her iron grasp!
Down went the Cumberland all a wrack,
    With a sudden shudder of death,
    And the cannon's breath
For her dying gasp.

Next morn, as the sun rose over the bay,
    Still floated our flag at the mainmast head.
Lord, how beautiful was Thy day!
    Every waft of the air
    Was a whisper of prayer,
Or a dirge for the dead.

Ho! brave hearts that went down in the seas!
    Ye are at peace in the troubled stream;
Ho! brave land! with hearts like these,
    Thy flag, that is rent in twain,
    Shall be one again,
And without a seam!

HENRY WADSWORTH LONGFELLOW.

JONATHAN TO JOHN.[1]

It don't seem hardly right, John,
   When both my hands was full,
To stump me to a fight, John, —
   Your cousin, tu, John Bull!
     Ole Uncle S. sez he, " I guess
     We know it now," sez he,
" The lion's paw is all the law,
     Accordin' to J. B.,
     Thet 's fit for you an' me!"

You wonder why we 're hot, John?
   Your mark wuz on the guns,
The neutral guns, thet shot, John,
   Our brothers an' our sons:
     Ole Uncle S. sez he, "I guess
     There 's human blood," sez he,
" By fits an' starts, in Yankce hearts,
     Though 't may surprise J. B.
     More 'n it would you an' me."

Ef *I* turned mad dogs loose, John,
   On *your* front-parlor stairs,

[1] This poem refers to the period of our difficulties with England after what was known as the " Trent affair." November 19, 1861, Captain Wilkes, in command of the Federal war steamer San Jacinto, boarded the British mail packet Trent, and took out the ambassadors of the Southern Confederacy, Mason and Slidell, who were on their way to England. This was a gross infraction of neutral rights, and President Lincoln wisely gave up the prisoners. But the hostile attitude of England and her sympathy with the South excited just and deep indignation on the part of the United States. England, after the war, expiated her conduct by the treaty of Washington and by the award of the Geneva arbitration.

Would it jest meet your views, John,
  To wait an' sue their heirs?
    Ole Uncle S. sez he, " I guess,
    I on'y guess," sez he,
" Thet ef Vattel on *his* toes fell,
    'T would kind o' rile J. B.,
    Ez wal ez you an' me!"

Who made the law thet hurts, John,
  Heads I win, — ditto tails?
" *J. B.*" was on his shirts, John,
  Onless my memory fails.
    Ole Uncle S. sez he, " I guess
    (I 'm good at thet)," sez he,
" Thet sauce for goose ain't *jest* the juice
    For ganders with J. B.,
    No more 'n with you an' me!"

When your rights was our wrongs, John,
  You did n't stop for fuss, —
Britanny's trident prongs, John,
  Was good 'nough law for us.
    Ole Uncle S. sez he, " I guess,
    Though physic 's good," sez he,
" It does n't foller thet he can swaller
    Prescriptions signed ' J. B.,'
    Put up by you an' me!"

We own the ocean, tu, John:
  You mus' n' take it hard,
Ef we can't think with you, John,
  It 's jest your own back-yard.
    Ole Uncle S. sez he, " I guess,
    Ef *thet* 's his claim," sez he,
" The fencin'-stuff 'll cost enough

To bust up friend J. B.,
Ez wal ez you an' me!"

Why talk so dreffle big, John,
Of honor, when it meant
You did n't care a fig, John,
But jest for *ten per cent?*
Ole Uncle S. sez he, " I guess
He 's like the rest," sez he:
" When all is done it 's number one
Thet 's nearest to J. B.,
Ez wal ez t' you an' me!"

We give the critters back, John,
Cos Abram thought 't was right;
It warn't your bullyin' clack, John,
Provokin' us to fight.
Ole Uncle S. sez he, " I guess
We 've a hard row," sez he,
" To hoe jest now; but thet, somehow,
May happen to J. B.,
Ez wal ez you an' me!"

We ain't so weak an' poor, John,
With twenty million people,
An' close to every door, John,
A school-house an' a steeple.
Ole Uncle S. sez he, " I guess
It is a fact," sez he,
" The surest plan to make a man
Is, Think him so, J. B.,
Ez much ez you or me!"

Our folks believe in Law, John;
An' it 's for her sake now,

They 've left the axe an' saw, John,
  The anvil an' the plough.
    Ole Uncle S. sez he, " I guess,
    Ef 't warn't for law," sez he,
" There 'd be one shindy from here to Indy;
    An' thet don't suit J. B.
    (When 't ain't 'twixt you an' me!) "

We know we 've got a cause, John,
  Thet 's honest, just, an' true;
We thought 't would win applause, John,
  Ef nowheres else, from you.
    Ole Uncle S. sez he, " I guess
    His love of rights," sez he,
" Hangs by a rotten fibre o' cotton:
    There 's natur' in J. B.,
    Ez wal ez you an' me!"

The South says, " *Poor folks down!* " John,
  An' " *All men up!* " say we, —
White, yaller, black, an' brown, John:
  Now which is your idee?
    Ole Uncle S. sez he, " I guess,
    John preaches wal," sez he;
" But, sermon thru, an' come to *du*
    Why, there 's the old J. B.
    A crowdin' you an' me ! "

Shall it be love, or hate, John?
  It 's you thet 's to decide;
Ain't *your* bonds held by Fate, John,
  Like all the world's beside?
    Ole Uncle S., sez he, " I guess
    Wise men forgive," sez he,
" But not forget; an' some time yet

Thet truth may strike J. B.,
Ez wal ez you an' me!"

God means to make this land, John,
Clear thru, from sea to sea,
Believe an' understand, John,
The *wuth* o' bein' free.
Ole Uncle S., sez he, " I guess
God's price is high," sez he;
" But nothin' else than wut He sells
Wears long, an' thet J. B.
May larn, like you an' me!"
JAMES RUSSELL LOWELL.

BARBARA FRIETCHIE.

UP from the meadows rich with corn,
Clear in the cool September morn,

The clustered spires of Frederick stand
Green-walled by the hills of Maryland.

Round about them orchards sweep,
Apple and peach tree fruited deep, —

Fair as the garden of the Lord
To the eyes of the famished rebel horde,

On that pleasant morn of the early fall
When Lee marched over the mountain-wall, —

Over the mountains winding down,
Horse and foot, into Frederick town.

Forty flags with their silver stars,
Forty flags with their crimson bars,

Flapped in the morning wind: the sun
Of noon looked down, and saw not one.

Up rose Barbara Frietchie then,
Bowed with her fourscore years and ten;

Bravest of all in Frederick town,
She took up the flag the men hauled down;

In her attic window the staff she set,
To show that one heart was loyal yet.

Up the street came the rebel tread,
Stonewall Jackson riding ahead.

Under his slouched hat left and right
He glanced: the old flag met his sight.

" Halt ! " — The dust-brown ranks stood fast.
" Fire ! " — Out blazed the rifle-blast.

It shivered the window, pane and sash;
It rent the banner with seam and gash.

Quick, as it fell, from the broken staff
Dame Barbara snatched the silken scarf.

She leaned far out on the window-sill,
And shook it forth with a royal will.

" Shoot, if you must, this old gray head,
But spare your country's flag," she said.

A shade of sadness, a blush of shame,
Over the face of the leader came;

The nobler nature within him stirred
To life at that woman's deed and word :

" Who touches a hair of yon gray head
Dies like a dog! March on !" he said.

All day long through Frederick street
Sounded the tramp of marching feet :

All day long that free flag tost
Over the heads of the rebel host.

Ever its torn folds rose and fell
On the loyal winds that loved it well ;

And through the hill-gaps sunset light
Shone over it with a warm good-night.

Barbara Frietchie's work is o'er
And the rebel rides on his raids no more.

Honor to her ! and let a tear
Fall, for her sake, on Stonewall's bier.

Over Barbara Frietchie's grave,
Flag of Freedom and Union, wave !

Peace and order and beauty draw
Round thy symbol of light and law;

And ever the stars above look down
On thy stars below in Frederick town !
JOHN GREENLEAF WHITTIER.

THE OLD SERGEANT.

JANUARY 1, 1863.

THE Carrier cannot sing to-day the ballads
    With which he used to go,
Rhyming the glad rounds of the happy New Years
    That are now beneath the snow:

For the same awful and portentous Shadow
    That overcast the earth,
And smote the land last year with desolation,
    Still darkens every hearth.

And the Carrier hears Beethoven's mighty death-march
    Come up from every mart;
And he hears and feels it breathing in his bosom,
    And beating in his heart.

And to-day, a scarred and weather-beaten veteran
    Again he comes along,
To tell the story of the Old Year's struggles
    In another New Year's song.

And the song is his, but not so with the story;
    For the story, you must know,
Was told in prose to Assistant-Surgeon Austin,
    By a soldier of Shiloh:

By Robert Burton, who was brought up on the Adams,
    With his death-wound in his side;
And who told the story to the Assistant-Surgeon,
    On the same night that he died.

But the singer feels it will better suit the ballad,
    If all should deem it right,

To tell the story as if what it speaks of
Had happened but last night.

" Come a little nearer, Doctor, — thank you, — let me
take the cup:
Draw your chair up, — draw it closer, — just another
little sup!
May be you may think I 'm better; but I 'm pretty well
used up, —
Doctor, you 've done all you could do, but I 'm just
a-going up!

" Feel my pulse, sir, if you want to, but it ain't much
use to try " —
" Never say that," said the Surgeon, as he smothered
down a sigh;
" It will never do, old comrade, for a soldier to say
die ! "
" What you *say* will make no difference, Doctor, when
you come to die."

" Doctor, what has been the matter? " " You were
very faint, they say ;
You must try to get to sleep now." " Doctor, have I
been away? "
" Not that anybody knows of ! " " Doctor — Doctor,
please to stay !
There is something I must tell you, and you won't
have long to stay !

" I have got my marching orders, and I 'm ready now
to go;
Doctor, did you say I fainted? — but it could n't ha'
been so, —

For as sure as I 'm a Sergeant, and was wounded at
    Shiloh,
I 've this very night been back there, on the old field
    of Shiloh!

" This is all that I remember: The last time the
    Lighter came,
And the lights had all been lowered, and the noises
    much the same,
He had not been gone five minutes before something
    called my name:
' ORDERLY SERGEANT — ROBERT BURTON!' — just
    that way it called my name.

" And I wondered who could call me so distinctly and
    so slow,
Knew it could n't be the Lighter, — he could not have
    spoken so, —
And I tried to answer, ' Here, sir!' but I could n't
    make it go;
For I could n't move a muscle, and I could n't make it
    go.

" Then I thought: It 's all a nightmare, all a humbug
    and a bore;
Just another foolish *grape-vine* [1] — and it won't come
    any more;
But it came, sir, notwithstanding, just the same way
    as before:
' ORDERLY SERGEANT — ROBERT BURTON!' — even
    louder than before.

" That is all that I remember, till a sudden burst of
    light,

[1] A false story, a hoax.

And I stood beside the River, where we stood that
Sunday night,
Waiting to be ferried over to the dark bluffs opposite,
When the river was perdition and all hell was oppo-
site!—

"And the same old palpitation came again in all its
power,
And I heard a Bugle sounding, as from some celestial
Tower;
And the same mysterious voice said: 'IT IS THE ELEV-
ENTH HOUR!
ORDERLY SERGEANT — ROBERT BURTON — IT IS
THE ELEVENTH HOUR!'

"Doctor Austin!—what *day* is this?" "It is
Wednesday night, you know."
"Yes,—to-morrow will be New Year's, and a right
good time below!
What time is it, Doctor Austin?" "Nearly Twelve."
"Then don't you go!
Can it be that all this happened—all this—not an
hour ago!

"There was where the gunboats opened on the dark
rebellious host;
And where Webster semicircled his last guns upon the
coast;
There were still the two log-houses, just the same, or
else their ghost—
And the same old transport came and took me over—
or its ghost!

"And the old field lay before me all deserted far and
wide;

There was where they fell on Prentiss — there Mc-
    Clernand met the tide;
There was where stern Sherman rallied, and where
    Hurlbut's heroes died, —
Lower down, where Wallace charged them, and kept
    charging till he died.

" There was where Lew Wallace showed them he was
    of the canny kin,
There was where old Nelson thundered, and where
    Rousseau waded in;
There McCook sent 'em to breakfast, and we all began
    to win —
There was where the grape-shot took me, just as we
    began to win.

" Now, a shroud of snow and silence over everything
    was spread;
And but for this old blue mantle and the old hat on
    my head,
I should not have even doubted, to this moment, I
    was dead, —
For my footsteps were as silent as the snow upon the
    dead!

" Death and silence! — Death and silence! all around
    me as I sped!
And behold, a mighty Tower, as if builded to the
    dead,
To the Heaven of the heavens lifted up its mighty
    head,
Till the Stars and Stripes of Heaven all seemed wav-
    ing from its head!

" Round and mighty based it towered up into the in-
    finite —

And I knew no mortal mason could have built a shaft
    so bright;
For it shone like solid sunshine; and a winding stair of
    light
Wound around it and around it till it wound clear out
    of sight!

"And, behold, as I approached it — with a rapt and
    dazzled stare, —
Thinking that I saw old comrades just ascending the
    great Stair, —
Suddenly the solemn challenge broke of — 'Halt, and
    who goes there!'
'I'm a friend,' I said, 'if you are.' 'Then advance,
    sir, to the Stair!'

"I advanced! That sentry, Doctor, was Elijah
    Ballantyne! —
First of all to fall on Monday, after we had formed the
    line ! —
'Welcome, my old Sergeant, welcome! Welcome by
    that countersign!'
And he pointed to the scar there, under this old cloak
    of mine!

"As he grasped my hand, I shuddered, thinking only
    of the grave;
But he smiled and pointed upward with a bright and
    bloodless glaive:
'That's the way, sir, to Head-quarters.' 'What
    Head-quarters?' 'Of the Brave.'
'But the great Tower?' 'That was builded of the
    great deeds of the Brave!'

"Then a sudden shame came o'er me at his uniform
    of light;
At my own so old and battered, and at his so new and
    bright;
' Ah!' said he, ' you have forgotten the new uniform
    to-night, —
Hurry back, for you must be here at just twelve o'clock
    to-night!'

"And the next thing I remember, you were sitting
    there, and I —
Doctor — did you hear a footstep? Hark! — God bless
    you all! Good-by!
Doctor, please to give my musket and my knapsack,
    when I die,
To my son — my son that's coming, — he won't get
    here till I die!

"Tell him his old father blessed him — as he never
    did before, —
And to carry that old musket" — Hark! a knock is at
    the door! —
"Till the Union" — See! it opens! — "Father!
    Father! speak once more!"
"*Bless you!*" — gasped the old, gray Sergeant. And
    he lay and said no more!

FORCEYTHE WILLSON.[1]

---

[1] FORCEYTHE WILLSON was born in Ohio, and died in Cambridge a few years since. His fame rests wholly on this poem.

THE ARSENAL AT SPRINGFIELD.

THIS is the Arsenal.   From floor to ceiling,
  Like a huge organ, rise the burnished arms;
But from their silent pipes no anthem pealing
  Startles the villages with strange alarms.

Ah! what a sound will rise, how wild and dreary,
  When the death-angel touches those swift keys!
What loud lament and dismal Miserere
  Will mingle with their awful symphonies!

I hear even now the infinite fierce chorus,
  The cries of agony, the endless groan,
Which, through the ages that have gone before us,
  In long reverberations reach our own.

On helm and harness rings the Saxon hammer,
  Through Cimbric forest roars the Norseman's song,
And loud, amid the universal clamor,
  O'er distant deserts sounds the Tartar gong.

I hear the Florentine, who from his palace
  Wheels out his battle-bell with dreadful din,
And Aztec priests upon their teocallis
  Beat the wild war-drums made of serpent's skin;

The tumult of each sacked and burning village;
  The shout that every prayer for mercy drowns;
The soldiers' revels in the midst of pillage;
' The wail of famine in beleaguered towns;

The bursting shell, the gateway wrenched asunder,
  The rattling musketry, the clashing blade;
24

And ever and anon, in tones of thunder,
  The diapason of the cannonade.

Is it, O man, with such discordant noises,
  With such accursed instruments as these,
Thou drownest Nature's sweet and kindly voices,
  And jarrest the celestial harmonies?

Were half the power that fills the world with terror,
  Were half the wealth bestowed on camps and courts,
Given to redeem the human mind from error,
  There were no need of arsenals or forts:

The warrior's name would be a name abhorrèd!
  And every nation, that should lift again
Its hand against a brother, on its forehead
  Would wear forevermore the curse of Cain!

Down the dark future, through long generations,
  The echoing sounds grow fainter and then cease;
And like a bell, with solemn, sweet vibrations,
  I hear once more the voice of Christ say, "Peace!"

Peace! and no longer from its brazen portals
  The blast of War's great organ shakes the skies!
But beautiful as songs of the immortals,
  The holy melodies of love arise.
                HENRY WADSWORTH LONGFELLOW.

BEFORE SEDAN.

Here, in this leafy place,
　　Quiet he lies,
Cold, with his sightless face
　　Turned to the skies;
'T is but another dead;
All you can say is said.

Carry his body hence, —
　　Kings must have slaves;
Kings climb to eminence
　　Over men's graves:
So this man's eye is dim, —
Throw the earth over him.

What was the white you touched,
　　There, at his side?
Paper his hand had clutched
　　Tight ere he died;
Message or wish, may be ;
Smooth the folds out, and see.

Hardly the worst of us
　　Here could have smiled!
Only the tremulous
　　Words of a child, —
Prattle, that has for stops
Just a few ruddy drops.

Look.　She is sad to miss,
　　Morning and night,
His — her dead father's — kiss;
　　Tries to be bright,

Good to mamma, and sweet.
That is all.   " Marguerite."

Ah, if beside the dead
  Slumbered the pain!
Ah, if the hearts that bled
  Slept with the slain!
If the grief died, — but no, —
Death will not have it so.

AUSTIN DOBSON.[1]

AN ENVOY TO AN AMERICAN LADY.

BEYOND the vague Atlantic deep,
Far as the farthest prairies sweep,
Where forest-glooms the nerve appal,
Where burns the radiant Western fall,
One duty lies on old and young, —
With filial piety to guard,
As on its greenest native sward,
The glory of the English tongue.
That ample speech! that subtle speech!
Apt for the need of all and each:
Strong to endure, yet prompt to bend
Wherever human feelings tend.
Preserve its force, expand its powers;
And through the maze of civic life,

[1] AUSTIN DOBSON, born in 1840, is an English poet, who has
recently come into notice and acquired reputation as the author
of two or three volumes of graceful verses.

In Letters, Commerce, even in Strife,
  Forget not it is yours and ours.
                    LORD HOUGHTON.[1]

THE END OF THE PLAY.

THE play is done ; the curtain drops,
  Slow falling to the prompter's bell:
A moment yet the actor stops,
  And looks around, to say farewell.
It is an irksome word and task;
  And, when he 's laughed and said his say,
He shows, as he removes the mask,
  A face that 's anything but gay.

One word, ere yet the evening ends,
  Let 's close it with a parting rhyme,
And pledge a hand to all young friends,
  As fits the merry Christmas time.
On life's wide scene you, too, have parts,
  That Fate erelong shall bid you play;
Good night ! with honest gentle hearts
  A kindly greeting go alway !

Good-night ! — I 'd say, the griefs, the joys,
  Just hinted in this mimic page,

[1] RICHARD MONCKTON MILNES is an English statesman
and writer. He was born in Yorkshire in 1809, and graduated
at Cambridge University in 1831. He was elected to Parliament in 1837 for Pontefract, which he continued to represent
until 1863, when he was raised to the peerage as Baron Houghton.

The triumphs and defeats of boys,
  Are but repeated in our age.
I 'd say, your woes were not less keen,
  Your hopes more vain, than those of men;
Your pangs or pleasures of fifteen
  At forty-five played o'er again.

I 'd say we suffer and we strive
  Not less nor more as men than boys;
With grizzled beards at forty-five,
  As erst at twelve in corduroys.
And if, in time of sacred youth,
  We learned at home to love and pray,
Pray Heaven that early Love and Truth
  May never wholly pass away.

And in the world, as in the school,
  I 'd say, how fate may change and shift ;
The prize be sometimes with the fool,
  The race not always to the swift.
The strong may yield, the good may fall,
  The great man be a vulgar clown,
The knave be lifted over all,
  The kind cast pitilessly down.

Who knows the inscrutable design?
  Blessed be He who took and gave!
Why should your mother, Charles, not mine,
  Be weeping at her darling's grave ?
We bow to Heaven that will'd it so,
  That darkly rules the fate of all,
That sends the respite or the blow,
  That 's free to give, or to recall.

This crowns his feast with wine and wit:
  Who brought him to that mirth and state?

His betters, see, below him sit,
  Or hunger hopeless at the gate.
Who bade the mud from Dives' wheel
  To spurn the rags of Lazarus?
Come, brother, in that dust we 'll kneel,
  Confessing Heaven that ruled it thus.

So each shall mourn, in life's advance,
  Dear hopes, dear friends, untimely killed;
Shall grieve for many a forfeit chance,
  And longing passion unfulfilled.
Amen! whatever fate be sent,
  Pray God the heart may kindly glow,
Although the head with cares be bent,
  And whitened with the winter snow.

Come wealth or want, come good or ill,
  Let young and old accept their part,
And bow before the Awful Will,
  And bear it with an honest heart,
Who misses or who wins the prize.
  Go, lose or conquer as you can ;
But if you fail, or if you rise,
  Be each, pray God, a gentleman.

A gentleman, or old or young!
  (Bear kindly with my humble lays);
The sacred chorus first was sung
  Upon the first of Christmas days :
The shepherds heard it overhead —
  The joyful angels raised it then:
Glory to Heaven on high, it said,
  And peace on earth to gentle men.

My song, save this, is little worth;
  I lay the weary pen aside,

And wish you health, and love, and mirth,
  As fits the solemn Christmas-tide.
As fits the holy Christmas birth,
  Be this, good friends, our carol still, —
Be peace on earth, be peace on earth,
  To men of gentle will.
                    WILLIAM MAKEPEACE THACKERAY.

SAY NOT THE STRUGGLE NOUGHT AVAILETH.

SAY not the struggle nought availeth,
  The labor and the wounds are vain,
The enemy faints not, nor faileth,
  And as things have been they remain.

If hopes were dupes, fears may be liars;
  It may be, in yon smoke concealed,
Your comrades chase e'en now the fliers,
  And, but for you, possess the field.

For while the tired waves, vainly breaking,
  Seem here no painful inch to gain,
Far back, through creeks and inlets making,
  Comes silent, flooding in, the main.

And not by eastern windows only,
  When daylight comes, comes in the light,
In front, the sun climbs slow, how slowly,
  But westward, look, the land is bright.
                    ARTHUR HUGH CLOUGH.

INDEX OF AUTHORS.